ENDORSEMENTS

PRICELESS

Priceless is a great Christian novel with a large hint of reality. It shows the realistic and poignant struggles of a floundering Christian trying to find his true commitment and how this journey affects his life. The unexpected twists to the story only add interest and captivate one's imagination, leaving you guessing into the next chapter.

—Carla S. Hall, Ordained Deacon, Church of the Nazarene

I eagerly recommend *Priceless* for all Christians. Mark Gudmunson is a masterful storyteller! I couldn't help but connect with the characters.

—Pastor Ray Morris, Renaissance Foursquare Church

Priceless will remind you that being a "good" Christian is not counted by the number of times you go to church or the list of rules you keep, but rather by the place you give to Christ in your life.

—Donna Phillips Youth Leader, Nazarene Church

A fascinating storyline bound to capture your imagination. The insightful originality of the volume rank it a classic piece of work.

—Dave Roe, Layman

Priceless keeps you in suspense while at the same time establishing awesome moral principles for strong, healthy relationships.

—Pastor Don Moore, Church of the Nazarene, Colfax, WA

Priceless is one of the best Christian romance novels I have read. It has enough suspense and romance to keep the reader involved in the story until the end.

—Tina Kincheloe, Finance Specialist

Priceless held our interest and kept us reading to the surprising end. We appreciate the clear Christian message.

—Walt and Eunice Rasch, Elders, Prescott Valley Church of God

An easy-to-read book with a compelling plot. It carries a profound message of the greatness of God's love and grace for His children.

—Caryl Lemon, Homemaker

Priceless presents a thought-provoking set of questions and challenges through the lives of the well-developed characters and events in their lives. The characters are so realistic I found myself drawn into their lives as if they were real people.

—Thelma Morris, Business Manager

Priceless issues a challenge to all who call themselves Christians to ask themselves the hard questions, "What is my 'pearl of great price'?" and "Whom or what do I really serve?" Mark Gudmunson leads the reader through the whole range of human emotions from laughter to tears, from disappointment to immense joy.

—Rev. Thomas C. Gudmunson, Pastor,
Miles City Wesleyan Church and Terry, MT Wesleyan Church

PRICELESS

Your your family are Priceless Alaythea, and God loves you dearly.

With Love,
Uncle Ron + Aunty Judy

MARK A. GUDMUNSON
PRICELESS

TATE PUBLISHING & *Enterprises*

Priceless
Copyright © 2010 by Mark A. Gudmunson. All rights reserved.

No part of this publication may be reproduced, stored in a retrieval system or transmitted in any way by any means, electronic, mechanical, photocopy, recording or otherwise without the prior permission of the author except as provided by USA copyright law.

This novel is a work of fiction. Names, descriptions, entities, and incidents included in the story are products of the author's imagination. Any resemblance to actual persons, events, and entities is entirely coincidental.

The opinions expressed by the author are not necessarily those of Tate Publishing, LLC.

Published by Tate Publishing & Enterprises, LLC
127 E. Trade Center Terrace | Mustang, Oklahoma 73064 USA
1.888.361.9473 | www.tatepublishing.com

Tate Publishing is committed to excellence in the publishing industry. The company reflects the philosophy established by the founders, based on Psalm 68:11,
"The Lord gave the word and great was the company of those who published it."

Book design copyright © 2010 by Tate Publishing, LLC. All rights reserved.
Cover design by Tyler Evans
Interior design by Stephanie Woloszyn

Published in the United States of America

ISBN: 978-1-61566-836-6
1. Fiction / Christian / General   2. Fiction / Coming Of Age
10.02.24

THIS BOOK WAS WRITTEN IN DEDICATION TO MY WIFE, LORI, WHO NEVER ONCE LOST FAITH THROUGHOUT THIS JOURNEY. I LOVE YOU!

ACKNOWLEDGMENTS

Throughout the long journey of this story, from a God-breathed inspiration to a crudely written manuscript, and finally, to a story worthy of publication, more people than I can count have been there for me along the way. Although I undoubtedly will fail to mention every person worthy of mentioning, I will give it a try.

To my big brother Tom, what can I say? Your dedication and enthusiasm made me hope, even realize, that I had something special here. You polished the edges off and brought the story up to respectability. You're a great big bro and I love ya!

To Author Jody Conrad: Thanks so much for all your help. Your insistent prodding led me to take a huge step of faith that I probably never would have taken on my own.

To Lori: Wow, this never would have happened without you. You've been patient, encouraging, and so unselfish throughout this whole ride. So many times, you've reminded me that this is God's story and that it would be shared with many. Thank you for encouraging me and putting up with me throughout this process. You are priceless to me!

To Sarah: Thank you for those four little words, "*You* write a book!"

To the rest of my family: Thank you for encouraging me every step along the way!

To Megan: God's timing is perfect. He puts people in our

lives exactly when we need them, gifts and blessings from God. You are absolutely incredible! Your work and tireless dedication on this project are priceless. I can't imagine ever getting this far without your guidance and help. You are a great friend and a true professional. You encouraged, corrected, edited, and polished your way through this story. What would I ever have done without you?

To God: For giving me this story to tell.

To Jesus, my Savior: For making your grace more than sufficient.

To the Holy Spirit: For your still, small voice that compelled me to put pen to paper to record the message God placed on my soul.

INTRODUCTION

"Write a book," a small voice resonated inside my head as I made my daily commute from my home in Colfax, a small farming community in Washington, up to Spokane, where I am a project manager for a large development company. It was early spring, and the job I was managing was in the final stages of construction.

"Write a book," resonated again as my mind wandered back to the previous evening's commute, specifically to the story that had materialized, appeared, made its grand entrance—beginning, middle, and end—into my daydreams and thoughts during my trip home.

I chuckled as I pushed the thought from my mind, "I can't write a book," I said to myself as I wheeled down the highway toward work. The story continued to enter my thoughts for the next several weeks, taking shape and form as I ran through the story scene by scene, front to back, back to front.

"Write a book," the voice persisted in my thoughts.

"I can't write a book! I don't know how," I reasoned to myself. "I'm nearly forty years old. I have no training. I've never written a book before," I argued with the voice in my head. Still, the voice persisted, unrelenting, on a daily basis. "Write a book," it continued unabated.

"I can't write a book," I said with finality, determined to put the issue to rest once and for all. Still the voice persisted. "Write a book!"

By now, more than a month and a half had passed since the story first came to me. I felt as if the Lord was the source of the voice, since the book had a Christian theme, but I wasn't sure. "Lord, why me? I have no religious training. I can't write a book. I'll be the laughing stock of my family and friends if I try to write a book," I reasoned.

Still the voice persisted, "Write a book!"

"Have my brother, Tom, write the book. He's a pastor," I argued to no avail, as the voice continued in my mind on a daily basis. Still I resisted the Lord. "I have no credentials, no agenda, no importance. No one will read what I write. I'm a nobody."

The story continued to abide inside me like a weight that pressed down on my soul. On more than one occasion, I made my way to the computer, where I sat staring at a blank screen, afraid to obey the voice in my head. *I'm going crazy*, I thought each time as I turned off the computer and went on my way, pushing the voice from my head.

Finally, near the end of May, as my family and I prepared to go out to our ranch to plant some evergreen trees, my thirteen-year-old daughter informed my wife and me that she had only one English assignment left before the end of school.

"Write a book," I suggested to her.

"You can't just sit down and write a book, Dad," she said disgustedly.

See, Lord, even a thirteen-year-old knows that, I thought to myself. Undeterred, I continued on. "Sure you can, if you try." She rolled her eyes before answering sarcastically, "Then you write a book!"

"Alright, I will," I answered as I sat down at the computer and began to type. About fifteen minutes later I nervously handed the first chapter to my daughter and watched as she read the words I had written. My nervousness grew as she handed it to one of my sons, who handed it to my wife when he was finished reading. My heart soared when each of them asked me repeatedly what would happen next. They were showing an honest interest in what I had written!

I continued to write over the next several months. The words tumbled out of my mind, through my gnarled fingers on the keyboard, showing up on the screen in front of me. Chapter by slow chapter the story began to emerge into print just as it had in my mind. I continued to write, through two bouts with pneumonia and a gall bladder attack that required surgery, until joyfully, the Tuesday before Thanksgiving, I printed off the final chapters of the book the Lord had given to me just before heading out to my brother's house thirteen hours away for the holiday.

During the trip, I couldn't help but reflect on the greatest book ever written and the men who wrote it. I wondered if God told them to write a book, persisting over and over until they obeyed in spite of their own misgivings and fears. I thought about the words they had written and the lives that had been changed by those words and was thankful they had heeded the Lord's call.

I know that in the grand scheme of things my book is unimportant. It's merely a work of fiction, written for people's enjoyment, but with a clear Christian message. I'm not sure why God gave the story to me or asked me to write it, but I hope and pray that my efforts in this endeavor glorify God and that it touches all who read it in a positive way just as the experience of writing it has touched me.

"Write a book," the voice said. So I did.

PROLOGUE

That stupid letter, Jay thought. *That stupid, annoying, exciting letter.*

It lay there on his computer desk, crumpled and stained from coffee spilled earlier in the day. It was only inches from his big toe as he sat with both feet propped up, arms folded behind his head. His eyes were fixed on the letter.

A grin spread uncontrollably across his face. Trying to reach the letter without sitting up, he lazily scooted it closer with his right foot. Instead, the letter slid to the edge of his desk and onto the floor, out of sight. He shot up.

Unwarranted panic stabbed through him, unchecked. Jay quickly slid his chair back, leaned down and grabbed the letter, banging his head on the way back up. He angrily threw the letter back on top of the desk, where it landed between an empty Coke can and a Ding Dong wrapper, the skeletal remains of his dinner.

Jay rubbed his head and stared at the letter for a few moments before retrieving it from the desk, his anger abating. He slowly turned the letter over, inspecting everything and seeing nothing. Having read the letter dozens of times already, every jot of ink, each baffling word was ingrained in memory. His eyes scanned the desk, coming to rest on the alarm clock sitting next to a dusty NIV Bible. Jay watched as the clock on the desk changed to 1:38 a.m., and then rubbed his eyes. He was always in bed before 10:00 p.m. Not tonight.

Slowly shaking his head in disbelief, Jay began to re-read the letter as somewhere nearby a neighborhood dog barked. *Just one more time.*

A few minutes later, he slowly stood up and walked down the hall to the kitchen in the dark. He opened the freezer and placed the letter on top of a nearly empty carton of mint chocolate chip ice cream, the paper flipping open so that the top corner arched up into the accumulated frost. After closing the door, he stood there for a moment before retrieving the letter on impulse. Walking across the room to a cupboard, he removed a sandwich bag and placed the folded letter in it. Jay returned to the freezer and once again placed the letter on top of the ice cream and closed the door. *Never can be too safe,* he thought, and then felt foolish for thinking it.

Jay took one last look at the freezer door, turned and walked back to his room, flipped off the light switch, and went to bed. But it was to no avail. Sleep eluded him as he tossed restlessly, thinking about the changes that single piece of paper had brought to his life—and wondering about the even greater changes it might bode for his future.

CHAPTER ONE

The letter arrived on a Monday, regular mail, with no return address. The postmark showed it was mailed just down the road. His name and address were handwritten, in precise calligraphy.

After a casual thought about who might have sent it, Jay tossed the letter onto the coffee table along with his other junk mail. The lack of return address made him a bit leery. Making envelopes appear handwritten seemed to be the latest trick for both credit card offers and charities. He wasn't about to get tricked into opening the letter just to be shamed into donating money.

Over the next several days more junk mail and old newspapers joined the letter on the coffee table, where it became part of an accumulated mess that was the decorative theme to his small home. Without anything to mark the transition, Monday became Friday in Jay's monotonous, every-day-the-same routine that he called life: up at 6:00 a.m., shower, make coffee, watch a little news and Sports Center, eat breakfast, and leave for work at 7:30. Jay always walked to work, rain or shine, hot or cold—and in Eastern Washington, the weather was an adventure every day.

The evening schedule was much the same following his walk home from work at 5:15 p.m. Saturday's main highlight was sleeping in, with the addition of a church service to denote Sunday morning before heading home to waste the rest of the day and then start the weekly cycle once more.

Seven years working as a salesman at the local lumberyard blurred together in just such a fashion. Beginning as a yard boy in high school, Jay had rapidly advanced to counter sales and stayed there ever since. Bob and Nancy Rosemont, who owned the yard and treated him more as a surrogate son than as an employee, encouraged him to attend management classes. They even offered to pay his way and his salary during the six-week course. He always politely declined the offer.

Jay had a lazy, boring life. He wouldn't change a thing.

Except, maybe, Anna.

※

Anna Johnson came into Jay's life three years ago, when she moved in with the Rosemonts to study for a doctorate at the local university. Charming, committed, and motivated, she was Jay's opposite in many ways. Yet despite their differences, she and Jay hit it off right away.

"Glowing with life," was how he described the petite young woman to a friend. "Raven hair, dark brown eyes, the face of an angel—but what you remember is how *alive* she is." In her presence, even if she was only there in his thoughts, Jay also felt more alive.

For nearly a year, Jay and Anna were inseparable. But that had all changed one evening sometime between Thanksgiving and Christmas two years ago, as Jay still painfully remembered.

Early in the evening their church had had a special speaker, a missionary from Ghana. He spoke of the work the church and God were doing to dispel the darkness in that country, bringing hope to the hopeless. A slideshow was filled with images of new homes being built to shelter families and children with bright eyes and smiling faces, eager for the food and love handed out with equal generosity. Jay, while initially moved by the powerful images and admiring the work of the volunteers, found himself drifting off to sleep toward the end of the presentation. There always seemed to be the same pictures of poverty and mud-covered workers in these talks.

After the service was over, Anna excitedly engaged the missionary in conversation. Jay tried his best to seem interested, but his mind wandered away to the NFL playoffs. His favorite team had made the playoffs, and was slated to play that night. Neither Anna nor the missionary seemed to notice his mental absence.

When Anna was finished talking to the missionary, she turned to Jay and asked, "Would you like to go out for dinner tonight, or do you need to return to your lair? I know how you need your beauty sleep and all."

"Sure," Jay replied as a fleeting look of disappointment spread across his face. He quickly looked at his watch, half wishing that Anna hadn't asked him this night. After all, his favorite team was playing, and with any luck he'd catch at least half of it.

"Then it's settled," said Anna, undeterred by his less-than-enthusiastic response. "Lets go!" she exclaimed as she led him out the door of the church by the arm.

Before they had even ordered at the restaurant, Anna started reflecting on the church service, her eyes aglow with passion. "Wasn't that a wonderful service?" Without waiting for an answer, she continued eagerly. "It's just amazing all the miracles that God has given those poor people of Ghana."

Jay scanned the overhead televisions that the restaurant had placed around their establishment to lure sports-crazy people like him out from in front of their TV sets at home. With any luck, he would catch the current score of the playoff game his team was in as it scrolled across the bottom of the TV.

"It really makes me excited to go over there to get started spreading God's Word."

Jay only halfway heard Anna. The score to the game he was interested in was starting to scroll across the bottom of the screen. His favorite team had just scored to take the lead, and he barely repressed an enthusiastic cheer.

Anna continued animatedly, her pretty face awash with emotion. "With my education and training in hydro-purification, it will be very easy to gain access to Ghana, or any other country God leads me to."

Jay nodded halfheartedly in agreement, too engrossed in the highlights to even realize what he was agreeing with.

"You should take some courses in a foreign language, or maybe a science course or two, and you could come with me." Thinking of her dreams, and sharing them with Jay, Anna didn't notice as the appetizers were delivered to their table.

"Uh-huh," Jay muttered back unintelligibly. "Sounds interesting."

The restaurant was starting to get very busy. Several different couples from church had shuffled in and greeted Anna and Jay with a nod or a wave. As the food arrived, Jay realized he was famished. He took a quick look around and uttered a short, hurried blessing for their meal. It seemed as if everyone turned to watch him pray. Which was the main reason that the only time he actually prayed in public was when Anna was with him. He thought it would disappoint her if he didn't pray, so he forced himself to utter a few words of thanks before ravenously attacking his food.

Anna slowly started to eat her salad. After a few moments, she put down her fork and looked across the table inquiringly. "Jay!"

No response.

"Jay!" Anna exclaimed.

Jay sat up straight. "What is it?" he asked as a look of confusion and guilt crossed his face.

"Were you even listening to me? Can you remember a single thing I've said?"

Jay just sat there and tried to remember what she had been saying earlier. He could feel his face growing red as his heart started to race. "Sure I remember. You were talking about the wonderful job the missionary was doing over in Ghana," Jay meekly responded in an attempt to placate Anna.

"And?" Anna shot back with the same intensity of a prosecutor cross-examining a witness.

Jay fidgeted with his fork, trying to remember anything, all the while searching Anna's face for any sign that might trigger his memory. His quick glances at her were met by a challenging stare from her large dark eyes. He could feel the back of his neck start to heat up. He wasn't used to being on the spot like this. Try as he might, nothing came to mind. Jay realized that he was busted. Once again, it felt as if the whole restaurant was looking at him.

Seeking a respite, Jay looked out the window into the parking lot. Leaves were swirling around on the pavement as a light rain started to fall, making everything glisten and shine under the lights of the parking lot. He noticed a steady stream of headlights as college students were lined up to turn onto the main highway out of town, ready to start their winter break. Try as he might, nothing else came to mind.

"Jay," Anna broke in again. "You weren't paying attention, were you?" she pressed on, her face set with determination.

"Well, I um ... was actually kind of ... um ... checking out the score of the football game, and kind of got excited over that," he replied with a sheepish half-smile on his face. "I know what you were talking about though," he added quickly as a brief glance at Anna revealed a disappointed look on her face. He took a drink of water before continuing, "It is wonderful what God is doing over, um, there." In his anxiety, Jay had forgotten which country they were talking about.

An indulgent smile relaxed Anna's face. "Oh Jay, what will I ever do with you?"

Jay felt relieved and started to eat again. "I guess I was kind of engrossed in the football scores and highlights," replied Jay in a feeble attempt at an explanation. "I'm sorry; I should have been listening to you."

Anna took a bite from her salad. After a few moments she started again. "What I was trying to say... was how excited I was to go over to Ghana and start my ministry after seeing the slide presentation tonight."

Jay's fork stopped in mid-air as disbelief and shock spread across his face. "What?" he asked incredulously. After a few moments he added, "You've got to be kidding, right?"

"Why would I be kidding?" Anna asked with an earnest, searching look on her face.

"To teach me a lesson for not listening."

"No," Anna answered. "I am totally sincere about this."

Jay was stunned. He set his fork down on his plate. The waitress came over to their table and asked if anything was wrong with the food. "No, it's just fine," Jay answered.

Jay looked around the restaurant as if searching for help. He wasn't sure what to say next. "What makes you all of a sudden want to up and go to Ghana, or some other remote part of the world for that matter? Was the slide presentation really that emotional to you?"

"It wasn't all of a sudden," Anna said, looking down at the table. "I've been planning this most of my life."

"I thought you were planning on being a scientist," Jay replied, still uncertain where this was going to end up.

"I am a scientist," Anna replied. "But I'm working on my doctorate so I can gain easy access to a foreign country to help them build their infrastructure. Most of these third world countries make it very difficult for a Christian missionary to enter the country, but welcome a scientist who happens to be a Christian."

"I thought you wanted your doctorate so you could get a really good paying job," Jay answered, his voice faint.

Anna sat quietly looking at Jay, dejection beginning to dominate the many emotions playing across her face. "When have you ever heard me talk about wanting a high-paying job? I've never even mentioned trying to get a high-paying job before."

By now, both dinners were completely forgotten. Jay nervously sipped on his soda. "I'm sorry," he said. "I guess I just assumed you wanted to teach or work for a big company or something like that."

The scenes on the television above Anna's head went completely unnoticed, the playoffs losing all appeal in the face of this startling news. "It's just that you've never mentioned anything before about being a missionary, at least not that I can remember."

"I haven't mentioned anything about being a missionary to you, but I have told you many times that I'm a servant of God."

"I know, but we are all servants of God, aren't we? At least we try to be. That doesn't mean that we have to be missionaries, does it?"

"Well, Jay, it does mean that to me," Anna answered patiently.

"Why does it mean that to you? Why would it be any different for you?" The question was importuning but sincere.

"Because He told me, Jay, because God told me," Anna replied solemnly. "I have been called to be a missionary since I was twelve years old, and I've been following His plan for my life ever since."

"Why can't you just be a missionary here, in Pullman? I think a lot of people right here need missionaries, and here we are sending good people off to all corners of the world to do over there what they could be doing right here in our own backyard." Jay's confidence started to rebound with the logic in his argument. "You could be a missionary right here, and I could help you," he said with a smile.

"That's what churches are for, Jay." Anna's steady gaze never left Jay's eyes. "I was kind of hoping maybe you would help me wherever God sends us."

"Sends *us?*" Jay asked incredulously. "You think I'm going to follow you all over the globe?"

"I thought maybe God was calling you to go too," Anna replied, her voice soft and questioning.

"Well He hasn't asked me to go anywhere." There was a hint of irritation in his tone. "Besides, what would I do, sell them lumber?" Jay asked sarcastically.

Anna was not to be deterred. "You could learn their language and spread God's Word while teaching them to build homes."

"I'm not going to run off and try and save the world, and I don't think you should waste your life trying to either." Jay regretted saying that the minute it came out of his mouth. He looked away to avoid seeing the pain that immediately sprang up in Anna's eyes.

Why did I have to say that? Well, at least Anna knew where he stood. This whole line of conversation was making him uncomfortable. True, there had been times when Jay had sensed that maybe he had the call of God on his life, but he had decided it was all just his emotions running away with him. Now he just wanted to move on to some safer topic.

"I gave my life to the Lord," Anna continued slowly. "Whatever God asks of me is what I'm going to do. I am willing to 'waste my life' if it pleases Him. I feel God has led me here, to this town, to prepare to go to the mission field when it's time. I also feel God led me to you, Jay. I feel you are the person God intends for me." Anna's voice dropped almost to a whisper. "You are the love of my life, Jay."

Jay sat there, stunned beyond words. He recognized his feelings for Anna were growing, but had often wondered how she felt about him. She was always kind and loving to him, but she was that way to everyone. Somehow the elation that should have come with Anna's revelation evaded him. She seemed so vulnerable in her admission, and part of him wanted to respond to that, wanted to be who she needed him to be, but he just sat there wondering if this was what being hit by a train felt like.

Their dinners were hardly touched. Somehow his hunger had completely left him. The noise of the other patrons, combined with the televisions, was starting to really annoy Jay. He didn't know what to say. Resorting to staring out the window once more, he watched as the rain began to intensify. Each drop seemed to fall twice, crashing down from the heavens and then rebounding up into the air before falling back to the pavement. They joined the rest of the drops that had become a small lake flowing into the storm drain.

Jay looked back at Anna. She had her head down, her eyes focused on her food. Slowly she raised her fork and started to take little bites, never raising her eyes to match his. Jay followed suit, but his steak and potatoes seemed to turn to chalk in his mouth. After what seemed like an agonizingly long time, their waitress came over.

"Is everything all right?" she asked.

Jay managed a quick "uh-huh" along with a short glance and a spiritless attempt at a smile.

"Could I interest either of you in dessert?" she asked with an irritating over-abundance of enthusiasm.

"None for me," they answered in unison.

The waitress set down a black book with the bill inside. "I'll be your cashier whenever you're ready," she told them with a smile.

Jay reached out and picked up the bill. He took enough money out of his wallet to cover the tab for both of them, along with enough for a generous tip.

"I'll get that," Anna said, holding out her hand.

"No, it's alright. I already got it," he answered as he handed the little book back to the waitress. "Keep the change."

The waitress thanked him, and wished them a cheerful "Happy Holidays."

Ugh, it is almost Christmas, Jay thought. He hadn't yet gotten into the holiday spirit, and would have a difficult time now, it seemed to him. He and Anna stood up at the same time and slowly put their coats on and walked to the door without saying a word to each other.

The pouring rain was nearly cold enough to have snow mixed in as they walked the mile or so home. Jay thrust his hands all the way into his pockets, and hunched his shoulders up as he dropped his head down, focusing on the ground in a vain attempt to keep the rain out of his eyes. His ears were starting to ache from the chill. Yet he barely noticed, so intent was he on sorting out the conversation that had so shaken his world.

In truth, Jay was very thankful for the rain. He knew they would both be soaked, but it prevented them from talking to each other all the way home.

They reached Anna's first. She turned to him slowly. "Would you like to come in for a while to warm up?"

"Not tonight. I need to get home and get some rest for work tomorrow."

"I could ask Uncle Bob to give you a ride. I'm sure he wouldn't mind."

"No, I'll be alright. I feel like walking."

"Are you sure?"

"Yeah, it'll be okay."

Anna looked at Jay, clearly unable to think of anything else to say to him. The rain had obscured the tears that escaped from her eyes on the walk from the restaurant, but the telltale signs were still obvious for anyone who cared, or had the courage, to see them.

"Maybe I'll call you tomorrow sometime," Anna said numbly.

"Yeah, okay, maybe," Jay answered with no enthusiasm.

"Be careful, and get yourself dry as soon as you get home."

"I will," Jay replied without ever making eye contact. With that he turned and walked out into the cold, wet night, welcoming the rain and thankful to be alone at last with his dark mood.

After that night Anna began to immerse herself in her school work with a renewed fervor, while Jay simply withdrew into himself, falling into the repetitive pattern of solitude that was now normal to him.

CHAPTER TWO

Twelve days had passed since Jay had received the letter. It now lay forgotten under a mountain of newspapers that had been accumulating on his coffee table along with other unopened junk mail and empty Coke cans. Every day, Jay added to the pile, and every day new papers and unopened mail slid off the table, over a pair of lost sneakers and onto the floor, forming a veritable river creeping outward toward the center of the living room. True to his bachelor status, the nagging thought that he should clean up the mess hadn't quite materialized into reality.

Day twelve started out the same as usual. Since it was a Saturday, Jay got up around 10:00 am and leisurely started his coffee. He loved Saturdays. He always read the paper front to back. After the paper, he would watch the news and then put in some serious channel-surfing time—unless he needed to break for a nap.

Keeping to schedule, Jay finished his breakfast of toast with strawberry jam at about 1:00 p.m. Channel surfing proving fruitless, he sauntered down the hallway to his bedroom, where he plopped himself onto his unmade bed and buried his face into his pillow.

Oh the life, he thought as he covered himself up with the blankets, enjoying the coolness of the sheets on his feet and legs. He slowly moved them around the bed, using up every bit of coolness, until the entire mattress was heated up to near body temperature. It didn't take long for him to drift off to sleep.

Bang, bang, bang… Bang, bang, bang…

Jay rolled over.

Bang, bang, bang…

He was barely conscious of the persistent noise bringing him out of a deep slumber.

Bang, bang, bang. There it was again.

This time Jay knew it was someone knocking at his door. He looked at his clock, 3:18 p.m.

Where's the day gone? he thought groggily, and then reluctantly rolled over and swung his legs over the edge of the bed. Jay held his head in his hands, trying to get his bearings.

Bang, bang, bang.

"I'm coming!" he yelled out blearily.

Whoever was at his door hadn't heard him and began obnoxiously pounding on his door again. *Bang, bang, bang.*

"Hold your horses!"

Jay was starting to get annoyed at whoever was knocking. He rose up off the bed and started across the floor, out the hall, and into his living room to the front door.

"Come in," he yelled out, wondering just who it might be. The door knob started to turn back and forth, but the door didn't budge.

"It's locked," came the muffled reply from the other side of the door.

The voice seemed very familiar to him, but if any bells went off in his head, they were subdued by the lingering vestiges of sleepiness. Jay had locked his door after getting his morning paper. "A sign of the times," he always told himself. It was a habit he had picked up over the years, even though there was very little crime in his hometown. He walked the short remaining distance to open his front door, his mood souring with every waking moment.

When he saw who was standing on the other side of his door, his heart raced a little and his ugly mood lifted. It was Anna.

CHAPTER THREE

"Hello there sleepy head," Anna greeted him with a smile. "Are you up for all day?"

"Um, well yeah, I was just taking a short nap," Jay said as he futilely tried to smooth his disheveled and matted hair with his fingers.

"Are you going to invite me in, or what?"

Suddenly self-conscious of the fact that he looked absolutely slovenly, Jay answered stiffly. "Sure, sorry 'bout that," he said as he awkwardly moved out of the way to let Anna come in. He was annoyed with himself for feeling so twitterpated at the mere sight of her.

"Sorry about the mess," he sheepishly added as they walked into his living room.

Anna surveyed the house. "From the looks of things, I would guess you forgot the singles' group is slated to meet here this evening for Bible study and snacks." There was a bit of humor in her voice. "I figured you'd forget. That's why I came early."

Jay placed his hands on his head in frustration and closed his eyes. "Oh, no!" he responded with a sense of dread in his voice. "I completely spaced it off. There's no way I can be ready by... what 5:00 p.m.?!"

"Sure you can, I'll help you get ready," she stated enthusiastically as she continued to assess all she could see of his house.

Her eyes focused on the mound of papers on the coffee table before following the cascading pieces of mail and sections of paper that had fallen and spread out onto the floor. There were at least twenty empty Coke cans, along with empty Danish or cupcake wrappers. Picking her way across the floor and into the kitchen, her eyes were met with an overflowing sink of dishes and a garbage can unable to hold all of its trash. If she was mad or disgusted, she didn't show it at all.

Jay was thoroughly embarrassed, seeing the mess with fresh eyes. "There's no way in the world I can be ready," he stated and pleaded with her all at the same time.

"We can be ready in no time if we get busy right now."

"I haven't even taken a shower or anything," Jay argued in vain. He knew Anna wouldn't take no for an answer. She was a take-charge kind of person with a "can do" attitude. While he was complaining, she was already taking a garbage bag from his pantry to deal with the overflow.

"You go ahead and take a shower and get cleaned up, and I'll tidy up in here until you're done. Then you can help me finish up." She bent to the task of picking up the loose garbage.

Jay just stood there looking around like a lost and bewildered sheep.

"Go on, hurry up, shoo, shoo," Anna directed him out of the kitchen and down the hall toward the bathroom.

Jay stopped at the hall closet to grab a towel and washcloth. He dashed into his bedroom to get some clean clothes, and looked around at the mess he lived in. "I have to change my ways," he muttered as he retreated out of his room.

Once in the little bathroom, he started the water and adjusted the temperature until it was just right. He could hear Anna singing to herself as she cleaned. *How can she always be so cheerful?* he asked himself. He recognized the song by a Christian rock band they had seen in concert together. Before he knew it, he was singing the lyrics right along with her while he took his shower. He put his head under the water and let it simply cascade down over his body, starting to come fully awake for the first time that day.

He couldn't believe he'd forgotten the Bible study was that night. He wasn't wild about hosting it, but it was hosted on a rotating basis every eight weeks, and this was his week. The leader of the group, who just happened to be Anna, passed out the schedules around the first of February and everyone was encouraged to write down their hosting dates on a calendar at home. But true to form, Jay had simply thrown his schedule onto his coffee table and subsequently scooped it into the trash.

Anna almost always reminded him when it was his turn. The problem this time was that he had missed the last two or three Bible studies and had failed to return the many calls she had made to him. *Oh well, that's what I get,* he thought.

The steam from the hot water rose up around him. Jay leaned his head on his forearm and closed his eyes. A large smile spread across his face. He couldn't help himself. Just the thought of Anna in his home made him extremely happy. He could imagine her vacuuming his living room carpet while humming a praise song. She was always so cheerful and lifted the spirits of everyone she came into contact with. Jay knew it was because of Anna's personal relationship with Christ. She was one of the few Christians he knew who totally lived up to their witness, not that he was judgmental. After all, the thought occurred to him, he was probably guilty of being a "Sunday Christian" himself.

Slowly his smile faded away. *Why does she have to be so intent on being a missionary? Can't she see how perfect we are for each other?* His mood started to spoil as his thoughts turned to the fateful conversation that had driven them apart. He had debated this issue over and over in his mind for the past two years. Every now and then he caught himself thinking about becoming a missionary, just so he could be with Anna. Luckily, he always came to his senses and pushed those thoughts out of his head. He felt some shame at admitting it, but he had even prayed that God would change Anna's mind just so he could be with her.

Pushing all thoughts of his broken dreams with Anna out of his mind, he vigorously shook the water out of his eyes and began shampooing his hair. His conscience urged him to hurry so he could help Anna clean, but he found he had an insurmountable lack of motivation.

❧

Jay finished his shower and turned the water off. He grabbed the towel from the towel rod and quickly dried off. Waiting for the steam to clear out, he dressed before trying to check out his hair in the mirror. The mirror was still fogged, so he just ran his fingers through his hair and slapped on some aftershave, perhaps a little too liberally. Stepping back into the living room, he felt instantly guilty. He had taken a much longer shower than he had intended.

"Feel better?" Anna asked from the couch.

"Yes, a lot," he answered with surprise and appreciation at the sight that greeted him. The room was completely spotless. "Sorry I took so long. I never intended to leave all of this clean-up for you."

"That's alright, I didn't mind at all. After all, that's what friends are for."

"Really, so all this time I've had it wrong. I thought friends were for fellowship and fun," Jay said teasingly.

Anna smiled. "Oh, I had fun helping a friend out, and now it's time for fellowship."

"Well thank you very much, Mademoiselle! I am forever grateful." Jay grinned back and bowed with a flourish before walking into the kitchen to retrieve a Coke. "Would you like a soda or something?"

"Sure, if you have an extra one, please."

He opened the refrigerator and grabbed two cans of Coke. Out of the corner of his eye he noticed a neat little pile of mail on his counter under his phone and the True Value calendar that hung on the wall. Jay hesitated, then turned and picked up the stack of mail.

There were three items. The first was the power bill that he hadn't been able to find earlier that week when he was paying his bills. *Well this is late,* he said to himself as he opened up the envelope and looked at the bill. Sure enough, the due date was June sixteenth.

The second item was a renewal for the *Sporting News*. *Garbage,* he thought as he wadded it up and tossed it in the freshly emptied trash can.

The third item took him a few seconds to remember. It was a plain white envelope with his name and address handwritten and with no return address on it.

Anna came walking in to the kitchen. "What's taking you so long? Did you have to milk the Coca-Cola cow you keep in here?"

"I got distracted. The help forgot to tell me I had mail," he teased.

"Oh yeah, I meant to tell you I found some mail you had under your newspapers for safekeeping," Anna shot back sarcastically, followed by a smile and a roll of her eyes.

Jay smiled back. "Oh well, it's just two pieces of junk and one bill, nothing too exciting."

"I thought there were two bills and one letter, not that I was snooping or anything," Anna innocently replied. "Matter-of-fact, I'm sure of it."

"No, one was a power bill, one was a magazine renewal, and one was a solicitation for a donation or something. I never open magazine renewals or solicitations," he explained. "They're both a total waste of time." With that he tossed the unopened envelope after the magazine renewal notice.

Anna walked over and fished it out of the trash. "You're nuts. This is a letter if I've ever seen one. You can't just throw this away."

Realizing the only way to be done with the obnoxious piece of mail was to open it, Jay reluctantly took it back from Anna. Turning it over in his hands and really looking at it for the first time, he noticed the handwriting. It did look somewhat familiar to him. Just then someone started to knock on his door.

Anna ran from the kitchen to answer the door.

Jay looked back at the envelope in his hand and slowly opened the top edge. He slid the folded letter out, noticing it was typed on heavy stationary of some sort. *I knew it was a solicitation,* he thought as he unfolded the letter. *Only people soliciting money send expensive paper like this.*

Nevertheless, he slowly began to read the letter. His hands started shaking, slightly at first, and then much harder the further down he read. He finished reading the letter and re-examined the envelope, placing his right hand on his forehead in a posture of disbelief. After a quick scan he read the letter once again, holding it in one hand while rubbing his still-damp hair with the other. People were now talking and laughing in the living room, but he dashed over to the counter where his calendar hung on the wall and quickly scanned the days of the month. A sense of panic flooded through his entire body, stealing the breath from his lungs. He re-read the letter and looked at the calendar again.

"Jay, is everything all right?" Anna asked.

Jay spun around and shoved the letter in his pocket. "Yeah, I'm fine." His voice sounded unfamiliar even to himself.

"Is there something wrong? You look as if you've just seen a ghost." A note of concern was rising in Anna's voice.

Jay's right hand instinctively covered the pocket the letter was in. "No, I mean … yes, I mean no … everything is fine."

"We'd better get in there," he added before Anna had a chance to ask anything else. With that, he turned and walked into the living room, his right hand never leaving his pocket, guarding whatever was in it as if it were a treasure—or a plague.

CHAPTER FOUR

Jay walked into his living room. Before he could see who was there, he was greeted with, "Hey, Cous,' how's it going?"

The question stopped him in his tracks as his eyes squinted in a suspicious glare, searching for the source of the inquiring voices. Directly in front of him, sitting comfortably on his couch, were Jacob and Stewart. They were two of his uncle Milt's kids.

"What are you guys doing here?" His voice was heavy with accusation as he continued his challenging stare at the two young men sitting on his couch.

"Well, we're happy to see you, too," Stewart replied sarcastically, looking both shocked and hurt by Jay's rude greeting.

"What do you mean, what are we doing here?" Jacob replied at the same time, appearing confused by his cousin's cold greeting. "We're here for the Bible study, if that's okay with your highness."

Undaunted by their replies, Jay continued his assault. "Since when did you start being interested in these things?"

"Well, we've attended the last three Bible studies, if that's what you mean," Stewart replied defensively. "I noticed you weren't at any of them though," he added, his tone taking on an edge of accusation in return.

Anna stepped in between the two of them. "What in the world is wrong with you guys? You act as if you can't ~' other or something."

As suspicion gave way to shame, Jay looked down at the floor. "Sorry, I was just really surprised to see you here tonight."

Sensing an opening, Jacob took the opportunity to counter assault. Only seven months separated Jay and his eldest cousin, and they had never gotten along well over the years. "You could have at least welcomed us or something, or acted as if you were even a little happy to see your own family." He added with a tinge of hurtful admonishment in his voice, "But why pretend, right?"

Jacob's words hit home. Jay felt absolutely terrible. He couldn't think of anything to say. Evidently none of them could. Jacob and Stewart sat on the couch looking at the floor, while Anna and Jay awkwardly shifted their weight from one foot to the other. As the silence dragged on for what felt like forever, Stewart finally rose and headed for the kitchen. "Well, truth be told, I just came to see Anna, and to mooch free soda from my wealthy cousin," he joked as he opened the refrigerator.

What's he mean by that wealthy cousin crack? Jay wondered as suspicion flared into life once more.

"I am glad you're here," he replied less-than-convincingly. "I just wasn't expecting you, it's not that I mind."

"Thanks for the reassuring vote of confidence," Stewart said as he walked back into the living room. He tossed a full Coke to Jacob without missing a step. "We can feel the love just oozing out of you."

Jacob sat stone-faced, but at least he wasn't scowling anymore. Jay looked completely embarrassed, one hand jammed down into his pocket.

"Oh you guys," Anna exclaimed. "Enough is enough!" She was deeply puzzled by Jay's sudden mood change. His rude outburst was totally out of character for him. She knew he could be moody and opinionated, but she'd never seen him behave this way before. She made a mental note to call him on it later, after everything settled down.

Before anyone could respond, relief came for all four of them in the form of more knocks at Jay's door.

"You really need to get a door bell, Cous,'" Stewart kidded. "Maybe after our service tonight we can take up a collection to help you buy one."

"You're so funny," Jay answered back as Anna opened the door.

She ushered three more people into the room. "Come on in, you're almost late."

A young man with long frizzy black hair tied back in a pony-tail came over and gave Jay a big hug. "Happy to see you, man," he earnestly stated as the two of them separated. "It's been awhile."

"Yeah, Bill, I guess I've kind of been out of the loop lately," Jay replied. "Bible study was at your house last week wasn't it?"

"Yeah man, full house too."

"Sorry I missed it; I guess I'm turning into kind of a hermit in my old age."

"It's all good." Bill clapped Jay on the shoulder. "Solitude is good for the soul from time to time."

Jay found himself truly relaxing for the first time that strange evening. Bill always had that effect on him. Well, at least since his friend's winding road had brought him back home to Jesus after rebelling against his parents' Christian values. Starting with the usual teenage defiance at the age of sixteen, Bill was fully into every kind of drug there was by the time he graduated high school. He left home and wandered the streets of Spokane to live the "alternative" lifestyle, losing himself in the drugs, and devoting his life to anarchism as his parents looked on with broken hearts.

Like so many of his peers, Bill finally hit rock bottom and came back home to Pullman. He entered a drug treatment program and slowly started to put his life back together. That's when he became reacquainted with Jay. Every so often, he would have to stop in the lumber yard for parts needed for his new job as an electrician, and he always took the time to say "Hi" to Jay. After the third or fourth visit, Bill asked Jay if he remembered who he was. Jay just looked at him, unsure until Bill reminded him that they had grown up together and even attended the same church as kids. Jay was dumbfounded and apologized several times. He absolutely did not recognize Bill. He was nothing like the boy Jay remembered. He had gone from being a clean-cut, straight-laced conservative Christian boy to a long-haired, hippy-talking, chain-smoking rebel with tattoos up and down his arms. Both of Bill's ears were pierced several times, and his left eyebrow had some sort of weird spike through it. Bill was almost freakish looking, Jay thought at the time.

From that point on, they visited every time they saw each other and soon became best friends. Jay was actually Bill's only real friend at the time. Even so, it never crossed Jay's mind to invite Bill back to church. He just never even considered it. Bill probably still wouldn't be in church if it wasn't for Anna's witness two years earlier.

She and Jay had been out for one of their dinner dates when Bill walked in. Jay greeted Bill and introduced him to Anna. Before he knew what was happening, Anna had invited Bill to join them for dinner. Bill accepted somewhat reluctantly, but by the end of dinner he was completely at ease with both of them. They spent three hours together visiting as if they had always been the best of friends. Bill confided in them many of his life's troubles and trials, things he hadn't even told his drug counselor. Anna listened with complete sincerity, and afterward asked Bill if she could pray with him. Bill felt somewhat awkward, but said, "Whatever floats your boat." As they left the restaurant and said their good-byes, Anna invited Bill to the next day's Bible study for singles. Bill reluctantly accepted, and after a few months, recommitted his life to the Lord. He hadn't missed a Bible study or a church service since. As a matter-of-fact, he started a second chance outreach program through the church for people trying to get off of meth or other drugs.

Jay turned his attention to the other two people who had entered his apartment with Bill. Beth and Susan were two people Bill was helping. They were both in their late twenties, but looked much older as a result of their lifestyle. They were now regulars and had committed their lives to God, too. A lot of the older church attendees looked down their noses at Bill and his friends, but if he noticed it, he just ignored it. Bill was on fire for the Lord.

Beth and Susan ran up to Jay and gave him a big hug before handing him a bag. "Here are some cookies we made for the fellowship," Beth said as she handed them to Jay.

"Half are oatmeal with chocolate chips and the other half are oatmeal raisin," Susan added.

"What about peanut butter cookies?" Jay asked good-naturedly. "You know those are my favorite."

"We'll make peanut butter for you next time," Beth smiled. "But what kind will you make for all of us?"

"I don't make cookies. Maybe someone could help me, though," he hinted to Anna.

"Oh, I'll help you make some cookies, *if* your kitchen is clean," Anna teased back.

More knocks came at Jay's door. Surprised at the continuing influx of guests for the Bible study, he hurried into the kitchen with Anna to retrieve all of the chairs from around his table. There were a total of five kitchen chairs that were quickly claimed. By five-thirty there were twenty-one singles crammed into Jay's little living room. As he looked around, he realized that three quarters of the group were new people that Anna had brought into the church. *She is amazing,* he thought.

Jay had completely depleted his refrigerator of Cokes and had taken out two cases from his pantry. Luckily he had a lot of glasses, and his fridge had an ice maker. No one likes warm Coke. A few more people brought cookies that were quickly scarfed down by the large crowd.

"Man, I'm really sorry," Jay told Anna as they watched the last cookie being eaten. "Since I forgot about tonight, I didn't stock up on any refreshments,"

"That's okay. We're here mainly for your good company," she said with a wink.

"Sorry I was acting so funny tonight." Jay unconsciously felt at the letter through his pants pocket. "I'm better now."

"I noticed, and I'm glad."

Jay's house was starting to get very warm with all of the bodies in it. He walked through the maze of people and turned on the air conditioner. "That should be better."

"Hey man, thanks a lot. I was going from medium to well done in a hurry," Bill responded.

It was 6:30 p.m. They hadn't even started the Bible study yet. He looked around the room. His couch and loveseat were completely full. All of the chairs were full, and his recliner had two people in it. There were an additional nine people sprawled across his floor. Jay walked over to where his hallway met the living room.

"I want to thank everyone for coming tonight," he stated enthusiastically. "Anna is going to lead us in some praise songs, and then the lesson. First, I'd like to ask Bill if he would lead us in prayer, though."

"Sure, anything you want, man."

With that, the Bible study started.

Jay sat under his living room window, facing Anna. The descending sun was starting to shine through the curtains covering the window and onto Anna. It gave her the appearance of glowing. *Almost angelically,* Jay thought to himself.

The sun's rays were also shining into his living room mirror directly behind Anna and reflecting back onto Jay. For a moment, Anna's eyes locked with Jay's large, steel-grey eyes while she sang. She smiled at him as she let her eyes rove over his freckled face, dark and curly hair, and strong square chin. Jay felt his pulse quicken when their eyes met again, Anna's shining with warmth. There was no denying the chemistry between them even now.

As Anna started the Bible study by reading 1 Corinthians 13, Jay was having a hard time focusing. He ran his hand back and forth over the distracting letter in his pocket and then self-consciously scanned the room to see if anyone had noticed.

His gaze stopped on his cousins. His smile left his face and he shook his head slightly from side to side, still confused about their presence. Stewart he could almost understand. His much younger cousin was extremely good-natured and got along with just about everybody. Although Jay had never really spent that much time with him, he usually enjoyed his company whenever he was around.

He continued to feel the letter in his pocket and in spite of himself broke into a huge grin. Jay quickly glanced around to see if anyone noticed him. *Get a grip on yourself,* he thought. But no one seemed to notice.

Jay looked at Anna. She was talking about the power of God's love. Almost everyone was listening intently. As always, there were a few people who had checked out mentally as soon as the lesson started, and Jay felt a little guilty as he realized he was one of those people tonight.

Jay did his very best to give Anna his full attention. He kept his eyes focused on her intently for fifteen or twenty minutes. She was so pretty, he felt as if he could watch her all day. Every now and then Anna would make eye contact with Jay, causing his heart to leap with joy. *Why am I doing this to myself?* he thought. *There is no way we will ever be a couple again.* Jay determinedly looked away from Anna.

He slowly looked around the room. He was surprised at the number of people he didn't know. *I guess it's been few and far between, as far as my attendance goes.* Another pang of guilt hit Jay. Then he realized he had hardly eaten anything all day.

Trying not to make a disturbance, he rose up and gingerly made his way to the kitchen. Anna looked at him questioningly, but continued on with her lesson.

Several people were interjecting their thoughts, and then the group would discuss whatever point was trying to be made. It sometimes made for interesting debate. It was amazing how many different meanings could be taken out of one small passage of the Bible. *I guess that's why there are so many different denominations,* he thought to himself as he began rummaging through his cupboard drawers.

After a few moments, he pulled out a phone book, an old ballpoint pen, and a scrap piece of paper he had saved for reasons long forgotten. He started flipping through the yellow pages of the phone book until he found the section he was looking for. It was a well-used section of the book. He scanned down the columns and quickly jotted down a number before placing the phone book back into the drawer. After scribbling down a few more lines, Jay picked up the phone, dialed, and then waited until someone answered.

"Pizza Pipeline," the voice on the other end of the line said.

"Yes, I'd like to place an order," Jay said into the receiver, cupping his hands around the phone so he could talk quietly into it.

"Just one moment sir," the female voice said on the other end.

Jay could hear Anna talking. "Hurry, hurry, hurry," he said into the receiver.

Finally the voice on the other end of the phone came back on. "Sorry for the delay."

"That's alright," Jay replied.

"I can take your order now."

Jay proceeded to order ten large pizzas of various kinds. He also ordered forty eight cans of assorted soda pop.

"That will be $228.50 sir."

Jay gasped. "Um, okay, can I pay for it over the phone?"

"Sure, credit or debit?"

"Debit," Jay answered as he reached for his wallet, retrieving his debit card. He read the numbers to the voice and added a thirty dollar tip.

PRICELESS

The voice read the order back and said, "The total is $258.50 with tax and tip."

Jay swallowed his regret over the compulsive purchase he just made. "Yes, how long will that be, Miss?" This was a lot of money for him. He did make a decent living, but he spent it almost as fast as he made it.

"It'll be thirty minutes sir. Could I get your address and phone number?"

Jay gave the young woman his address and phone number, checked the time, and hung up.

Wow, that's a lot of money, he thought again and giggled nervously. He looked at the clock on his kitchen wall. It read 7:45 p.m. The Bible study was almost always over by 8:00. Hopefully tonight Anna would be long-winded, or he'd have a lot of pizza to eat.

Jay walked back to the living room. He leaned against the wall, just next to his living room mirror. The room was finally starting to cool down. Beth was asking how it was possible for her to love the people that had sold her and her friends meth, knowing there were kids that were being introduced to the drug for the very first time every single day by these people.

This ought to be interesting, Jay thought. Anna stood there a moment before answering.

"You have to forgive them, and love them the same as Jesus did for each one of us. All sin is equal in God's eyes, and these people are lost to Him. Jesus died for each one of our sins, no matter how despicable or terrible they were, no questions asked, and He loved us while dying. To fully accept the gift of grace that he extends, we must both ask for forgiveness, and forgive those that have sinned against us. Not only forgive them, but love them wholly." No one said anything for a few moments. People were starting to fidget around, becoming restless and tired.

"I hear what you're saying, but it's just so hard. These people have hurt me and my family so badly," Beth responded, bursting into tears. She stood up, all hunched over. Not one person moved or said anything. Anna walked over to Beth and put her arm around her.

"I know it hurts, and I know it's hard, but you have to be able to forgive and love those who wronged you, with the help of Jesus. You have to take responsibility for your actions and trust God to come into your heart and make your soul as pure and as fresh as snow. If you forgive them, love them, and pray for them every day, somehow, by the grace of God, they may be saved. They may be in the same position you are today, leading others whose lives seem hopelessly lost to the love of Jesus Christ."

Shaking his head in agreement, Bill affirmed Anna's message with a heartfelt "Amen!"

Jay looked around. Some of the people were crying, some of them were laughing, and some of them were nodding their heads in agreement. One thing was certain though, they were all paying attention.

"I love you, I love all of you!" Beth exclaimed, tears running down her face. "Thank you so much for accepting me and for helping me to get from where I was to where I am today."

Anna gently pulled Beth's head to her chest. "We love you too!" she responded as tears welled up in her eyes.

She really is a servant of God, Jay thought as he watched Anna with admiration. Why did she think she had to go off to a foreign country to do His work? She was making such an impact right here.

"I think we should pray now. It's getting kind of late, and we do have Sunday school and church tomorrow!" Anna reminded them, emphasizing the Sunday school part. Everyone bowed their heads as Anna offered a prayer of thanksgiving to God.

After the prayer, people starting visiting and milling around as much as they could in the limited space.

"Are we having refreshments tonight?" Jacob asked.

"I think we had most, if not all of them, before the Bible study started," Anna replied.

Jay raised his hands out in front of his face, "Hold on, hold on, I ordered some pizza for everyone."

His proclamation was met with enthusiastic exclamations, "All right!" "Yeah, Cool."

"Hey Cous, did you win the lottery or something?" Stewart yelled at Jay.

Jay whirled around and glared at him. As soon as his brain caught up to his actions, his neck and face began turning red in embarrassment. Anna raised her eyebrows at him in surprise. She walked over to him, "You didn't have to do that."

"I know. I just wanted to."

The knock on the door from the pizza delivery man was greeted with cheers. Someone opened the door and exclaimed, "Man, are we glad to see you! Come in, come in." The delivery man set his carrying case down, opened it and started passing out large steaming pizza boxes.

"Take them to the kitchen," Anna directed.

"I have two cases of soda pop in the car," the pizza man told them.

"I'll come give you a hand," Bill offered. Out they went to the idling car.

"Are you having some kind of party?" Jay heard the delivery man ask Bill.

"We're having a celebration, man" Bill responded.

"What kind of celebration?"

"Well bro, let me tell you…" Bill stated as the delivery man opened his trunk.

Jay walked into the kitchen. Half of the pizzas had already disappeared out of the boxes. Several people came up and thanked Jay.

Anna came into the kitchen, walked over to Jay, and tried to hand him some money. "Here, I want to help with the pizza."

"No, that's all right, I already got it."

"That was a lot of money, Jay!"

"It wasn't that bad," Jay answered. "Nice lesson tonight." He tried to change the subject.

"Thank you, but I would feel a lot better if you would at least let me help a little."

"Anna, I wanted to do this for the group tonight. Besides, it's not that big of a deal."

Anna stood looking at Jay, trying to figure out what had come over him. His mood had gone from being almost grumpy to downright giddy. It just wasn't normal for him. And now, with him buying all this pizza and pop, well it was just out of character for him.

Jay worked his way back through the throng of people and into the living room. About half of the people had cleared out and the remaining people were busy talking to each other. Jay spotted an empty spot on his couch next to Bill. He slid around two people on the floor deep in conversation with each other, sidestepped a third, and fell onto the couch with a thud. Bill raised his right fist up toward Jay in greeting. Jay responded by banging his right fist against Bill's.

"Hey dog, nice party," Bill greeted Jay.

"No problem, man."

Bill extended his left hand, fingers clenched shut on something. "Let me slip you a little jingle to help out with din." Jay could see bills of unknown denomination between his friend's fingers.

"No, it's no problem. Just something I wanted to do. Thanks for the offer though."

Bill let his left hand hang there elevated slightly over Jay's right arm for a few moments, then slowly pulled it back and slid the money into his pant's pocket.

"Right on bro, I ain't going to argue with The Man." Jay felt self-conscious, almost embarrassed, and he wasn't sure why. "Love, love, love. That's the theme for tonight, and I'm diggin' it."

Jay just sat there. He found it hard to respond to Bill at times.

His hand rested on the pocket that contained the letter, and his fingers traced around the bulky outline of the envelope through his pants. Jay hated to admit it, but on more than one occasion when he was by himself he would try to talk like Bill. "Hey dog, what's happenin'?" He would say to his image in the mirror. He sounded funny to himself and looked foolish too. He resigned himself to the fact that he just wasn't cool.

"Speakin' of love, dog, how's that little love interest of yours doing?" Bill asked as he nodded toward Anna.

"There's nothing happening on that front," Jay responded somewhat downcast.

"What? You have to be kidding. Everyone knows she's the alpha to your omega."

"She has her own life and goals, and I have mine. Unfortunately they don't match. I wish they did, but they just don't."

"What do ya mean? You two are a perfect couple, man." Bill continued to press the issue. "What goals do you have anyway that are that much different from hers?"

Jay didn't answer. *What are my goals?* He thought to himself. The truth was, he didn't have any discernable goals.

"Anna has a definite set of plans for the foreseeable future. Where she's going and what she's going to do are very different than what I want to do," Jay stated in a feeble attempt to satisfy Bill's inquiry.

"Yeah but, I mean, what are your goals, man?"

Jay was becoming annoyed at Bill's relentless questioning. "She wants to become a missionary and I don't, okay?" Jay responded with more than a hint of irritation in his voice.

"No problem."

"I'm sorry. The whole thing just kind of annoys me. Sorry I snapped at you."

"It's all good," Bill answered, unfazed by Jay's outburst. "But what are your goals?"

Jay just shook his head, unsure of what to say next. "I don't know for sure, I really don't know. Not being a missionary is all I'm sure of."

Most of the people had said their good byes and gone on their way. There were still five or six people sitting around talking to each other. Jay and Bill were the only two left on the couch. Anna was in the kitchen. Jay could hear her cleaning up in there.

"You gotta get some goals for your life. You aren't getting any younger man."

"Why the sudden interest in my life, anyway?"

"I just wandered around wasting my life for several years looking for something, but having no idea what it was I was looking for. Then I came back home, became re-acquainted with you and met Anna, and the two of you helped lead me back to Christ. Since then, since I recommitted my life to the Lord, I've had clarity in what I'm supposed to do with my life. Believe me brother; the truth has set me free."

"Maybe I have a clear direction for my life already," Jay responded unconvincingly.

"All I'm askin' is what your clear vision is," Bill persistently questioned.

"What's your clear vision, then?" Jay replied tersely.

"Well, man, I've been instructed to reach down, grab my lost brothers and sisters from despair, from the monster that grips their lives, and raise them up to the light. Raise them up to the Son, and to help them keep the monster from getting its death grip on them. Anyway necessary, anyhow possible!" Bill finished his statement by slamming one hand with a clenched fist into the palm of his other hand.

"I know, and you've done a remarkable job. We're all proud of you," Jay answered, not sure what else to say.

"I haven't told anyone else this, but I feel as if the Lord is leading me to open a clinic or a home. You know, a kind of halfway house, second chance pad or something like that. I don't know where I'll get the money for it, but I know the Lord will provide one way or another if that really is His plan for me. You see, I look at myself as a fisher of men, and I'm here to tell you, the schools of fish are getting bigger day by day."

They both fell silent. Jay didn't know what to say. He admired the things Bill was doing, but those things weren't for him, were they?

CHAPTER FIVE

Everyone had gone home with the exception of Anna, Jacob, Stewart, Beth, and Susan, who were all in the kitchen. Of course Jay and Bill were still on the couch. Slowly the group in the kitchen started to migrate out into the living room.

Jacob and Stewart headed for the front door. "See ya'll tomorrow," Jacob said as he half bowed, tipping his imaginary hat to the rest of the group.

"Catch ya on the flip side," Stewart chimed in, rolling his fingers down into a fake pistol, pointing at the group as if he were a gun slinger, then holstering his hand pistol into an imaginary holster.

"Thanks for coming over," Anna responded. "See you in church tomorrow."

"We'll try to make it," Stewart half-promised.

"Thanks for having us over, Cous," Jacob said somewhat sarcastically. "We'll be seeing you later."

"Yeah whatever," Jay answered with annoyance in his voice, his hand firmly resting over the letter in his pocket. With that, Jacob and Stewart closed the door with a thud.

Anna turned and looked at Jay. "That was kind of rude of you," she stated matter-of-factly.

"Oh well, they're big boys, they'll get over it," Jay replied with no hint of remorse in his voice.

"It still wasn't very nice, or Christian-like." Anna wouldn't give up on it.

"They have a way of annoying me is all. They don't take me seriously anyway."

"I hope we don't annoy you too," Susan said shyly.

"No, everyone is just fine, it's just me. I've been kind of uptight lately."

"Uptight? You've been downright moody, I'd say," Anna chided him.

"Yo, ease up on my man. The big dog has a lot he's working out, you know, with the main Man upstairs." Bill attempted to defend Jay but only succeeded in annoying him even more.

"No, really I'm sorry if I made anyone feel uncomfortable or unwelcome. It really wasn't my intention," Jay offered meekly.

For a few moments nobody said a word. Anna had a small frown on her face and fixed her gaze out the window on nothing in particular. Susan just looked at the floor. She was a very shy girl and really didn't know how to act in uncomfortable situations. Bill fiddled around with the top to his Coke can. Rarely was he at a loss for words. Beth had a very bubbly personality. She was the one that broke the tension of the moment.

"Well I for one am very appreciative of your wonderful hospitality. You allowed us the use of your home and even ordered pizza for us. What more could a person ask for? As a matter-of-fact, I'm going to give you a great big hug."

That's when disaster struck. Beth started to lean down to give Jay a hug with one arm while balancing her cup of coffee in her other hand. As she leaned down, her left foot caught Jay's tennis shoe on his left foot and over she went, falling right onto Jay's leg, dumping her half full cup of hot coffee onto his lap and the hand that covered the letter in his pocket. Jay could feel the warm liquid run through his fingers and onto his pants directly over the letter. Complete instant panic erupted inside of Jay. He looked like a wind up Jack-in-the-box that had just been wound one turn past the maximum tension point, exploding up into the air, landing in the center of his living room floor.

Poor Beth, who was very petite, went flying off of Jay's leg as if she was a feather. She landed on the arm of the couch before toppling onto the floor on her head and shoulder, coffee cup still clutched tightly in her hand, a slight screech escaping out of her mouth.

In the mean time, Bill reacted just as quickly as Jay, sliding out of the couch and down onto the floor in an attempt to keep from getting wet from the coffee. During his acrobatic moves, his legs flew out and hit Susan right above the knees, knocking Susan backwards into Anna, who fell against Jay and slid down onto the floor.

Jay hardly noticed Anna falling into him. He was still in a state of panic and flung her off of him as he started to run down the hallway and into his bedroom, slamming the door closed and locking it behind him while simultaneously pulling the letter out of his pocket and flinging it across the room. It hit the wall above his bed and slid down and out of sight next to his bed onto the floor and into no man's land.

Jay quickly climbed out of his wet pants and flung himself onto his bed, reaching his arm down to the floor in the same spot where the letter had disappeared only moments before. He felt around on the floor. Nothing but carpet and lint. He quickly rolled off of the bed and onto the floor. He reached his arm under the bed as far as he could until his shoulder bumped up against the frame. Slowly, he moved his arm back and forth hoping to feel even a tiny portion of the letter. The only thing he felt was carpet and his dress shoes that he hadn't been able to find for a couple of years. Carefully, Jay withdrew his arm.

Dread was slowly replacing his initial panic. Unwarranted and illogical as it was, Jay's gut was starting to constrict with a feeling bordering on pure terror. Hesitantly, he got to his feet. He couldn't figure out where the letter could be. He fought off the urge to completely tear his bed apart until he found it. Jay forced himself to take a big breath and exhale slowly. He knew the letter had to be right there under his nose.

Slowly he climbed back onto the bed and pulled his covers back until he could see down onto the floor. It was very dark, but his eyes began adjusting to the light. Carefully he scanned the floor until he caught a glimpse of something white and somewhat shiny. It was near the end of the bed. Jay reached down until his fingers felt wet paper and cautiously slid the letter to himself until he could get a finger on either side of the envelope. He pulled it up until it was clear of the bed, and held it in front of him.

The envelope was wet around the edges. Slowly he opened it and gingerly removed the letter. It was a good thing the letter was written on expensive stationary. The stock was about three times as thick as regular paper. About half of the letter was wet with coffee and was starting to turn mocha brown. Jay was very careful to not smudge the writing. He slowly unfolded the letter and set it on his bed, inspecting it for damage. It was wet, but otherwise intact.

Jay started to read the letter again. A smile slowly emerged on his face followed by a relieved chuckle. He couldn't help himself. He shook his head in disbelief. Suddenly a loud series of bangs on his door startled him back to reality.

"Jay, are you alright in there?" Anna asked, concern in her voice. "Jay, are you okay?"

"Yes, I'm fine. I'll be right out." Jay responded, turning to locate some dry pants. He grabbed up the letter and placed it on his desk and then set his Bible on top of it. Jay spotted a pair of shorts and quickly slid them on. He turned and, with one quick glance back at his letter, opened his door and went down the hall and into the living room.

"Oh Jay, are you all right?" Beth and Susan chimed in at the same time.

"Yes I'm okay, I just overreacted is all."

"I'll say," Anna exclaimed as she looked at Jay wide-eyed. "You looked like a wild man for a minute."

"I'm so sorry, Jay. I hope I didn't burn you," Beth exclaimed, tears welling up in her eyes. "I'm such a klutz."

"Hey sister, the dog says he's top notch," Bill added. "Don't sweat it."

"Yeah, it was just an accident. It could have happened to anyone. Besides, I probably deserved it, the way I was acting earlier."

"Yes, you probably did," Anna chided.

They all laughed, except for Beth, who was still struggling to keep from crying. Slowly she came around.

"Well, I hate to leave a good party, but my ride is going to turn back into a pumpkin soon, so I'd better take these ladies and be off." Bill walked to the door followed by the three girls. He opened the door and gestured for the girls to go out first. After they had all gone outside, Bill bowed to Jay and walked out. "That was one wild and crazy time," he said as he closed the door.

Anna yelled back at him, "See you in church tomorrow," and away the four of them went.

Jay sat down slowly in his recliner. He was tired and famished. He hadn't eaten a single thing. He rose up off his chair and walked into his kitchen and turned on the light. It made a very distinct humming sound, as do most fluorescent lights. Slowly Jay looked around for some pizza. The light blue counter tops were all cleared off and washed. Not a sign of pizza to be found. Jay walked over to his refrigerator and opened the door expecting to find some pizza, but to no avail. The pizza was all gone.

"Man, I can't believe they ate all of that pizza," Jay said to himself as he moved things around in his refrigerator.

After a few more moments, he grabbed a cold Coke and closed the door to the fridge. He reached inside his cupboard next to the microwave and removed a Hostess Cupcake.

"Dinner of champions," he said as he left the kitchen, flipping off the light as he headed down the hall to his bedroom. He walked the short distance across the floor to his desk and plopped down on his chair. In moments he had the wrapper off of his cupcake and ate the chocolate frosting off the top. After the frosting was gone, Jay took a big bite of the cake, revealing the filling on the inside. Slowly he licked the cream out of the center of the cupcake until it was gone. He then ate the remainder of the cupcake in one bite. Jay always ate his cupcakes in this manner. Try as he might, he couldn't bring himself to eat them any other way.

After a few minutes he opened his can of Coke. Raising the container to his lips, he chugged over a third of the liquid in one drink. He loved the way the Coke burned all the way down his throat and into his stomach when it was really cold, especially the first drink of the can. The carbonation was very best at the top of the can, it seemed. Jay drank the rest of the Coke, enjoying every sip, thinking about the letter the whole time. Several times he chuckled to himself, once even clenching his fists and raising his arms up into the air until his fists were about head high. He fought the urge to bring the letter out from under the Bible.

"I'm going to finish this Coke and relax for a few minutes," he thought aloud, fighting the temptation to grab the letter.

After what seemed like an hour, but was more like fifteen minutes in reality, Jay moved his Bible and placed the letter next to his computer on his desk. Reaching across his desk, he turned on his lamp next to his computer and slowly examined every inch of the letter. He didn't know what he was looking for, but it didn't prevent him from looking. After a thorough inspection Jay started to read.

June 9

Dear Jay,

This is not a joke.

I have decided to give you a gift from my estate. The gift will be monetary and will be for the sum of one million dollars

($1,000,000.00) U.S. currency. You will receive this gift in one lump sum.

There are stipulations you must follow to receive this gift. They are very simple and are listed below.

1.) You must tell absolutely *no one* about this gift or this letter. If you do tell anyone, you will forfeit your right to this gift. (Believe me, I will find out if you tell anyone.)

2.) Under no circumstance are you to contact me. Not by mail, e-mail, phone, or in person. There must be *absolutely no contact whatsoever.*

3.) You must present yourself to The Bank of Whitman on Bishop Boulevard in Pullman, Washington, at 10:30 a.m. on July 6. You must ask for George Gillis, branch manager, and must not be late! If you fail to show up on the above date at the aforementioned time, you will forfeit your right to this gift.

God Bless,
Milt Bilston

CHAPTER SIX

It was a beautiful morning. The dawn broke in the eastern sky, unobstructed by clouds. Slowly the sun rose, warming the air and the earth. The light glistened brightly on the thin potato chips that someone had either thrown or dropped on the sidewalk and street.

A thin dark line formed from somewhere in the grass across the street. It stretched across the sidewalk and out to the nearest potato chip in the middle of the road. Slowly, it picked at the pieces of the chip until small pieces broke free. It then appeared as if the small particle of chip was moved across the line in some sort of brigade. Upon closer examination, it was apparent that there was a rather large army of ants, all in a single line, working feverishly to gather up the carbohydrates and transport them back to the nest, where they would be food for the masses.

Overhead, on a power line almost directly above the potato chips, one could hear *Ka, Ka, Ka*. If one looked for the noise maker, one would see a large black crow sitting up on the wire. If one were even more diligent in their observation of the crow, one would witness the crow flying down to the road, where he picked at the glistening potato chips until approached by a car. At the very last moment, one would see the crow frantically fly off, barely avoiding the car and lifting himself back up to the waiting wire overhead while the black line of ants reformed where the tires had broken it. Once the crow landed, one would again hear *Ka, Ka, Ka*, and then the whole game would start all over.

So that's how the morning progressed up to that point. *Ka, Ka, Ka, Ka*, march, march, march, *Ka, Ka, Ka*, and so forth and so on. It was the *Ka, Ka, Ka* that finally roused Jay from a fitful slumber. He had been unable to sleep for most of the night, falling asleep sometime well after dawn. Rubbing his eyes as he slowly rose from bed, he enjoyed a huge yawn. He felt absolutely terrible, and a glance at his clock showed why—it was only a quarter to eight. *So much for sleeping in even a little.*

Remembering what was to blame for his lack of sleep, Jay headed into the kitchen, where he flipped on the light and walked to the refrigerator, opening the freezer door. He then removed the ziplock bag that contained his frozen letter, closed the door, and turned and walked out of the kitchen and down the hall to his room. After he entered the room and sat at his desk, he opened the zip lock bag and carefully removed the frozen letter. After a few moments he unfolded the letter and read it slowly. His fatigue was quickly replaced with elation. "Wahoo hoo!" Jay hollered, raising his arms into the air. "Wahoo hoo," for a second time as tears of joy filled up his eyes. Jay walked around the room rapidly, not quite knowing what to do. "Wahoo hoo!"

He decided a long hot shower would be his next course of action. After the shower, Jay grabbed a towel and dried. He slipped his shorts back on and proceeded to comb his wet hair. After a few moments, he set the comb down and grinned at himself in the mirror. Without restraint, he laughed and shook his head at his reflection in the foggy mirror.

"I can't believe it, I just can't believe it."

He repeated that several times to himself and then just stood there looking at himself.

"What do I do now?" he asked the image in the mirror. "This is just unbelievable, unbelievable." After a few moments Jay thought, *I have to get a hold of myself. I need to calm down.*

With that, he took a couple of long, deliberate breaths and ran his hands through his hair. Slowly his composure returned.

"That's more like it," he said to himself as he turned and walked out of the bathroom and back into his room. He decided he would go to Sunday school and church since he was already up, a rare event for sure. A quick search of his chest of drawers turned up a pair of khaki shorts and a fairly wrinkle-free polo shirt. He then searched around his room until he found his flip-flops and slipped them on over his bare feet.

Before he left the room he walked over to his desk and quickly read the letter again, even though he had it memorized. His finger traced down the letter slowly, stopping at every line, which he read and re-read before moving down the letter. When he was finished, he folded the letter, first in half, and then in half again, and placed it inside his Bible.

Jay walked to the kitchen and flipped on the light. Somehow the hum, hum of the fluorescent light had a comforting effect on him. He proceeded to make a pot of coffee and bent to the task of finding something to eat for breakfast. Jay surveyed his countertops. Nothing. He rifled through the cupboards until he found a partial loaf of whole wheat bread. All that remained of the loaf was one small piece of bread sandwiched between two heels.

"This will have to do," he muttered to himself as he searched for some butter. Jay placed the lone slice of bread and one heal into the toaster and pushed down the lever, still unsure if there was any butter in the house. He could hear the coffee finishing its brew cycle and poured himself a steaming cup, the heat uncomfortably warm against his hands as he carried it into the living room.

After switching the television on to keep him company, Jay returned to the kitchen for his toast, which still hadn't popped up. When he hit the manual eject button, the bread was a little more done than he liked. A small step from burnt to be more precise. "It'll have to do," he said to himself for the second time that morning. Another inspection of his kitchen satisfied him that he had no butter, or jam for that matter. Jay thought briefly about spreading yellow mustard on his toast, just so it would have something on it, but quickly decided against it. "It'll have to be dunked in my coffee dry," he said out loud.

Jay returned to the living room and placed his dry toast on the coffee table, picking up the remote by his recliner to turn up the volume on the Sports Center broadcast. Baseball highlights dominated the show, since it was summertime. A test of his coffee found it to be just right for drinking. He gulped down half of the cup at once, loving the way the hot liquid warmed him up inside out. The toast, on the other hand, was hard and crusty and seemed less appetizing than ever. With a shrug, Jay dunked it in his coffee, letting it soak up the heat and the flavor, and then in two bites devoured the whole piece. He repeated the process with the burnt heel and then finished off the coffee, all except the very bottom of the cup, which contained crumbs from the toast. For some reason, Jay had never been able to make himself drink that last bit after dunking toast. The sight of those wet crumbs gave him the willies.

After a second cup of coffee in a freshly rinsed cup, *Sports Center* lost his interest and he shut it off. His mind kept drifting back to the letter and his newly found fortune. He smiled in spite of himself, visualizing the whole letter in his mind. For some reason he couldn't get over the first line. "This is not a joke" ran through his mind over and over.

Why had his uncle put that line in the letter at all?

Suspicion ran rampant through his mind. He knew from his dad's stories that his uncle had been known as a practical joker in his younger days. Personally, he had never seen that side of Uncle Milt, but the stories had made a huge impression on Jay. They were all funny, and his uncle seemed to be very clever with his elaborate practical jokes, but they had always been just stories.

Could I be the victim of one of his jokes now? He couldn't bear the thought of it. Uncle Milt couldn't play that cruel of a joke on someone, could he? His earlier elation was quickly morphing into fear and suspicion. The first stipulation of the letter added to his growing paranoia, the one that stated he could tell absolutely no one or he would forfeit his gift. The most disturbing part was the assertion that his uncle would know if Jay told anyone. It was very matter-of-fact.

How could he know if I told someone? He's not an all-powerful, omnipresent being. Yet a frown began spreading across his face. His mind quickly flashed back to the previous evening: Jacob and Stewart both showing up at his house for the Bible study. Was it coincidence, or were they there to spy on him, eyes and ears for his uncle, so to speak. But Stewart said they had attended the last three Bible studies.

Interesting, Jay thought. *Three weeks… about the same time frame the letter was being written and sent.* His suspicion was growing stronger by the minute.

They would have absolutely no idea that I hadn't opened the letter when I first received it. His sleuthful mind was now in full gear. Jay's mouth dropped open a little as a sudden realization struck him. He never would have opened the letter if it wasn't for Anna. Disbelief and the feeling of betrayal now dominated his consciousness. *She wouldn't be part of this, would she?* Jay just sat there not knowing what to do. He was becoming paranoid, and he knew it.

He looked at the nearest clock. 10:00 a.m., straight up. Realizing he was going to be late, he jumped up and ran down the hall to his room, where he flung open the door and practically jumped across the room to snatch up his Bible. Locking the door to his house behind him, Jay headed off down the sidewalk toward the church, which was a good ten minutes away by foot. Ten whole minutes that Jay could ponder the letter. Plenty of time for his mood to go from elation to suspicion, again and again.

CHAPTER SEVEN

It seemed to Jay that he had just started walking when he found himself at the door of the church. He looked around in surprise, opened the door, and walked inside the foyer. A lot of commotion came from the nearby Sunday school classrooms, voices from multiple teachers, men and women, drowning each other out. The distinct high shrill of children's voices rose above all of the others, creating a strange harmonious effect, out of tune of course.

Jay continued down the hall, to the room where the young adult singles met for class. He could hear the teacher talking and hesitated a moment before opening the door. Everyone turned and looked at him as he walked in. A quick scan of the thirteen faces in the room revealed Anna, wearing a purple and white dress that set off her complexion nicely. Her gaze and a huge smile greeted him, causing any doubt about her to fade away. The light radiated brightly from her black shiny hair and caused her huge dark eyes to sparkle.

"Sit here," Anna whispered to Jay as she pulled out an empty chair right next to hers. It was the same chair that she reserved every Sunday morning for Jay, just in case he was to make one of his rare appearances. Obediently, he sat next to her and placed his Bible on the table in front of him. "Hi there," he mouthed to her.

Ami was teaching the class today, and as she opened the attendance book to mark Jay's presence, he glanced around the room to see who else had abandoned the comfort of their beds this morning. Next to Beth and Susan, Bill was giving Jay a thumbs-up signal. He was too distracted by the presence of his cousins at the far end of the table to respond to Bill, his brow furrowing into a scowl born of confusion and uncertainty.

I won't let them get to me, he told himself as he looked away.

Despite his better intentions, he tuned Ami's voice out and started thinking about the letter again. Enthusiasm overrode sensible precautions, and he started spending the money in his head.

A car would be nice for a change, he thought. *I could even take a year or two off work if I wanted.*

Jay started to get excited at the prospect of no work. *I could sleep in every morning and stay up as late as I want.* The fact that he didn't normally enjoy late nights never entered his mind.

Anna will be thrilled, Jay thought hopefully. He could see her in his mind's eye falling into his arms, totally committed to him now that financial security was assured for the two of them.

Jay snapped back to reality when Ami started to pray, a sure sign that class was ending. When she finished, everyone began visiting as they gathered their Bibles and other possessions. Anna turned to Jay and grabbed his upper arm. "I'm so happy to see you here this morning." She beamed a large smile up at him.

He smiled back at her. "I couldn't resist coming to visit you—and the wonderful fellowship."

"You're staying for church, aren't you?" It seemed almost as if she was pleading with him.

"Maybe, if you beg me a little more," he teased, hoping to see just how much she wanted him to stay.

Bill walked over and extended his fist for their usual greeting. "Great to see ya bro'; what pried you from the rack this fine a.m.?"

"Why the thought of fellowship with all of you, of course," Jay responded, straight-faced. Feeling a hand on his shoulder, he turned to see his cousin, Jacob, standing there. Jacob extended his hand, and Jay reluctantly took it in his own in greeting.

"I just wanted to thank you for a good party last night," Jacob said sincerely. "I was kind of quick to develop an attitude, so I want to apologize to you and thank you properly."

"That's all right. I'm sorry too," Jay responded, not sure what else to say.

"Are you staying for church?" Jacob asked.

"Well, I was planning on it."

"Cool. Stewart and I and a couple other people are planning on going down to the river after the service to go water skiing and swimming, and well, you're invited to come along if you'd like."

Jay was totally shocked. He wasn't expecting anything like this from Jacob. Now he wasn't sure how to respond. "Thanks man, um, I'll have to see what's going on, but maybe," he said as he looked down at Anna.

"You could bring Anna, too," Jacob added, clearly noticing that they seemed to be together today.

"Maybe, that sounds kind of fun," Jay said, knowing that there was little chance he would go anywhere with his cousins.

As they left the classroom and headed down the hall to the foyer, Anna noticed Jay looking down at her and smiled back at him. Just seeing her again made his day worthwhile, and he instantly had butterflies in his stomach. *Get a grip on yourself,* he thought as they entered the foyer.

"Jay and Anna, how are you?"

Jay spun around at the familiar voice. It was his boss, Nancy Rosemont, coming into the foyer from the middle hallway.

"We're just fine," Anna responded enthusiastically.

Bob Rosemont, dressed in a pinstripe suit, stood just behind Anna and looked very uncomfortable to Jay. His boss was seen in jeans, plaid shirts, and his work boots six days a week, but always wore a nice suit to church.

He extended his hand to Jay. "Good to see you, Son." Bob

greeted him as he pumped Jay's hand up and down in a strong handshake.

"Good to see you, too," Jay responded sincerely.

While the two couples chatted, the crowd by the doors thinned down to just a few people. Anna turned to Jay. "Are you ready to go in?"

"I need to use the restroom first," Jay answered quietly.

"I'll save you a seat," Anna assured him. With that she turned and entered the sanctuary.

Jay's good mood evaporated into sheer panic when he sauntered into the restroom—and ran smack dab into his Uncle Milt. Jay didn't know what to do or where to go.

Milt reacted first. "Well, how are you young man?" he asked, much to Jay's surprise.

"I'm fine, thanks," was all he could think to say after a long moment spent searching for his voice.

"Well, I haven't seen you forever, what have you been up to lately?" Milt prodded.

"Not much, just some work. That's pretty much it." Jay felt very small next to his uncle. He didn't know why, as his uncle was always warm and cheerful to him.

The organ music started in the sanctuary, signaling the beginning of the service.

"Well, we'd better get in there before we get in trouble," his uncle said as he walked out into the hallway.

Still shaken from the encounter, it took Jay several minutes to pull himself together and find his seat next to Anna. "I thought you must have gone home or something," she whispered to him.

"I'm sorry, I ran into my uncle and we lost track of time visiting," he explained.

After a few minutes of listening to a sermon on the importance of obedience and the destruction caused by deceit, Jay was lost in his own troubled thoughts.

Why did my uncle talk to me today? he wondered as he glanced across the congregation to where his uncle was seated. *The letter said absolutely no contact whatsoever, and Milt didn't seem one bit phased at seeing me.*

Although he couldn't think of anyone who would be that mean, the theory that the letter might be a prank began to strengthen. Instantly, his cousins came to mind, with their strange behavior and sudden appearance in his life.

The room became uncomfortably warm as an even more frightening possibility presented itself in his mind. *Maybe I just forfeited all of the money by talking to my uncle.*

This speculation was getting him nowhere. Jay took a deep breath and tried to focus—on the sermon, thoughts of Anna, anything but the letter.

The pastor was nearing the end of the sermon. Anna touched his shoulder, motioning to him that she wanted a pen. Jay took one out of the little holder that was on the back of the seat directly in front of him. They usually wrote each other notes in church when they wanted to communicate with each other. Jay looked for some paper as well but couldn't find any. His heart leaped into his throat when Anna opened his Bible and took out a coffee stained piece of paper and proceeded to write a note to him

He couldn't just grab the letter out of her hand, but he couldn't let her open it and read it either. All he could do was sit there, heart racing, until she finished her note and handed it to him.

The message simply asked if he wanted to go to the potluck this afternoon. Jay took the letter and pen from Anna, working hard to keep his hands from shaking. Instead of writing a reply to her, he simply nodded his head in the affirmative and slid the letter into his pocket.

Less than a day had passed since he read the letter. July sixth suddenly seemed very, very far away.

CHAPTER EIGHT

The potluck was a busy commotion of friendly people all enjoying home cooked meals and good Christian fellowship. Jay instructed Anna to stay away from the pots of food that absolutely couldn't be identified. "Mystery meat surprise," he told her, ushering her away to more appealing fare, particularly the dessert section.

By the time they settled at a table across from Jay's parents, Jay had been given fifty hugs if he had been given one. He didn't care for hugs at all, so he felt that his food had been thoroughly paid for.

This was the first time he'd had a chance to visit with his parents in several weeks, so it took even longer than usual to find out what his large family had been up to. His dad seemed very reserved, talking very little and lost in his own world. Jay couldn't help but notice that his parents seemed to have aged noticeably. He made a mental note to ask his mother privately if his father's health was okay. Something wasn't right, and for the first time all day, thoughts of *the letter* were banished from his mind.

"Well son, what's new with you?" Jay's father asked him as the potluck was slowly winding down after nearly an hour. Jay had an almost unstoppable urge to blurt out to his dad everything about the letter, but managed to restrain himself.

"Not too much, but things are looking up markedly," was all he allowed himself to say of the biggest event in his recent life.

His dad looked genuinely interested for the first time that day. "Really, are you getting a promotion or something?"

"No, nothing like that," Jay replied, not knowing what else to say. Then his mother and Anna turned their attention to him, looking on with great curiosity.

"It's nothing definite. I shouldn't have even brought it up at all," Jay said, irritated with himself for bringing anything up at all. "Anything new with you?" Jay asked his dad to deflect any further questions.

"Been thinking along the lines of retirement some," his dad replied, mood lifting noticeably.

"Really? I thought you still had five or six years to go."

"It'd be nice to retire when your mother and I could still enjoy ourselves," his father proclaimed.

Jay was really starting to worry now. There must be something wrong with his dad, what with his talk of early retirement "so they would be able to enjoy themselves." Jay couldn't think of anything to say. Fortunately, he didn't have to try very hard. His sister Lisa came over from a couple tables away and took charge of the conversation.

Lisa was eleven years older than Jay. She had grown up and moved out when he was still a young boy, so he could remember only enough of their shared life together to know that she had a type A personality and was very opinionated—and she wasn't afraid to share her opinion with any and all.

"How are you two?" she asked Jay and Anna. "I haven't seen you forever," she stated to Jay without waiting for an answer.

"We're alright," Jay replied. "Well, at least I am," he added, deferring to Anna.

"I'm just fine," Anna replied with a smile. "How are you doing?" she added earnestly.

"Good, good. I've been so very busy looking at floor plans for a new house, what with Dan's promotion to junior high principle and everything," Lisa bragged. "We've been cramped up in that little house of ours for so long now, I won't know how to act once we build a new home."

This was the first Jay had heard about a new house for his sister. He wanted to butt in and tell her about his good fortune, but resisted the temptation. This didn't keep him from imagining her envious look as she congratulated him. *That'll be the day,* he thought to himself with a satisfied grin on his face.

Jay quickly tuned out as his sister, mother, and Anna caught up on all the local gossip. Actually, Jay's mother and Anna just listened as Lisa went on and on, sharing her vast wealth of knowledge with them.

Jay's thoughts zoomed back to the letter and to his unfortunate encounter with his uncle. He couldn't get over the fact that his uncle acted completely normal. A tiny flame of hope that refused to be extinguished, that the letter was somehow legitimate, kept him from marching right up to his uncle and asking him about it. He knew if it was real, he would forfeit any claim to the gift on the spot. *Maybe I already have,* he thought gloomily. "Absolutely no contact whatsoever" kept racing through his mind, over and over.

෴

After promising Anna a return visit to the church for the evening service, Jay walked home. "Eleven more days," he said to himself as he unlocked the door. "Two hundred and sixty-four more hours, give or take. I can survive that long, can't I?"

Once inside, he went directly to the kitchen, set his Bible on the counter, and dug a pen out of his junk drawer. A moment later, July sixth was circled on his calendar, along with the reminder: "10:30 B.W." Not that there was any chance he was going to forget the biggest day of his life. He looked at the intervening two weeks between now and then and let out a long sigh, sure that the coming fourteen days would be the longest of his life.

Jay turned the air conditioning on before settling down on the couch and covering his eyes with his arm. Before the room even began to cool down, he was fast asleep, but it was a fitful sleep filled with unfriendly dreams.

First, Anna was forced onto a large ship by men in fluorescent green jumpsuits. He couldn't understand a single word they said, but he could clearly understand Anna as she repeatedly cried out to Jay, "Don't leave me, Jay. Don't leave me!" Try as he might, he could never reach the ship to get to Anna. The dock that led to the ship had a large steel pole that dropped directly into his path whenever he came within thirty feet or so of the ship. First he would move one way, and then another, but the pole stayed directly in front of him at all times, obstructing his path completely. Slowly the boat pulled away from him and sailed out of the harbor as all of the men in green jumpsuits pointed at him and laughed, all the while uttering something he couldn't understand. Still, Anna called his name.

The second dream placed Jay and Anna in a forest of oak trees. Three inches of snow blanketed the ground, but it was warm out. Even more confusing, the snow wasn't cold. All of the oak trees had lost their acorns, which were now lying on top of the snow. For some reason, Jay was picking up all of the acorns and placing them in a large bucket that never seemed to fill up. In the meantime, Anna started to slide down the mountainside on the snow. She yelled out for Jay to help her, but he couldn't stop picking up acorns. He told her repeatedly that he was working his way over to her and that she should just hang on for a little longer. She continued to slide away, unable to catch anything to slow her descent. Jay continued to frantically pick up the acorns, all the while working his way toward Anna. He could hear her voice fading away as she called out his name over and over as she slid down the mountain. Once she was completely out of sight, a large beaver came out of the woods, looked at Jay, then headed down the mountain in Anna's direction. His front teeth rotated until they were like a large snowplow. The beaver then started eating all of the snow, but not the acorns. When the snow was all eaten, the beaver turned and looked at Jay and then slowly melted into the earth.

Jay's dreams continued tormenting him until a shrill ringing startled him back to reality. He grabbed the receiver of his phone and glanced quickly at the time on the microwave: 5:40 p.m. Almost time for evening church.

The male voice on the other end of the line was familiar, but he couldn't quite place it.

"Who is this?" Jay finally asked, totally clueless as to whom he was talking.

"Why, I'm hurt," came the reply. "My own little brother doesn't even recognize my voice."

"Todd? Is that you?" Jay asked, still not 100 percent certain it was his brother.

"Of course it's me. Who else would it be?" Jay hadn't heard from his oldest brother for a long time. In fact, as he did a quick calculation, it had to have been at least two years since their last conversation. Not really a surprise, as Todd was more than seventeen years older and had moved out of the house and gotten married while Jay was still in diapers.

"What's up? Is there something wrong?" Jay asked, concern evident in his voice.

"No, I just felt like calling my little brother to see what was new."

"Wow, I haven't heard from you for a long time," Jay exclaimed, little caution bells going off in the back of his mind.

"Well, it's been too long," Todd answered. "I'm going to make it a point to talk to you at least once a month from here on out."

"You aren't sick or anything?" Jay asked, chuckling a little as he said it.

"No, I'm serious. I just want to get to know my kid brother better," Todd answered, laughing at Jay's previous remark. They visited for another five minutes or so, catching up on family news, talking about the weather, predicting how the Mariners' season would end up, and then they ran out of anything to say to each other.

"Well, I'd better go," Todd finally said after an awkward pause.

"Thanks for calling," Jay replied, and that was that.

Jay hung up the phone and began rubbing his eyes. He looked at the clock. It was 5:53 p.m. "Man, I'm always late," Jay said to himself as he rushed out the door to meet Anna.

Heavy thunderclouds were massing over the southern horizon as he arrived at church; a blend of whites, grays, and nearly blacks with just a glazing of red fading into various shades of pinks on the very top fringes of the clouds. The different colors and shapes gave the clouds an almost eerie, life-like quality. The wind was picking up slightly from the south; a hot sticky wind that only added to the misery of anyone unfortunate enough to be outside. Jay reached out and grabbed the door handle, almost in desperation to get out of the heat. The door opened with ease, and he was greeted with a huge gust of cool air from the air conditioner inside the church.

Jay instantly felt refreshed, but he detoured to the restroom to wipe the sweat off his face with a wet paper towel before heading into the sanctuary. He looked at his reflection in the mirror and was startled to see dark bags under his eyes. The combination of stress and lack of sleep was beginning to show. Shrugging, he threw the used towel into the garbage bin in an overhand style. "Two points," he said to himself as he walked out the door and down the hall.

An elderly lady was giving her testimony as he entered the sanctuary. He could see that Anna had saved him a spot just like always. The lights were shining off of her black hair, giving it a satiny hue. When he reached her pew, Anna greeted him with a smile that made him weak in the knees. For that moment, Jay knew exactly where he belonged.

The service let out fifteen minutes early. Jay felt doubly lucky since he had arrived late enough to miss the evening tithes and offering.

"For a minute I thought you weren't going to make it," Anna said as she turned toward Jay.

"I wouldn't have made it either if I hadn't received a phone call from Todd. I fell sound asleep on the couch, and the only thing that woke me was the ringing of the phone."

"How's Todd doing? I haven't seen him for a long time."

"He's okay I guess. I was sure surprised to hear from him."

They walked down the aisle until they reached the foyer, where the pastor was greeting everyone.

"Well, Mr. Bilston, we sure have been blessed with your presence today."

"Yeah, I should come more often," Jay said awkwardly.

"He's going to start coming more regularly," Anna added firmly.

"Well, we're very happy to see you," the pastor added with a friendly handshake.

Jay and Anna milled around the foyer for a few more minutes, visiting with some of the other churchgoers. It occurred to Jay that everyone there really loved Anna. Again he was startled by the realization that he had never seen anyone as genuine to everyone as she was. Each and every person, no matter how young or how old, was left with a word of encouragement followed by a hug. She was worth loving, and old feelings began to awaken in his heart.

The clouds were still ominous overhead as they finally exited the church, and thunder rumbled in the background. Surprisingly, the heat was still rising up off the sidewalk, even though there was no sun. "Let's go have ice cream," Jay suggested as a means to prolong his evening with Anna.

"Aren't you too tired?" Anna asked Jay.

"Never for ice cream," Jay responded eagerly. "Besides, it's still early."

"Well, okay," Anna agreed with mock hesitation. "But only if I can buy."

"I'm buying, we're going, and that's final," Jay insisted with overstated confidence, eliminating any chance of further argument over the issue.

"We might get wet," Anna pointed out as she eyed the threatening sky.

"Not if we hurry." Jay picked up the pace accordingly, and they reached the ice cream store in record time. Jay ordered a mint chocolate chip milkshake with hot fudge mixed in, and Anna ordered a single scoop of chocolate mousse royale on a sugar cone.

The wind was starting to gust and swirl, first from one direction and then from the other. Large drops of rain plunged through the dust, and other debris kicked up by the wind and smeared whatever they hit with a blend of mud and water. Soon the wind was blowing so hard that the rain appeared to be falling sideways. Jay and Anna watched the storm, mesmerized by its sheer strength. Lightning flashed as they silently enjoyed their ice cream, lighting up the sky brighter than the brightest part of any day. The sound of thunder exploded around them, sounding like bombs going off. All of the storm drains were quickly overwhelmed, little whirlpools of draining water soon the only proof they even existed below the surface.

The storm continued its savage assault on the city for about fifteen more minutes and then stopped as rapidly as it had begun. After a few minutes, wet pavement along with a few large puddles were all that remained.

"That was cool," Jay commented, eyes still fixed on the sky.

"More like scary," Anna added in.

"There's nothing like a good thunder storm on the Palouse," Jay said excitedly. "I just love them."

"They aren't that bad as long as you don't have to be out in them." Anna was eyeing more large clouds that were approaching from the south. "Maybe we should take this opportunity to head home."

"All right, party-pooper," Jay teased as he got up and tossed his empty cup into the garbage. "Let's head for home."

Jay held the door open for Anna as she threw her trash away. She smiled up at him and walked out the door. The wind was still blowing from the south. It was a steady wind now, punctuated frequently with large gusts. The air was still warm, although it had cooled considerably from earlier in the day. They could see lightning in the sky, remnants of the strong storm that had moved on its way. The approaching clouds appeared to hold promise of more lightning.

"Isn't this great" Jay asked enthusiastically. "If we're lucky we'll be in the next storm."

"Lucky? You have to be crazy."

ೂ∽ಲ

Anna's house was a good ten minutes away, even walking at a brisk pace. Walking across a side street, they had no choice but to go through a large mud puddle to reach the other sidewalk. Jay jumped, landing in the middle of the puddle with one foot and then on the sidewalk with the other, suffering only minor wetness. Anna wasn't so lucky. She tried to jump or skip her way through the puddle, but started to lose her balance and had to put both feet down to keep from falling. The water was more than eight inches deep and went halfway to her knees.

"Oh goodness," she exclaimed. "I'm getting soaked."

She gingerly placed each foot one in front of the other in the dark water, unsure of any obstacle that may lie ahead of her. When she was a little more than half way across, Jay walked back into the water to help her rest of the way.

"I may as well join you," he said as she grabbed onto his arm.

"Aren't you a gentleman tonight," Anna responded.

He gently squeezed her hand clasped around his arm. "Just for you."

They made it less than a block and a half before they felt the first large rain drops. Lightning flashed almost directly overhead, lighting up the street and sidewalk all around them, followed immediately by a huge clap of thunder. The rain beating steadily down on them was wet, but not extremely cold.

"We're getting soaked," she yelled to Jay, who was a step ahead of her.

"Really, I hadn't noticed," he replied sarcastically. After a few moments he dashed into a doorway of one of the dark buildings and pulled Anna in alongside him.

"Let's wait it out in here," he explained to her.

"We could be here awhile," she answered.

"No, these storms never last very long. We have them every year, and they leave just as fast as they arrive," Jay assured her.

They watched the rain pour down out of the heavens, pounding the pavement with a relentless fury. Every few minutes the rain was highlighted by both flash and bolt lightning dancing across the sky in all directions, followed by blasts of vibrating thunder that shook the large pane glass windows with every clap.

"This is the best night ever," Jay said to Anna after several flashes of lightning.

"You sure are in a good mood," she answered him.

"Why do you say that?"

"Because you are. I'm not complaining though. I've had a wonderful time today."

"Well, if I am it's because I have some wonderful news, and I've been able to spend most of the day with you," he explained.

"I'm not so sure about the last part," Anna teased. "What's your 'wonderful news'?"

"I'm not supposed to tell anyone for about two weeks, but if you promise not to tell anyone, I'll tell you," he eagerly offered.

"Did you promise not to tell anyone?"

"Well, sort of," he hesitated. "But nobody'll find out if you don't say anything."

"Jay, I don't want to be responsible for any broken promise. You'd better not tell me anything. I'd rather wait the two weeks to find out the news," Anna replied sternly.

Jay was disappointed for a moment or two. He really wanted to tell Anna of his newfound good fortune. He was too pumped up about the money to stay disappointed very long.

"Alright, two more weeks it is, but you'll be the first person I'll tell," he promised.

Anna looked at him through the dark rain. She had prayed every night for the past three years that God would give her clarity concerning their relationship. She had been given a reassuring calmness about Jay once she turned it all over to God. Even so, those old feelings were drumming up old emotional pains along with guarded fear of more pain. She decided to be very careful.

"I really have had a good time today," she started out slowly. "I just want to remind you, Jay, nothing has changed with me. I mean, we do have a history together, and it hasn't been all that easy these past few years. I don't want to give you any false ideas or hopes."

Jay was shocked by the sudden turn of conversation. He wasn't sure if he had just been rejected by Anna. He wanted to be cautious about what he said to her next. He didn't want to mess it up again.

"Anna, just give me a chance, that's all I ask. I know it's been really hard for you the last few years. It's been hard on me too. I promise you this, the good news I have is good news for both of us. I love you Anna, and I know you're the right person for me. Can you give me the benefit of the doubt?"

Tears were welling up in Anna's eyes. She had prayed for two years to hear those words, and now that she had, her emotions were on the verge of exploding. She took a few deep breaths to gain her composure. The rain blowing into the doorway and wetting her hair and face felt very refreshing. She wanted to have a clear head and not let her emotions run out of hand.

Lord, please give me wisdom. Help me know what to say. Help me to not be influenced by my emotions. Amen.

Almost immediately Anna knew what she was going to say. She felt a calming reassurance in her soul just as if the Lord was reaching down his hand and touching her. With renewed confidence she turned her face up to look into Jay's eyes.

"I love you too, Jay, and I will give you the benefit of the doubt. But I want to make this clear to you: I won't be here forever. I should be finished with my schooling about the first of the year, and then I'll be moving to Colorado Springs to start ministerial school. It'll last a little over two years and then I'll be sent on my mission." She paused to let her last statement sink in before continuing on.

"I just need to know that we're on the same page so we can avoid any kind of conflict or suffer any kind of misunderstanding." *Like before.*

Jay was speechless. He couldn't tell Anna about his news, yet if he did it would simplify everything. From the first moment he finished reading the letter, he kept telling himself this over and over. Now doubt had gained a foothold in the back of his mind. He quickly shoved it as far back as possible, but it still lingered there creating an uneasy feeling.

"I understand you completely, Anna, really I do. I just need a chance to prove it to you." His voice was pleading.

"This is your chance, Jay," she said softly. "This is your chance."

After a long hug and a final dash through the rain, Jay left Anna on her doorstep. He couldn't believe how good he felt. This walk home in the rain was much better than the last.

Anna made her way up the stairs to her room. She quickly changed out of her wet clothes and into a dry warm flannel nightgown. She couldn't stop thinking about Jay. Her large dark eyes sparkled with joy and a broad smile seemed permanently etched on her round, petite face.

"I do love you, Jay Bilston! For better or worse, I really do." She said these words out loud as she climbed into bed and turned on the lamp sitting on the nightstand. Thumbing through her Bible, she found the bookmark she had made two years earlier. After reading the scripture on the front, comforted as usual by the words of the twenty-third Psalm, she turned it over. The back side of the bookmark was plain with a small, block style script inscription in her efficient handwriting. Tears filled her eyes once more as she ran her fingers back and forth over the familiar words, evidence of her girlish dream of romance. "Oh Lord, please let it be true. I really want it to be true," she prayed silently before placing the bookmark back into her worn Bible.

CHAPTER NINE

As Jay got ready for work the next morning, he was still thinking about the previous evening. He couldn't believe his good fortune. He was getting both the money and the girl. That letter was changing his whole life for the better. *Ten more days.*

In the shower, he found himself singing as he rinsed the shampoo out of his thick curly hair. Jay rarely sang in the shower and, when he realized what he was doing, smiled and continued singing, "Song to the King."

"Man, it sure feels good to be in love!"

As if in response to the exuberant outburst, the phone rang. Quickly toweling off and racing into the kitchen, Jay noted that he really should invest in a cordless phone. When he picked up the receiver and said "Hello," there was a short pause on the other end. Then he heard a familiar female voice.

"Jay, is that you? This is your sister Barbara."

Jay was shocked. Barbara was four years older than him, and he hadn't spoken to her for some time.

"Barbara? Is everything alright?" he asked as his brow creased in concern. "Is something wrong with Mom or Dad?"

"No, nothing's wrong with anybody. I just thought I'd call you before you left for work to tell you to have a good day," she said in her most sincere voice.

Jay wasn't buying it. He and Barbara had fought like cats and dogs their whole lives. She was probably the last person in the family he would willingly call, and he was fairly certain the feeling was mutual.

"Oh come on, you expect me to believe you would actually call to tell me to have a good day?" he answered in disbelief.

"That is why I'm calling," she answered, a hint of irritation in her voice.

This was just too out of character for Barbara. Jay was certain something else had to be the motive for this call, and he was going to find out exactly what it was.

"Why are you really calling? I haven't heard a word from you since Christmas, when you were too busy with your new boyfriend to even be polite to me. Sorry if I'm skeptical, but I just can't believe that's the only reason you're calling."

"You're such a jerk! You always have been! I just wanted to call and tell you to have a good day and to see what was new in your life. Forgive me for caring!"

Jay didn't know what to say. The phone was silent. He decided he'd better apologize to her. "I'm sorry. I didn't mean to hurt your feelings." His sister didn't say a word. "Barbara, are you there? Barbara, Barbara!"

She had hung up on him.

Jay tossed the phone back into its cradle. His face contorted with anger. "What in the world is going on?"

First Todd, calling out of the blue yesterday, and now Barbara; he was growing more suspicious with each passing minute. It was nearly time to leave for work, but Jay had half a mind to call his sister back to try and get to the bottom of this. She probably had caller I.D. and wouldn't answer anyway. He was sure this had something to do with that letter.

What if it's not real? Panic started to creep back into his mind. *This could ruin everything with Anna.* He started pacing around the room, trying to wear off some of his nervous energy. Heading back to his room, he picked up the letter and started to read it again, looking for anything that might indicate whether it was either a joke or was the real thing. It smelled like old, stale coffee. It didn't give up any new secrets.

"This is ridiculous, I'm being ridiculous," he said as he placed the letter back on his desk. He looked at his alarm clock. Time to leave.

The phone started to ring again. "Who could it be this time?" he said as he rushed to the kitchen for the second time that morning. He reached the phone before the third ring and just stood there, not sure if he wanted to answer it. It rang again. Jay reached his hand out and placed it on the receiver, not yet picking it up. It started to ring for the fourth time. If he didn't pick it up now the answering machine would answer for him. Jay hesitated for a split second more then lifted the receiver up. "Hello."

"Jay? Is that you?" It was a very familiar voice on the other end.

"Yes, it's me," he said, confidence returning to his voice.

"I almost didn't recognize your voice. It sounded like something was wrong."

"No, everything is fine. It's a lot better now, actually."

"Really, was something wrong?" The voice asked with discernable concern.

"No silly, it's better just because I'm talking to you."

And when Anna told him she was just calling to tell him to have a good day, he had no trouble believing her.

There were several impatient people waiting to be helped at the counter when Jay came in the back door. Bob was the only one there, and he was frantically writing down orders and working the two-way radio to keep things flowing smoothly. Jay looked at the clock and realized he was five minutes late. He usually tried to get there at least five minutes early, especially on Mondays. He set his coffee on his desk and walked up next to Bob.

"Sorry I'm a little late," he offered meekly.

"Better not let it happen again," Bob teased, clearly not upset.

Jay grabbed a computer terminal and logged on. "I can help the next person here," he offered to the people in the front of the line.

"It's about time," came the reply of a grumpy contractor who'd been waiting all of five minutes.

Jay didn't let the grumpy man, or any of the other impatient customers, put him in a bad mood. He knew most of the guys from waiting on them for the past several years and had even become friends with some of them. It seemed like they were always in a huge hurry, especially on Mondays, which put most of them in an impatient and grumpy mood.

Before Jay knew it, noon had arrived. The steady flow of customers had hardly slowed at all. During the first lull in activity, Bob approached. "Are you going to take your lunch now, Son?"

"Why don't you go now, and I'll go when you get back."

"I will go, if you don't mind; I'm kind of worn out from all the running this morning," Bob said as he logged off of his computer terminal. "You've sure been a ball of energy today. What got into your water this morning?"

"It's just a really nice day," Jay answered, not wanting to go into any details. He wasn't sure how Bob would react to the news about him and Anna, since she was his niece. His concern was probably unnecessary. The last time he and Anna were together, Bob and Nancy both seemed happy about it. They had never butted in when things were going well between Anna and him, and didn't say much when they had their falling out either. Jay often wondered if Anna had ever given them any details of their disagreement. If she had, they never acted like it.

Now that work had slowed down, Jay wondered what Anna was doing. He could picture her in his mind smiling up at him, and he wished he could call her right then. Immediately he decided that he was going to get cell phones for the two of them as soon as he got the money.

If I get the money. The dark thought recalled the early morning phone call from his sister. Something funny was going on, but he couldn't quite put his finger on what it might be. There had to be more to the letter than met the eye. Somehow his sister and brother, along with his two cousins, had to be involved. Somehow, he was going to make it the next ten days without going crazy. He had already decided he'd play along for now. At least long enough to figure out what was really going on.

                                                                                     ❧❧

At lunch, Jay walked outside and was met by a brilliant sunny sky. He slipped on his shades and headed down the road toward the burger joint. When he reached the restaurant, most of the lunch crowd had already cleared out, leaving Jay to himself and his conflicted thoughts as he took a seat facing the road and waited for his order. He watched the cars drive up and down the road, everyone hurrying to one place or another. *Who in their right mind would just give away a million dollars? Worse, what kind of idiot would believe they were going to receive a gift like that? Nothing comes free.*

"I have to just put this whole thing out of my mind!" But he decided that was easier said than done.

"Number seventy-four," the cashier said into a microphone. Jay looked around. No one else was even in the restaurant. He walked up to the front, picked up the tray and returned to his seat. He opened his hamburger package and realized he'd forgotten to ask them to hold the tomato.

"Bummer." He gingerly took the tomato off his burger and placed it on his napkin. Then he added about a dozen French fries to the top of his burger and doused them with ketchup before replacing the bun. It was the way he always ate his burgers. He didn't mind the funny looks it sometimes earned him.

He saved the huckleberry milkshake, his favorite flavor, for the walk back to the lumberyard. The clouds had built up considerably during the short time he was inside. Jay walked along slowly. His thoughts drifted back to Anna. She was probably almost finished with school for the day. He couldn't even imagine what it was like to go to school as many years as she had. Yet he also couldn't believe her schooling was almost complete. It seemed as if he had met her just a short time ago.

He didn't know what he was going to do if that letter proved to be a hoax. *Lord, let it be real,* he prayed quickly, and then felt guilty for praying it.

☙❧

Jay arrived home about ten after six. His answering machine was blinking. The first message was left at five-thirty. It was Anna checking to see if he was home yet. He smiled at the sound of her voice.

The second call was from his brother Dan, who said he was just calling to see what was going on, if anything. He left his number and asked Jay to call him back if he had a chance. Jay just shook his head, a frown worrying his face again. This was the third sibling out of seven to give him a call out of the blue, "just to see how he was doing." This was no coincidence. Something was going on.

Well, I'm not calling him back, Jay decided as he picked up the phone. He dialed Anna's number instead.

"Hello?" Anna said as she picked up the phone. Hopeful anticipation filled her voice.

"You rang?" Jay did his best to not sound grumpy to her. He failed.

"Jay? Is something the matter?" Anna asked with genuine concern.

"No, just a long day," was Jay's short reply.

"Well, I was going to see if you were busy tonight, but it sounds as if you're probably tired out."

"No, I'm sorry, my mind was just preoccupied. I'd love to do something with you tonight. What do you have in mind?" Jay answered, his mood beginning to lift.

"Bible school. This week is Bible school and I'm teaching a class. I thought maybe you could be my assistant."

Jay hesitated. He didn't really want to help out with Bible school, but he did want to see Anna. Sitting at the church with a bunch of little kids singing Sunday school songs wasn't his idea of fun. But after a minute, he decided he could stand it. It would be worth it to see Anna.

"Fine, I guess I could help," he finally answered her. "How long do I have to get ready?"

"You have about fifteen minutes until I pick you up," Anna replied.

"Fifteen minutes? I just got home," Jay complained.

"I have to be there by six-thirty," Anna explained. "I have to unlock the church."

"All right, I'll be ready," he promised.

As he changed clothes, Jay's mind started to wander. Prank or not, it would be fun to plan what to do with the money. He decided the first thing he was going to do was pay all of his bills. There really weren't that many. Then he definitely wanted to get cell phones for him and Anna. It wasn't as if he couldn't afford one now, but he had never needed one. Maybe he could pay an entire year's worth of his lease in advance, or just buy a house of his own. He couldn't really think of too much he needed, and aside from the cell phones, none of the ideas really excited him.

Then it hit him. He needed a car. That's what he would like to get, a new car. Although he had survived just fine without one, his previous thought of purchasing a car just would not leave his mind. The longer he thought about it, the more he wanted one. That settled it. Pay the bills off, pay a year's lease, get two cell phones, and buy a car. Those were the first things he'd do with his money.

Jay was still daydreaming when a knock on his door brought him up off the couch. He quickly turned off the TV, which had been playing unnoticed in front of him, and opened the door to a patiently waiting Anna.

"Are you ready to go?" she asked cheerfully.

"Wow, that was quick. You should have just honked," Jay said as he followed her down the sidewalk to the waiting car. Anna had borrowed Nancy's Buick LeSabre.

"I hope this rain doesn't keep the kids from coming," Anna yelled out as they ran to the car, dodging raindrops.

It didn't. The kids came by the dozens, and every one of them was jabbering at the top of their lungs. Or so it seemed to Jay. He watched Anna with admiration as they all rushed up to her for a hug or to show her some small treasure they had brought along with them. She didn't even lose her patience with the little boy who brought a garden snake with him. Anna declined to hold it, but she admired it enthusiastically along with the beaming boy.

"Hey dog, what's up?" Jay turned and banged Bill's waiting fist.

"Not much, just a little Bible school I guess," Jay answered. "What are you doing here?"

"This dog's the recreation engineer," Bill answered enthusiastically.

"In other words, they roped you into being here, too?"

"No, I volunteered for this duty," Bill said with pride.

Jay rolled his eyes and gave a little laugh. "Yeah, right."

"No really, it's my chance to get the kids while they're still like play dough. I can help mold them into the kind of upstanding citizens they should be," Bill replied enthusiastically.

That's a scary thought. Jay kept the thought to himself.

"What's your duty here?" Bill asked.

"I don't know. I guess I'll be helping Anna."

"Cool, I couldn't help but observe the two of you've been like this lately." Bill held up two fingers, one wrapped around the other.

Jay smiled in spite of himself. "Yeah, I guess you could come to that conclusion pretty easy."

"Cool dude, you and the Big Dog must've got things worked out," Bill said as he pointed up to the sky. For some reason this really annoyed Jay. He didn't have to go into details with Bill, or anyone else for that matter. His private life was his business, and his alone. He decided not to answer Bill.

"Well, we'd better get in there. The music is starting to play." Jay headed toward the sanctuary.

❧

When Anna dropped him back at his apartment, Jay had to admit he'd had fun. After promising to help the following night, he watched her drive away. "One day down, nine to go," he said to himself.

CHAPTER TEN

Days nine through five were pretty much a repeat for Jay. The busy schedule helped keep his mind off the letter, but his week was punctuated with moments of alternating panic and excitement. Anna was the glue that kept his sanity together. Even so, she had asked him on more than one occasion if there was anything wrong. She could easily see when something was bothering him. He always had an explanation, however unconvincing it was. Anna never pressed the issue, for which he was thankful.

Jay headed out early so he could keep his promise to make it to Sunday school. He didn't mind walking. It gave him a chance to enjoy the beautiful day and time to reflect on his previous whirlwind week. Anna was on his mind almost as much as the letter now. He wanted to spend as much time with her as possible. She seemed to be just as enamored with him. Virtually everyone was congratulating them on being back together. He worried occasionally about the letter and what effect it might have on their relationship, if it was all a hoax. Those instances were becoming fewer and further between.

He reached the church a few minutes early. From the looks of the parking lot, it appeared that a lot of folks were gone for the long holiday weekend. Once inside, he entered the church and headed down the hallway toward his Sunday school classroom. The door was open, and sure enough, Anna was already there saving a chair for him. She smiled at him as she pulled out his chair. "How are you this morning?" she asked.

"Superb," came his sincere reply.

Anna seemed surprised. "I thought you'd probably be sore today. You know, the way you and Bill tore around at the VBS picnic."

"It didn't really bother me that much. It's not like we played tackle football or anything."

"Hey dude, it's a record," Bill said to Jay as he walked in. "Eight days in a row for you, man." They went through their usual greeting ritual as Bill pulled out a chair next to Jay and sat down.

"Not a record yet. Back in the day I never missed a service for years," Jay explained, referring to his youth.

༺༻

When church was over, Jay's mother rushed over to give him a big hug, remarking how happy she was to see Jay and Anna as a couple again. As his dad slowly made his way over, Jay couldn't help but notice that he seemed much more reserved and withdrawn. He even had dark circles around his eyes. "Is everything alright, Mom?"

She seemed to draw back at the question. "What do you mean?"

"I don't know; Dad just looks as if he doesn't feel well. He looks really haggard and tired."

"He just has a lot of things on his mind right now. He'll be just fine." His mother's explanation was less than convincing. Jay couldn't imagine his mother would keep anything from him, but he decided to find his sister to see if she knew anything.

In the church parking lot, he could see Lisa starting to get into her minivan. "Hey, Sis," he yelled as he quickly jogged over to her. Lisa stopped and glanced around, trying to see who was yelling at her. She saw him and got back out of her van as he approached.

"Hi, Jay, what's up?"

"Not much, I was, um, well wondering if you knew what, if anything, is going on with Dad. He doesn't look good at all."

Lisa looked startled for a minute. "You know, I noticed that too the other day. I never asked anything though. You don't think he's sick or anything, do you?"

"I asked Mom, but she said everything's all right. She said he's just preoccupied with something. I think there's something she's not telling me though."

Lisa was genuinely concerned now. "We've been preoccupied ourselves the past few weeks. I should've asked Mom what's going on. Maybe I'll see them over the fourth. If I do, I'll get to the bottom of it."

"I thought you guys went camping over the fourth every year."

"We usually do, but we have something to do right after the fourth," Lisa answered without offering any more information.

"If you find out anything, give me a call." Jay hugged her good-bye.

He knew that if anyone could find out what was going on, it would be Lisa.

Jay and Anna went to a Chinese restaurant for lunch, along with a group of other singles from the church. Stewart and Jacob went too, which really annoyed Jay. He thought he was probably being paranoid, but he couldn't afford to trust anyone but Anna. Jacob tried to converse with him on a couple of occasions, but gave up after a number of one–or two-word answers. He was relieved when the afternoon was over, and since the evening service was canceled, Jay had a good excuse to go home and take a nap.

"Four more days, this is going to kill me," he said as he walked to his bedroom to lie down. The letter was still sitting on top of his desk. He had read it at least a hundred times. Re-reading it now gave him no new answers or ideas. He threw the letter down almost in disgust. "This should make me happy, not crabby and on edge," he said as he stretched out on his bed. "Unc, what in the world is going on? What are you up to?"

When Jay woke up it was already dark outside. He made his way down the hall to the kitchen and grabbed a Coke out of the refrigerator. He looked at the time on the microwave. It was 11:17 p.m. He couldn't believe it. He had slept for over six hours.

He walked into the living room, fell into his recliner and turned on the television. After catching the end of the nightly news, Jay watched the baseball highlights on *Sports Center* for about fifteen minutes before turning off the television. He got up, went back into the kitchen, and looked at the calendar. The answering machine was blinking again. He was sure it was a message from Anna.

"Eighty-two hours, eighty-two hours," Jay repeated over and over. "I can make that, no problem." With that he headed back to his room and got into bed for the remainder of the night.

CHAPTER ELEVEN

Jay woke up at five the next morning. He was wide awake and felt great. He got up and turned off the alarm clock so it wouldn't go off all day. After a quick shower, he headed to the kitchen for breakfast. In no time he had whipped up a nice three egg and cheese omelet and headed to the living room to enjoy his early morning feast.

After the morning news, Jay decided to take some initiative with the phone calls and went into the kitchen to dial a number he knew by heart.

"Hello," Jay heard on the other end of the phone. It was Anna.

"Hi there."

"What happened to you? I called last night but didn't get an answer."

"Man, I fell asleep and didn't wake up 'til after 11:00 p.m. I got up, had a Coke, and went back to bed until this morning. I feel great now."

"That's good, you needed the rest. You've been burning the candle at both ends lately." They talked a little more before deciding they'd grill some burgers at Jay's for dinner that evening sometime after six. There was no school until after the fifth of July, so Anna was going to spend the time working on her doctoral thesis. Jay told her to call him at work if she needed any help, and they both got a good laugh out of that.

Jay made his last preparations for the day and headed out the door. The morning air was still cool and refreshing, almost chilly if one didn't have a light jacket on, which Jay didn't. He shivered slightly as he walked from shade to sunshine along the tree-lined street. The walk heated him up in no time, and he was soon thankful to not have a jacket on. He was in a good mood, and he was fairly certain it would be a light day at work, since most of the regulars had headed for the mountains or some other far away place for the holiday.

Arriving at work nearly twenty minutes early, Jay helped Bob open the last few lumber bays and then turn on all the computers. Bob made coffee while Jay put out half a dozen boxes of donuts on the contractors counter. It was a small and inexpensive gesture of appreciation for their business. Jay wasn't really hungry, but he grabbed a donut anyway. He loved maple bars, especially when they were so fresh. Often times he had said that if he went into any other line of work, it would be as a baker.

He loved the smell of fresh baked breads and pastries. Every day on his way to work he could smell all those wonderful odors coming out of the bakery as he passed by. The particular smell of fresh pastry bread had stopped him on more than one occasion, rendering him either unable or unwilling to go any further until he had purchased a fresh donut or two. Even the knowledge that a large assortment of donuts awaited his arrival at work couldn't give him the strength to pass them up on those days.

True to his prediction, business was a trickle during the morning hours. Jay spent his time helping restock shelves and hardware bins just to pass the time. As noon approached, Nancy found Jay and offered him the rest of the afternoon off. He appreciated her offer and packed up his stuff to head home for an extra long holiday. On his way out the door, Nancy made sure to invite him and Anna to a Fourth of July picnic and barbecue the next evening. Jay quickly accepted and asked if he could bring Bill along too. Always the generous host, Nancy not only agreed but actually insisted on it. Jay headed out the door and up the sidewalk for home.

It was warm and sunny and he felt absolutely great. He and Anna were getting along superbly. And it was less than three days until his meeting with his Uncle Milt regarding the gift. He had his doubts about the validity of the letter, but had decided the only way to keep his sanity was to be completely positive.

The phone was ringing when Jay entered his house. He hurried over and picked up the receiver. "Hello," Jay said into the receiver, half-expecting it to be one of his siblings or relatives.

"Hey dog, what's up?" Bill answered him. "I stopped by your place of gainful employment this afternoon, and they told me you skipped out."

"Yeah, it was pretty slow in there today."

"Excuses, excuses!"

"What's up with you?"

"Some of my people and I were hoping you and Anna would join us for a movie or something."

"We kind of have plans. We were going to grill some burgers."

"Cool. Wining and dining the little lady sounds kind of serious to me."

"It's just a change of pace from eating out all the time. Hey, why don't you and your people come join us? We could have a party."

It only took Bill a second or two before he decided. "You know we'll be there. What time?"

"Six p.m."

"What should we bring?"

"Whatever you want to grill, let's just make it kind of a potluck."

"We'll be there with bells on, buddy!"

Anna arrived a little after five. She placed a couple of salads she had made in Jay's refrigerator and took out his hamburger. "How thick should I make these?" she asked Jay, who was busy dusting off and firing up his grill.

"Not knowing how many people will be here, you'd better make them thin enough to read through," Jay joked.

Anna took a plate out of the cupboard and started to pat out hamburgers that would make McDonalds proud. "I ran into Jacob and invited him and Stewart over for dinner. Hope you don't mind," she added, without giving Jay a chance to object.

For a moment he felt irritation rising as he digested this new bit of information. Then he realized it really didn't make any difference. He hadn't told anyone of the letter, and he had no control over whether it was all a big joke or not. "That's fine," he said as cheerfully as possible.

It wasn't long until people started arriving. Bill was the first one there, followed by Jacob and Stewart. They all brought along food of one sort or another.

Jay started grilling hamburgers and smoked bratwurst. Someone had brought spareribs that were partially cooked. He threw them on the grill to finish them off, slathering them in barbecue sauce right before they were ready to take off the grill.

"Yo dog, you're a real Chef Tell," Bill said to Jay as he handed him a cold Coke.

"You better not say that until you taste it," Jay warned.

Bill set up a folding table and several camp chairs too. He borrowed a sheet from Jay to cover the table before helping Anna place all of the food on it. There were more than a dozen different kinds of salads, baked beans, and a large assortment of grilled meats. Jay had a large igloo cooler filled with ice and everyone put their soda pop in it.

"Everyone, gather 'round for grace," Bill said as he headed

toward the table. He quickly prayed and everyone helped themselves to the abundant food before settling down on one of the many chairs, on Jay's steps, or on some blankets spread out on the grass. Jay sat next to Anna on a blanket, and they were soon joined by Bill and Beth. It was becoming apparent to Jay that Bill and Beth were becoming somewhat of an item. *They're a good fit for each other,* Jay thought to himself.

They traded small talk until Anna told them she had been contacted by the District Superintendent of their church earlier that day. It seems he wanted to have a meeting with Anna sometime before the first of August to discuss her upcoming mission and where they would like to send her. She kept her eye on Jay to see what his reaction might be, but he remained stone faced the whole time.

"That's top notch," Bill excitedly told Anna. "I have some breaking news of my own—well I will have some breaking news of my own very soon. I don't want to jump the gun, but you all can pray for me. I've made a big decision in my life, with help from The Big Man of course, and need all the prayer and support I can get."

Jay didn't say anything, but he wanted to very badly. He wanted to jump in and tell them all he had some really *big* news to tell them too, but he didn't. Instead he sat there sulking, annoyed that Anna had waited until everyone was there to tell them her news. Now he couldn't discuss it with her.

Oh well. He decided it wouldn't do any good until he could share his good news with her. *She would probably just argue right now anyway,* he thought to himself. Reluctantly, he joined in the visiting and congratulating Anna with everyone else. They all ate too much before heading inside to watch movies and have banana splits to round out the evening.

Jay woke up at about nine in the morning. He looked at the clock and smiled. *Two days to go,* he thought to himself. He rolled onto his back and stared at the ceiling. *Two short days to go!*

He soon found himself deep in his favorite pastime of late: thinking about the different ways he could spend the money. It was actually more difficult to think of things than he thought it would be. He definitely wanted a car. He couldn't decide what kind yet, but he decided that would be one of his top priorities right after paying a year's lease and then all of his bills. He could do all of that for fifty to sixty thousand. That left him a lot of money.

His thoughts slowly shifted to Anna. He wondered what her reaction would be. *She'll probably be reserved to start with, but I'm sure the excitement will overtake her. She wouldn't be human if it didn't,* he surmised.

Maybe we can pick out a ring, too. Jay started getting excited about the prospect. *That would really make her happy!* He rubbed his hands together over his head in excitement and quickly jumped up and headed out of his room.

He ended up in the kitchen and grabbed a drink out of the refrigerator. "No coffee today," he said to himself as he downed half a can of Coke in one swig. "Maybe I'll buy some stock in Coke," he laughed quietly. Jay grabbed a handful of Fig Newtons and headed into the living room to watch TV. He had kind of lost track of baseball with all the excitement of the letter, coupled with his renewed relationship with Anna. The highlights held his interest for all of fifteen or twenty minutes. *It's really going to be difficult to concentrate on anything,* he realized as he clicked off the television.

Jay just sat there looking blankly at the darkened set, without really focusing on it. His mind was running a hundred different directions at once. "This is worse than the anticipation of any Christmas I can ever remember," he said, as he got up and headed to the kitchen.

He opened and closed most of the cupboard doors looking for something, but not for any one thing in particular. Finally settling on a frosted cupcake, he headed down the hall to get ready for the barbecue. "I may as well go early," he thought to himself as he started to eat the cupcake in his ritualistic manner. After finishing the cupcake, he fumbled around his room for something to wear before heading to the bathroom to take a quick shower.

Jay finished his shower in short order. It was supposed to be hot out, so he dressed in shorts and a t-shirt. In case they decided to watch the fireworks display later that night, he also grabbed a hooded sweatshirt out of his closet. He hadn't decided if he wanted to stay up that long, since he had volunteered to work the next day.

It was already hot when he headed down the road toward Anna's, and after a few minutes of walking in the glaring sunshine, he broke into a good sweat. "I'll be traveling in cool comfort before long," he said to himself as he wiped the sweat from his forehead. "I just need to decide what kind to buy." Jay continued down the road toward Anna's, daydreaming about what make of car and what color car he should buy.

As he approached Anna's, he stopped mid-stride. "I was supposed to get a ride from Bill," he said as he smacked himself on the forehead. "Oh well, I'll just call him from Anna's and have him come over."

Jay turned the doorknob and said, "Knock, knock!" as he walked into the house. Nancy came running over and gave him a big hug.

"Happy Fourth of July!"

Jay walked into the house and followed Nancy into the kitchen. "Happy Fourth of July to you!"

"Have a cupcake." She handed him a chocolate cupcake frosted red, white, and blue. "I made them just for you boys," she said with a wink.

That reminded Jay that he had to call Bill. "Can I use your

phone really quick?" "You know where it is," Nancy said as she went back to making her potato salad.

Jay walked into the living room and picked up the cordless phone from its charger. He quickly called Bill and told him to head over whenever he wanted to. Bill gave him a hard time for not waiting for him and then promised he'd be there in twenty minutes or so.

Jay walked back into the kitchen. "Where might the others be?" he asked, as he sat down at the table.

"What others?" Nancy asked Jay with false innocence.

"Oh, I don't know, someone called Anna and someone called Bob, I think."

"Oh yeah, those others! Well, let's see. Miss Anna is showering and making herself pretty for some reason, and Bob is out in his shop getting the grill ready for later today. At least that was his excuse for getting out of the house."

Jay visited with Nancy for ten or fifteen minutes. She told him how happy she was that he was attending church more regularly and that she hoped he'd keep it up.

"Anna will keep me in line, I'm sure." He got up and walked around the kitchen. Jay grabbed another cupcake and headed out the kitchen door. "I'd better go see what the mister is up to out here."

"You guys behave yourselves!" she yelled through the window at Jay as he walked across the yard to the shop. She started to say something more, but closed her mouth and shook her head slightly before turning back to her work.

Jay reached the shop and opened the door. "Are you here?" he yelled into the dark building. "Hello, anybody home?" It took several seconds for his eyes to adjust. He scanned around the shop, barely able to make anything out. A flip of the light switch did nothing. His eyes continued to adjust to the low light, and he could soon see the grill in the back corner of the shop. It hadn't been moved.

Jay's heart began to race a little. His pulse sky-rocketed when he noticed what appeared to be the bottom half of a man lying on the floor behind the grill. The legs were clad in jeans with the familiar boots sticking up. The lower torso was pinned underneath a large homemade tool shelf that Bob had made years earlier.

The shelf was over ten feet tall and three feet deep. Its height and bulk had made it very unstable, and it took over four men to move it. On more than one occasion Bob had said he wanted to get rid of the thing.

Jay started to panic now. His heart felt like it was in his throat. He ran toward the body, his own voice sounding strange to himself. "Bob, Bob, are you okay?!"

There was no answer. Jay reached the body in just a few moments. Dark liquid pooled under the shelf. Acting on pure adrenaline, he tried to move the hutch. It wouldn't budge. It was too dark underneath the hutch to see much of anything, but tools and some books spilled over the upper torso.

Jay accidentally put his hand in the liquid. It was sticky. "Blood," he said to himself as he squinted at his hand. Bile and cupcake rose in his throat.

He knew it was futile, but he yelled for Bob again, begging for an answer. He was near tears. Under normal circumstances, no man would ever try to pull another out from under something this large and bulky. But by now he was acting totally on instinct and sheer panic.

Reaching down, he took a hold of the boots and pulled with all his might. The next thing he knew, he had flown backwards several feet across the floor and landed on his hind end, one boot and leg under each of his arms. Much to his horror, he had pulled the body in half.

"Ugh, ugh," he yelled in complete terror as he scooted across the floor as fast as he could, pushing the lower part of the body away from him.

Suddenly the light came on. Jay was disoriented as he looked around. He could hear someone laughing hysterically. It was Bill. *How could he?!*

Then he looked behind him. Bob was over by the light switch, bent over laughing so hard tears were running down his cheeks. Jay was confused as he looked first at Bob and then at the legs with boots on them. He had been pranked by his own boss and his best friend.

He got to his feet slowly and walked over to the boots. There were two sticks for legs with rags wrapped around them and then stuffed into a pair of Bob's old jeans. The bottom of the sticks had a board screwed to them at a perpendicular angle. They too were wrapped in rags and placed inside of a pair of Bob's old work boots. Jay kicked one of the boots. It came off the board and slid across the floor and under Bob's fishing boat.

It took him a few moments to gather himself. He was still visibly shaking. Bill was still rolling around on the concrete floor laughing. Bob was shaking his head laughing.

"All right, you guys got me," Jay said as he brushed himself off with one hand. He looked at the other hand. It was covered in an oily substance. Not blood. He reached down and wiped his hand clean on Bob's old jeans.

By now Bill had gotten up and come over to Jay. He was trying to contain his laughter, but just couldn't stop. "Dog, that was primo!" he said as he clapped Jay on the shoulder.

"Glad I could humor you," Jay said, feelings obviously hurt.

"Now Son, it was all done in good fun," Bob added.

"Yeah, we didn't intend for you to grab the legs," Bill added as he started to laugh again.

"How'd you get here anyway?" Jay asked Bill.

"Dude, I came over to your house to give you a ride and you were gone, so I tooled back to my pad and waited for you to call. I thought you must've just slipped down to the store for something real quick like. I didn't think there was any way you'd forget your ol' bud, Bill. Then when you called I headed right over. When I got out of my car, Mr. B motioned for me to come in to the shop and set up this elaborate scheme to fool the ol' Jayster."

"So you thought this whole ruse up?" Jay asked as he turned toward Bob.

"Now, don't get up in arms, it was all done in good fun. You've been walking around with your head in the clouds for the last few weeks, so I thought we'd bring you back down to earth."

Jay walked around shaking his head. They had made a big fool of him, but he decided he wasn't going to get mad. "You dirty dogs!" he said with a big grin on his face. "It looks like the two of you have a big mess to clean up." He looked at the overturned shelf and the oil on the floor.

"Yeah, the oil was Bill's idea. I knew that would make a mess," Bob said as the humor left his voice.

"Yo, Mr. B, you have to admit the oil made the whole prank believable," Bill said in his own defense.

Bob started to chuckle again to himself. "Yeah, it did at that."

"I wish we'd had a video camera for that," Bill added. "Instant classic, man!"

"I'm awfully glad you two are happy," Jay said as he headed for the door. "Have fun cleaning it up."

"It was worth it Mr. B." Bill repeated to Bob as the two of them started to laugh uncontrollably again.

Jay walked back to the house. He still felt vestiges of panic and shock. "I have to get a hold of myself," he said as he approached the kitchen door. He paused for several seconds, running his hands through his hair while shaking his head. "Those dirty dogs!" he said under his breath, smiling a little in spite of himself. Jay opened the kitchen door and walked in.

"Hi there!" Anna exclaimed as she walked over to him and gave him a big hug. Jay noticed her hair was damp and smelled of lilac as he hugged her back.

"Is the grill all ready?" Anna asked Jay.

"Oh, I guess so."

Anna pulled a chair out next to him. "You look kind of pale. Do you feel alright?" she asked, concern masking her face.

"I'm alright, I've just been a little jumpy is all," he explained without going into any details.

Nancy came back into the kitchen, "Are you boys all ready?" she asked as she looked at the clock on the wall. "We weren't planning on cooking for a few more hours."

"That's all right; I'm not that hungry right now anyway,"

"I don't think Jay's feeling all that well," Anna added.

Nancy walked over and put her hand on his forehead. "He doesn't feel hot," she announced in a motherly tone. She looked him over carefully. "Don't you feel okay?"

"I feel just fine," Jay answered sheepishly.

Nancy sat down at the table along with Anna and Jay. "At least you have today to rest up. You don't have to do a single thing but eat if you don't want to."

"I'm fine, really." Jay tried to convince the two women.

Nancy got up and poured Jay a large glass of iced tea. She put just a little sugar in it and stirred it vigorously. "Here, drink this slowly and cool down. After you finish that you can lie down for a little while and get some rest." Jay accepted the iced tea. It was useless to try and convince them that he was okay. He sure didn't want to tell them that he had just been pranked and that was all that was wrong with him. All he needed was to have them laughing at him, too.

Anna went to the fridge and took out some little Swedish cookies she had made earlier in the day. "Here, try these," she said as she handed Jay one. They were two little pastries about an inch square. They were put together like little sandwiches with some type of white cream filling. Jay picked up his little cookie and took a bite. The taste and texture were perfect. He took another small bite.

"These are unbelievable!" He popped the last little bite into his mouth. "What are they called?" he asked Anna as he took another one off the plate.

"I'm not sure. They're something my mother has made for as long as I can remember."

Jay quickly finished his second one and grabbed another off the plate. "I have to have one more of these," he said as he took a bite.

"They're really rich," Nancy added as she finished her second one.

It was clear Anna was pleased that they had gone over so well. She smiled when Nancy took her third one.

About that time the door swung open and in walked a meek Bob followed by a grinning Bill. "I suppose we're in big trouble now," Bob said as he leaned down and pecked Nancy on the cheek.

"In trouble for what?" Nancy asked, bewilderment crossing her face.

"You mean Jay didn't tell you?" Bob asked, looking at the two women.

"He didn't tell us anything. Why, what'd you two do?" Anna asked, her voice tinged with suspicion.

"Nothing, nothing at all," Bob answered slyly.

"Come on, you might as well tell us now," Nancy added.

"Jay, what'd they do?" Anna asked

"You'll have to ask those two geniuses," Jay said, beginning to enjoy their discomfort.

"Oh, I'll tell the sisters!" Bill finally said. And tell them he did. It was as if he had spent the last fifteen or twenty minutes rehearsing. He told the whole story with gusto, adding little bits and pieces to make the story more interesting. "Creative license!" he said when Jay objected to one or two fabricated details. If it had been a full length feature, Bill would have been in the running for an Oscar. Finally, when Bill was done with his tale and everyone was finished laughing, Anna stood up and told them how awful and terribly mean they had been.

"I sure wish I could have been there," she added between laughs.

"Hey!" Jay protested.

"For you, I meant," she added as she gave him a big hug while winking at the others behind his back.

The rest of the afternoon passed with very little excitement. Anna and Nancy finished preparing the afternoon meal while Jay, Bob, and Bill went outside and started a friendly game of horseshoes.

At around two in the afternoon, the pastor and his wife showed up for the barbecue. They were in their mid-fifties and had no family in the area, so Nancy generally invited them to all holiday meals and events. "We're all one big family anyway" was her favorite line.

The men all gathered out around the grill. Bob emerged from the house with large sirloin strip steaks over an inch thick, along with some Bratwurst sausages.

"Looks like you have enough meat there to feed over half the town," Pastor Doug said as Bob made his way to the hot grill.

"You can never have enough meat," Bob answered cheerfully. "I can feast on leftovers for the rest of the week."

It didn't take long for the meat to cook. The smell was unbelievably good. Jay hadn't felt hungry until he smelled the steak cooking. Now he was famished.

Bob and Nancy had a large deck on the back of their house with plenty of chairs for everyone and a couple of large picnic tables. Everyone migrated out there to enjoy the nice weather while they ate their meal and enjoyed the fellowship. The afternoon went rather quickly. Bill gave an encore performance for the pastor and his wife. Jay could already tell he'd never live this one down. It was one of those stories that just got better with each telling. Soon the afternoon was turning to evening.

"Are we going to watch fireworks?" Anna asked with anticipation.

"I don't know. I'm pretty tired," Jay said as the two of them walked across the yard looking at Nancy's beautiful flower gardens. He was amazed at how pretty and well kept they were.

"When does Nancy ever find the time to work in these?" he asked Anna in amazement.

"She works in them every evening for a couple hours just before dark. She says these gardens are her therapy," Anna explained.

"She is amazing!" Jay said in admiration. They continued to talk about the flowers and the many colors and shapes as they made it around the house.

"Are you sure you're too tired?" she asked again.

"Oh, I could probably be persuaded, maybe with some dessert or something."

"You can't be hungry!"

"I'm not, but I always have room for ice cream. It just fills in the cracks in my stomach."

"I think I can arrange some ice cream."

"Then I'll watch fireworks with you." They walked back to the deck and joined the others. Bill was talking to the others about his Second Chance program. They were all very supportive of Bill. The pastor often attended the weekly meetings. Bill was practically in tears as he told story after story of young people that needed help.

Jay soon lost interest in the conversation and started thinking about his upcoming meeting at the bank. He fought the urge to jump up and dance a little jig in excitement. "Let's go find a good vantage point to watch the fireworks," he quietly said to Anna as he stood up and headed off the porch.

"I already have someplace picked out," she answered as she led him into the house through the kitchen door. They went upstairs and headed into Anna's room. She walked over to her window and opened it. "We'll sit out here on the roof and watch them. Bob says it's the best view in town."

Jay quickly climbed out the window onto the shingled roof. He then helped Anna through the window and onto the roof. The roof wasn't extremely steep, which enabled them to navigate around fairly easily. They carefully climbed up to the peak and sat down, letting their legs extend downward just as if they were on a slide. The sun was setting in the west. Anna leaned her head on Jay's shoulder. "Isn't that sky beautiful?" she asked.

"Yes it is." The western sky was turning golden from the setting sun. It would still be a good half hour until fireworks. They could hear firecrackers going off all over town, along with music from a band playing in the city park.

"I love the fourth of July," Jay said as a Whistling Pete went off in the neighbor's yard. They sat there peacefully enjoying the ambience for another fifteen minutes or so, neither of them saying a word. It was getting dark, but was still very warm up on the roof. Jay was wishing he'd brought a cold Coke up with him. Every now and then a test firework was sent up into the air to test the light. They could hear them launched and would watch them advance up into the sky until they exploded. Ka-Boom! They were so loud and bright that the explosions shook the windows of the neighbors' houses.

"Mind if I join you two love birds?" Bill asked, startling the two of them as he climbed out through Anna's window. "Bob said I'd probably find you up here." He worked his way up the roof and sat down next to Anna, handing Jay an ice-cold Coke. "I figured you might want one of these."

"Thanks, man," Jay said as he popped the can open.

"I want the first drink," Anna said, holding out her hand. Even though the first drink was Jay's favorite part, he relented and gave the can to Anna.

"That's true love right there!" Bill teased. The fireworks started in earnest now, one shot after another rising up into the night sky. They lasted for a good thirty minutes before the grand finale. "Here it comes!" Bill announced as shot after shot could be heard. The mortars all rose up into the air in a choreographed masterpiece that lasted several minutes. Bright color after bright color lit up the black sky, each mortar exploding just moments before the one before it burned out all the way, until ten or more of them exploded simultaneously, signaling the end of the show. They sat there in total darkness.

"Well, it's over kids," Bill said to the two of them. "How do you propose we get off of this dark roof without killing ourselves?"

"I propose you fall off and then get us a light," Jay suggested.

"Ta da!" Anna said as she presented them with a small flashlight she had brought along in her pocket.

"You're my hero," Bill teased as they carefully worked their way off the roof.

They gingerly climbed down and through Anna's window before heading into the kitchen. Stifling a yawn, Jay took a raincheck on the ice cream. It was too late and he was too tired to walk, so he was happy to accept Bill's offer of a ride home.

"Thanks for being a good sport, dude," Bill said to Jay.

"Paybacks are rough, just remember that," Jay warned good-naturedly as they turned down the street toward his apartment. Several neighborhood kids were lighting fireworks in the road. Bill had to stop for a few minutes to allow a large fountain to burn out. Jay turned to Bill. "So what's your good news you've been dying to tell everyone?" he asked.

"I'd just as soon not say anything right now," Bill said, obviously uncomfortable talking about it. Jay felt like pursuing the matter but decided to let it drop for the night.

Bill nudged the car into drive and slowly maneuvered the car through the spent fireworks just like a pro through an obstacle course. In less than a minute, Bill pulled up out front and put his car into park. "Thanks for letting the old Billster tag along today, dude."

"No problem, I'm glad you came over," Jay said as he undid his seatbelt and climbed out of the car.

"Ten days," Bill said as Jay started to close the door.

Jay stopped, puzzled by what his friend had just said. "Ten days, what?" he asked Bill as he turned around and looked back into the car.

"Ten days and I can tell you my good news, I think," he added.

"Fair enough," Jay said as he closed the door.

In minutes he was in bed, welcoming the coolness of the sheets on his body. "Man this day flew by," he said to himself as he settled down for a good night's sleep. "Less than two days to go."

CHAPTER TWELVE

Jay was trying to defuse a bomb. Two wires armed the device, and he had to decide which wire to cut. He finally decided to cut the white one. It was the wrong wire, but instead of a huge explosion, the bomb started beeping a long obnoxious beep followed by a short pause and then another beep. This process kept repeating itself until Jay finally shook the cobwebs loose and realized it was his alarm clock that was beeping.

"Ugh, already?" he said to himself as he rolled over on his stomach and pulled his pillow up over his head. "That was one short night." He tried to muster the energy to get up out of bed. Jay lay there for several more minutes. He slowly stretched his arms and legs before getting up out of bed.

Just a little more than a day to go, he said to himself when he stood in front of his calendar. It was hard to believe he'd be a millionaire in one day. He stood there smiling. Butterflies were going wild in his stomach. "This is totally unbelievable!" he repeated to himself over and over again.

Jay filled his travel cup with the last of the coffee and headed out the door for work. The weather was absolutely beautiful, seeming to validate his stellar mood. There weren't many cars on the road at all. Many people had taken the day off so they wouldn't be exhausted from the fourth. With any luck, it'd be a slow day at work.

He was amazed at the large amount of spent fireworks still littering the streets. *I wonder who'll clean those up?* He turned the corner toward work. *Probably the poor city crew. Those guys should get a bonus for today,* he decided as he watched a city truck drive by.

Despite the groggy start to his day, Jay arrived at work a little early. Bob was already there and had unlocked everything. "Good morning youngster," he said as Jay walked to the back counter. "Find any bodies lately?" He started to chuckle to himself.

Yep, this'll definitely be a legend for years to come, Jay thought to himself as he turned on his computer. "I'm glad to see you're in such a cheerful mood today—at my expense of course," he added after a short pause.

"Couldn't be better," Bob replied, still laughing lightly.

Jay walked over and started the coffee brewing. Bob had brought several dozen donuts, just as he always did. Jay snagged a couple for himself. He hadn't taken time to eat breakfast before leaving the house. "Someday I'll probably be sorry for this," he admitted as he wolfed down the first donut and started on the second.

The business traffic was as light as Jay had thought it would be. Anna came down at noon and brought lunch to both Bob and Jay, leftovers from the day before. They didn't mind one bit, though. The assortment of salads seemed to taste better the second day than they did when they were first made. It was a delicious lunch made all the better by Anna's presence.

"Man you're in a good mood today," Anna said to him at one point over lunch.

"I feel great," he told her. He really wanted to tell her all about his meeting tomorrow and how it was going to change their lives forever, but he resisted the urge once again. *I can wait one more day,* he thought.

The rest of the afternoon dragged on slowly. Bob had a delivery, so Jay was left to man the store alone. He fronted all of the shelves, swept all of the floors, and even washed the windows.

He looked at the clock. *Two long hours to go.* He tried with all his might to will the hours away.

When Bob made it back to the store, he took one look around at everything Jay had accomplished and told him to get lost for the day. He was definitely pleased with the way everything looked.

Jay didn't have to be told twice. He gathered his belongings and headed out the door. When he was outside on the sidewalk, he stopped and looked at the building. *The next time I come here, I'll be a millionaire!*

He turned and headed down the sidewalk for home. The traffic was still very light. Jay practically ran the whole way. He seemed to have boundless energy, fueled from the excitement the next day promised to bring. He still had a few little doubts about the validity of the letter, but he'd pretty much shoved those to the back of his mind.

As Jay unlocked his front door, he could hear his phone starting to ring. *Is it going to ring every time I open the door?*

Flinging his empty cup into the sink, he quickly answered the phone.

"Hello," he gasped into the receiver, out of breath.

"Hello, Jay, this is Bob," the voice on the other end of the phone said.

"What's up?"

"I need to ask a huge favor of you. John called in sick for tomorrow, and I have a delivery I have to make first thing in the morning. I know I gave you the day off, but if there's any way possible, I really need you to come in tomorrow morning for a couple hours to watch the store."

Jay didn't say anything for a few moments while he digested this information. Usually he'd do anything Bob asked of him, but there was no way he could miss his meeting tomorrow.

"I would, but I have a meeting that's very important to me tomorrow morning at 10:30," he explained to Bob.

"I'll easily be back by then," Bob promised. "I should be back by 9:30 no problem."

"I don't know, I can't miss this meeting," Jay protested, knowing that deliveries seldom went as smoothly as planned.

"I know it must be important to you, Son, and I wouldn't ask if I wasn't in a tight spot here. You know you can trust my word though, don't you?"

Jay couldn't say no. Bob and Nancy had done so much for him over the years, never asking a single thing of him. It made him feel uneasy, but he finally agreed. "All right, but I really can't miss my meeting," he insisted.

"I'll tell you what, you can use my Tahoe after I get back to get to your meeting on time, and I'll even give you the rest of the week off for helping me out," he offered.

"Okay, I'll be there first thing in the morning," Jay said as he hung up the phone. He absolutely did not like this little wrinkle in his plans. He had anticipated getting to the bank at least a half an hour early, just to ensure that nothing went wrong.

Oh well, what could go wrong? Bob has never once let me down, he said, trying to convince himself that everything would be all right.

The evening dragged on and on. Jay watched a little television and paced a whole lot. He made several trips to his bedroom, where he took out the letter and read it over and over. His sanity was stretched to its limits. "How will I ever make it until tomorrow?" Every five minutes or so he looked at the clock. Time was barely crawling along.

Jay was so keyed up he almost had a heart attack when his door bell rang. He jumped up and flung open the door. It was Anna, Bill, and Beth.

"Hi, what are you doing?" Anna asked Jay.

"Nothing, absolutely nothing."

"Well, I was on my way over to see if you wanted to have dinner when Bill and Beth came along," Anna said as she walked in.

"Where did you guys want to go?" Jay queried.

"Somewhere that has ice cream, dude," Bill answered.

"Sounds good to me," Jay responded, thankful to have a distraction.

"It's settled then, let's go," Anna said as she headed out the door.

The four of them piled into Bill's car and headed out for the local burger joint. Jay was still bouncing off the walls. This was just what he needed to help pass the time.

They spent over an hour having dinner, including banana splits. Jay was absolutely stuffed.

"Do you kids feel like watching a movie?" Bill asked the others.

"No, I have to go into work tomorrow," Jay answered before the others could try to change his mind.

"I thought you had tomorrow off," Anna spoke up.

"Well I did, but that was before Bob called and asked me to work tomorrow morning."

Anna's eyebrows raised. "Oh, really?"

"Yeah, someone called in sick, and Bob has to make a delivery in the morning, so I told him I'd come in and man the store while he's gone. Besides, I'm still pretty tired from last night," he added.

They drove back to Jay's place to let him out. Anna gave him a hug and told him she'd see him the next day.

"Better go get your beauty sleep!" Bill called out as they drove off.

Jay watched them leave before heading inside. It felt like he was stepping into a furnace. He quickly turned on the air conditioner and stretched out on the couch. The sun was just starting to set, so Jay didn't bother turning on any lights. He started reflecting on the previous two weeks. It had been quite a roller coaster ride, emotionally. He still wasn't satisfied that all of the calls from his siblings had been coincidental. His cousins suddenly becoming an integral part of his life just added to the mystery. Instinct told him something was definitely up, but hope in the letter was what got him through the days. *Well, I guess the truth will come out shortly,* he said to himself as he got up off the couch and headed to bed for some calming sleep, which never came.

CHAPTER THIRTEEN

"Well, bud, this is the day you become a millionaire," Jay said to his reflection as he prepared for the day. *Or a fool!* he thought to himself.

His heart was beating rapidly. He took a long breath to calm down, but it had no calming effect on him. "Get a grip," he said to himself as he walked down the hall to the kitchen to make some coffee.

Jay closed and locked the door behind him, checking the folded letter in his back pocket. He looked around and headed off to work. *This is going to be a great day!* he said as he walked down the sidewalk.

When he got to work, Bob was ready and waiting to go. He met Jay at the door and told him he'd be back in about an hour.

The store was busy for a one-man shift, but Jay didn't mind. It helped time pass more quickly. Then time began to pass too quickly. By 9:45 panic was starting to set in. *Where in the world is Bob?* he asked himself as he started helping another customer.

His next customer wanted to purchase some paint. Getting the paint mixed just right could sometimes take up to a half hour, and today it did. Jay looked at the clock. 10:15. He was almost frantic as he tried to raise Bob on the two-way walkie talkies, to no avail.

"What am I going to do?" he asked himself. Tears were actually welling up in his eyes. He felt completely helpless. He couldn't leave the store unmanned, yet he couldn't miss this meeting. Sweat that had nothing to do with the heat began running down his back in rivulets. He looked at the clock.

10:23 a.m.

He couldn't believe it. There was no way he could make it across town in less than seven minutes. He remembered the letter said that he must be at the bank at 10:30 sharp. What would happen if he was late?

Jay turned quickly as he heard the back door open. It was Bob. He looked just as frantic as Jay felt. "Sorry, Son, the old truck died and wouldn't start. I tried to radio to let you know what was happening, but these Palouse hills wouldn't let my signal get out."

"That's okay. I should still make it on time," Jay called over his shoulder as he ran from the store.

He jumped in the front seat of Bob's Tahoe and started off across town. He looked at the clock on the dash.

10:29.

"There's no way I'll make it on time," he yelled at the dash.

Jay raced across town, getting stopped at two different stop lights. He turned onto Bishop Boulevard at 10:36 and headed for the bank. "Great, I'm way late!" he said in a complete panic. He reached the bank and pulled into the parking lot, jumping out, and slamming the door shut behind him.

Normally he would have looked around at his surroundings, but today he didn't have time. Instead he ran across the parking lot, up the steps, and into the bank. If he had taken the time, he would have noticed there were several familiar vehicles in the parking lot that day. Too many to be coincidental.

CHAPTER FOURTEEN

The Bank was a large red brick building that resonated wealth. Large white fluted pillars held up a parapet roof over the entryway. The doors were oversized and had large brass latches and hardware. The entryway floor was finished in Greek tile, hand cut. Maroon carpet with golden highlights was almost thick enough to lose a small child in. A tile walkway cut through the carpet and led up to cashier stations with polished granite countertops.

Jay noticed none of the grandeur as he came running into the foyer, out of breath. He looked around the massive bank with wide eyes. The large clock on the wall said 10:47. Jay's heart sank. He looked around for any sign of his uncle, but couldn't find him anywhere. Frantically, he clawed the letter out of his jeans pocket. *What was the name of that guy I was supposed to meet?*

A very pretty young woman with long blonde hair stood up from a nearby oak desk. She was wearing glasses that looked like they had been in style during the sixties, and the plaque on the desk said her name was Lilly. Seeing Jay's distress, she made her way over to him, smiling professionally.

"May I help you sir?" she asked as she approached Jay.

"I, um, I was supposed to meet someone here," he said as he fumbled around with his letter. His heart was beating about two hundred times a minute. It felt as if it was going to explode. His forehead had beads of perspiration running down it. Jay raised his hand and wiped the sweat away, suddenly very self-conscious. The young lady was looking at him with concern, waiting for him to reveal exactly who it was he was supposed to meet.

After an awkward pause she asked him, "Did you have an appointment with someone?"

He looked at the paper for a moment and then said, "I was supposed to meet a Mr. um, Mr. George Gillis and a Mr. Milton Bilston."

"And you are?" the pretty girl asked.

"Jay. Jay Bilston."

Lilly walked back to her desk and took out a sheet of paper with a lot of writing on it. She started to run her finger down the left hand margin of the paper.

"I'm kind of late," Jay offered as the girl kept looking for something on her paper.

"Oh yes, here you are Mr. Bilston," she said as she placed the paper back inside a leather jacket and closed it. "Could you wait here for just a moment?" she asked as she turned and headed toward the back of the bank and the lone open door that could be seen.

Jay watched as she reached the door and stepped inside, obviously talking to somebody. She looked out at Jay a couple of times, nodded her head, and started back over toward him. Jay was so nervous he was trembling. A knot of dread solidified in the center of his stomach. He just knew he had botched this one up. "One chance and it's probably all ruined," he said under his breath as the lady approached.

"Could you come this way please, Mr. Bilston."

His heart leapt with joy at the unexpected words. Maybe he wasn't too late. He obediently followed Lilly to the back of the bank and to the open doorway. She stood to one side and motioned for him to enter.

"Thank you," he said, barely able to recognize his own voice.

Jay walked into the brightly lit room and was immediately

shocked. There were about fifty or sixty chairs with desks, similar to the style, if not quality, used in high schools. At least thirty of them were occupied by people he knew.

He could see his parents and most of his siblings. The pastor and his wife, along with a number of other people from the church. There were also a few people he didn't recognize. He glanced around quickly, his wide-eyed expression reflected back from the myriad faces.

The desks had name plates on them. Jay scanned the empty desks until he found the one with his name on it. It was up front, next to his mother's desk. Jay sat down at the desk and looked at the clock. It was now 10:58, and eerily quiet. His mind was numb, and the joke theory began to gain credence. Slowly, and reluctantly, his hopes began to fade.

A rather large man standing in the corner, wearing a dark three piece suit kept looking at his wrist watch. The man had thick glasses and was balding on top. He looked nervous.

The time continued to slip by, second by agonizingly slow second. Jay kept looking at the clock. He was afraid to look around, for reasons he didn't even try to fathom. Nobody spoke. He didn't remember seeing his cousins when he came in. Someone started to cough behind him.

At 11:08, the nervous-looking large man walked across the room and opened a door. He started conversing with someone behind the door. After a few more moments he came back out into the room and stood at the podium, appearing to be doing a head count. He had a list that he kept referring to. After a few more moments he put the paper down and walked back to the closed door, opened it and walked out.

Jay managed to look over at his mother and father. They were pale and appeared as edgy as he felt. He heard his sister Lisa from somewhere in the background say, "Oh good grief!" under her breath just loud enough for everyone to hear.

After what seemed like a half hour, but in reality was more

like five minutes, the door reopened and the large man in the suit came back in, followed by none other than Milt Bilston. He was dressed in new Levi blue jeans and a blue button-down dress shirt with an open collar. The cuffs on Milt's sleeves were undone and rolled back to his elbows. His head was shaved bare, as it had been for as long as Jay could remember. It made it impossible to tell how old he really was. Milt was very fit and was close to six feet in height. He was an imposing individual.

Both the stranger in the suit and Milt approached the podium, clearly agitated. They were looking intently at a piece of paper and appeared to be conversing about something written on it. Try as he might, Jay found it impossible to tell exactly what Milt was saying. A few more moments passed before Milt nodded his head in agreement with the large man as they looked at the clock. The suited man, apparently satisfied, turned and walked back to his original place in the front corner of the room.

Milt stood at the podium, gathering his thoughts. After a few more moments he cleared his throat. "First of all, I'd like to thank each and every one of you for taking time out of your busy day to come down here. By now, I'm sure you've figured out that all of you have received a copy of the same letter." A hushed murmur could be heard around the room.

Jay was absolutely stunned. He knew his uncle was very wealthy, but he had absolutely no idea that he was this wealthy. He lived very modestly, after all. He wasn't a flashy dresser, he lived in the same home he had built twenty years earlier, and he even drove a two-year-old Chevy Silverado.

Then suddenly everything made sense to Jay. The phone calls from his siblings, his father's odd behavior and talk of retirement. They were all trying to see if anyone else had any information or knew anything at all about the letter. The problem was, everyone was afraid to say anything for fear of losing the money. Jay felt stupid for being so paranoid. He was sure they were all in the same boat.

The fact that his cousins were starting to come around must have been nothing more than a coincidence, since they weren't at the bank. At least that was the most logical explanation Jay could think of. He still didn't know what to think about his encounter at church with his uncle Milt. It must not have been a big deal since nothing had been said about it. At least not yet. Jay felt a huge wave of relief, even though he had long ago shoved most of his doubts about the letter aside.

"Second, I want to assure you, this is not a joke."

A collective sigh of relief could be heard spreading throughout the room. Some of the people started clapping, while others began to cheer. Jay heard his sister Lisa say, "It's about time!"

Milt stood looking out at the crowd, waiting for them to calm down so he could continue on. "I'd also like to take the time to apologize to you for the tardiness of this meeting. There's a good explanation for it, and I'll get to that point in a few minutes."

Jay couldn't help but notice that his uncle's grey blue eyes seemed to bore right into your soul when he looked directly at you. They were very intense, but somehow managed to be friendly at the same time.

"There was a portion of the letter that instructed that under no circumstances were you to discuss its contents with any other person without forfeiting your right to the gift." Milt paused. "I want to take the time now to ask if anyone here did tell anybody about the letter or will admit telling anybody about the letter."

The room was silent. Not a single person moved a muscle or said a word. Even though Jay hadn't told a soul, his heart started to race. He knew what was at stake. He glanced around the room but didn't see a single person respond to Milt's questioning. After all, no one wanted to lose a million dollars. Yet he was sure that somebody in that room had to have told someone else about the letter they had received. Human nature alone would have prompted them. Who knows if he would have held out if he had opened the letter when it first arrived.

Judging by his uncle's expression, Jay thought Milt must be having the same skeptical thoughts. "Now, what would you say if I told you that I had evidence that some of you have talked about the letter to others?" There was still no response.

Milt waited through a long period of silence, his eyes settling on each person sitting before him. Still nobody said a word. "I know that some of you have talked about the letter to others," he said emphatically as his voice rose an octave or two. There was no room for doubt.

Everyone was squirming in their seats. Jay found it difficult to even look his uncle in the eyes. He wondered if his sisters could. *I'll bet any amount of money they both told someone about the letter*, he thought to himself.

"I want everyone here to tell me the truth." No one moved or dared to look away for fear it would indicate guilt. Milt started again, slowly. "I'm going to tell you something now that will hopefully ensure that all of you will tell me the truth." He paused even longer.

Not one person said a word. Milt had everyone's undivided attention, and he intended to keep it.

"I've decided that whether you talked to anyone about the letter or the money doesn't matter. As of right now, you are all eligible for the money. You will not forfeit one dime of it." He waited and watched. Still no one moved a finger or said a word.

"I'm going to repeat myself. You will not forfeit the gift if you told someone about the letter or the money. All I'm asking is that you be honest with me about it. I hope that you can trust my word on that."

For several tense seconds no one moved. No one even looked around the room. It reminded Jay of prayer time in church when the evangelist or pastor opened the altar or asked for a show of hands if you wanted to be prayed for. Everyone was very uncomfortable.

Finally the preacher's wife timidly raised her hand. She looked absolutely scared to death, yet she raised her hand. Jay thought the pastor looked even more scared, if that was possible. *Probably the fear of losing the money.*

Everyone waited, still as statues, to see if she would garner the wrath of Milt. She didn't. Milt simply acknowledged her hand with a nod.

Slowly, one by one, more and more people raised their hands, twenty-one in all. Milt shook his head and smiled. Jay was stunned. He never would have predicted that so many people had talked, let alone would risk admitting it. He waited in nervous anticipation for Milt to jump up and down yelling, "Ah-Ha!"

Milt never did.

"Thank you for your honesty," he said as he motioned everyone to lower their hands. "Now, I'd like to address the issue of the tardiness of this meeting. I decided a few months ago to give away fifty million dollars. Consequently, I sent out fifty identical letters to some family and close friends. I spent a lot of time deciding to whom I would send a letter, the reason for which I will disclose at another time. The fact of the matter is that I committed the fifty million. I can only say that I was dumbfounded when only thirty two of you showed up today. I was sure there had to be some kind of mistake or explanation, so I waited and waited, holding the meeting off longer and longer hoping that more people would present themselves. Obviously, no one else did. I can only wonder in bewilderment why, given the opportunity, thirty-six percent of the recipients didn't show up. You would think that curiosity alone would have made them want to attend today." Milt stopped to gather himself. Everyone was still at full attention, waiting to see what he had to say.

"As I said earlier, the fifty million has already been committed. The eighteen million that has not and will not be claimed will therefore be split evenly between the thirty-two people who did show up." He paused to let this new revelation sink in. "That means each of you will receive an additional five hundred sixty-two thousand five hundred dollars."

Jay couldn't believe his ears. This was unbelievable news. *Their loss is our gain,* he said to himself with glee. The entire room was abuzz about this new revelation. Excitement was overriding caution, and everyone was starting to feel much more relaxed.

"What's going on Milt, are you dying or something?" Jay's sister Lisa asked.

"Yeah, is something wrong?" another lady at the back of the room asked Milt in concern.

Milt held his hands up, palms toward the crowd. He had a big smile on his face. "First of all, I forgot to set the parameters of this meeting." He paused while everyone quieted down. "The only questions that will be allowed will be ones asked by me to all of you. No exceptions!"

Everyone was quiet. Jay quickly looked around the group. Lisa looked really annoyed. *Milt sure put her in her place.*

"I will answer that question, though. There is absolutely nothing wrong with me physically, and contrary to popular opinion, there is nothing wrong with me mentally either," he said as the entire group, excluding Lisa, laughed out loud. Instead, she sat with a petulant look on her face and her arms crossed over her chest, pouting like a little child.

Milt stood there, gathering his thoughts before continuing on. "Now, about the money." Everyone was at full attention, hanging on his every word, waiting for him to continue on. In the air-conditioned room, the palms of Jay's hands were wet with perspiration. Even the large man in the corner seemed to be paying closer attention, and he didn't seem to have anything to gain.

"Let me back up a bit. I've neglected my duties by not introducing the man to my right." Milt turned and stretched an arm out to the large man in a suit. "This is my good friend and personal banker," he paused, "and now your banker too. Mr. George Gillis."

PRICELESS

The banker, obviously uncomfortable with the attention, half raised his hand, half waved at everyone. Some of the people clapped, some nodded, and others greeted him with a friendly hello.

Milt continued after the brief introduction. "Where was I? Oh yes, about the money." He paused. Jay didn't know if it was for dramatic effect or if Milt was simply gathering his thoughts.

"Mr. Gillis has already opened up an interest-bearing account in each of your names in the amount of one million five hundred sixty two thousand five hundred dollars."

Once again there was a collected gasp throughout the group. Jay could hardly contain himself. It still seemed too good to be true. Everyone in the room was smiling; some had tears in their eyes. Everyone was definitely overjoyed.

"Now, I'm going to explain to you how you can collect the money. I want everyone to listen very closely because you have to follow these directions precisely."

This was the part Jay was afraid of. He could sense some sort of hitch or stipulation attached to the money, some kind of terms that would prove impossible to meet.

Milt looked around the room. The once enthusiastic crowd had turned suddenly suspicious. "Each of you will receive a bank card, a credit card, or debit card of sorts. It will be in your name and will allow you to spend up to three thousand dollars a day, every day, for the next thirty days. At the end of the thirty days, if you follow all of the directions precisely, the money in your account will be exactly that: yours. If you don't follow the directions precisely, you will forfeit the money." He paused to let his audience absorb the new information before explaining further.

"The three thousand dollars a day will be yours to keep even if you fail to qualify for the rest of the money. I want to stress however that you can spend only three thousand dollars a day or less. Also, your card cannot gain in value. It will never be worth more than three thousand dollars a day. In other words, you cannot carry three thousand dollars from today over to tomorrow and then have six thousand." The room was silent but for a rustle of clothes as someone shifted in their seat.

"Are we all on the same page?" he questioned the quiet, somber group.

Everyone nodded their head in affirmation, but the pastor's wife raised her hand.

"Yes?" Milt asked her.

"What if we don't spend money on Sundays, since it is the Sabbath?" she asked.

"Good question. I have made provisions for that. Since Sunday is the Sabbath, your cards will be worth six thousand dollars on Monday. This is the only day any balance can be carried over. If on Monday you don't spend the six thousand, your card will only have a three thousand dollar value on Tuesday. If you aren't able to think of anything to use your card on, then you can simply go to any bank and withdraw three thousand dollars cash. You can do that every day except for Sundays. Basically, you have access to ninety thousand dollars by the end of the month."

"What kind of foolishness is this?" Jay heard his father ask Milt.

"Yeah, this isn't fair," Lisa chimed in. "You can't make us do this. We don't even know what the other stipulations are," she continued, her voice now tinged with anger.

"Yeah, we'll go the thirty days, and then you'll have some other stupid stipulations or rules that we have to follow to get the money!" Jay's sister Barbara joined in.

Several nodded in agreement, but nobody else had anything to say. Milt just stood there, waiting to continue until he was sure everyone was through talking.

"First of all," he started, "I don't think getting ninety thousand dollars is foolishness. Secondly, fair is a relative term. Fair to whom?

"I want to make it clear: you all are the receivers of this gift. I am the giver of this gift. Only the giver can make the rules, which are neither fair nor unfair. They are simply the rules. You are right in that I can't make you follow any directions or stipulations. All I can do is set the rules for you to follow to receive the money. It's very simple: if you don't want the money, don't follow the rules."

He stopped and consulted the papers in front of him. Satisfied, he began again. "On my honor, if you follow all of the directions I'm about to give you, at the end of thirty days the money will be yours with no strings attached. Now, I'm going to give you the stipulations or rules you must follow to receive the money:

"First, under no circumstances are you to contact me whatsoever.

"Second, you cannot tell a single soul about this money for the next thirty days. Not your friends, your bosses, your co-workers, your enemies, no one. Not even your long-lost relatives in Europe or other parts of the world.

"I know this was a stipulation I made prior to today and I let you off. Let me assure you now, I will not let you off the next time. I also want to assure you that if you tell anyone, I have the resources, and I will find out.

"Third, you cannot discuss this amongst yourselves. Even though you all know each other and the opportunity will present itself, you must refrain from talking, or else..."

There was complete silence. No one moved. *That doesn't sound too bad to me,* Jay thought. *But what can I say to Anna?*

Milt started again. "I hope you'll believe my sincerity when I say I want all of you to be successful. I don't feel that I am asking too much of you. I know you all are probably thinking I'm crazy, but I have my reasons for having you go through this. I promise you, it'll all make sense when we meet back here again in thirty days and I have the opportunity to explain everything to you. Now, I want to turn the meeting over to Mr. Gillis."

Milt stood back and waited for the banker to reach the

podium. He shook his hand, turned, and walked through the far door without glancing back.

The banker cleared his throat. "I'd like to take the time to thank all of you for your patience. In a few moments, Mary and Lilly will come in with some paperwork for each of you to fill out to receive your debit card. Now, are there any questions?"

The room was quiet for several seconds until Lisa raised her hand.

"Can you tell us, or do you know, exactly what Milt is up to?"

The banker looked uncomfortable. If he did know anything, he wasn't about to tell them. "I'm afraid that is the one question I can't help you with."

As if on cue, Mary and Lilly appeared with their paperwork. They quickly set up a workstation at the back of the room and motioned that they were ready, but over half of an hour passed before it was Jay's turn at the desk. He had rested his head on the desktop and dozed off. Lilly had to come and tell him it was his turn. Jay looked up, his mind dull with sleep.

"Everyone else is done, Mr. Bilston. It's your turn now."

Jay quickly covered up a pool of drool on his desk top. He didn't want her to see it. If she had, she never indicated so. After verifying his identity, Lilly had him sign his name on the form and on the back of his new green debit card.

"Here you go sir, you're all done."

Jay thanked her and walked out into the foyer of the bank. "I may as well see if this works," he said to himself as he walked up to the cashier.

"May I help you?" the young lady behind the large granite countertop asked.

"I'd like to withdraw three thousand dollars, ma'am." Jay handed her his new debit card and his driver's license.

The young lady punched some buttons on her keyboard. She waited a few moments, told Jay she'd be right back, and walked over to her supervisor. Jay watched the supervisor look something up on her computer screen and then check the debit card and license thoroughly. After a few moments, evidently satisfied, the supervisor handed Jay's card and I.D. back to the young lady. The teller returned to her station in front of Jay and asked, "How would you like that sir?"

Jay hadn't thought that far in advance. "Um, I guess in hundreds."

The efficient teller counted out thirty crisp, new one hundred dollar bills, had Jay sign a withdrawal ticket, and handed him his money.

"Thank you," he said with a big smile, then turned and headed for the door. Jay walked outside into the bright sunlight, cash in his pocket, and smile on his face. It felt like a whole new day.

CHAPTER FIFTEEN

Jay returned home immediately after leaving the bank. He was uncomfortable with all that cash in his wallet so he put it in a plastic bag and then placed it in the freezer. He decided that he needed to have a plan of attack, so he sat down at his kitchen table and started to write down all of his bills. A full year of rent up front would take $7,200 dollars. Three days before he could withdraw enough money. Next he'd pay off all of his credit cards. He would call and pay them by phone on Sunday, since the bank wouldn't be open. Besides, it would save him the trouble of withdrawing cash and then purchasing cashier checks and stamps to mail the payments. The rest of his bills wouldn't take him long at all to pay off. All told, his bills, including rent, came to a grand total of $14,620. He'd have enough money by the middle of the following week.

Jay smiled and sat back from the table. He couldn't believe this day had finally arrived. After a Coke run to the kitchen, he resumed working on the list. "New car" went under the list of bills. He wasn't sure what he wanted to get, but it was going to be red. He'd wanted a red car since he was a little boy.

Jay wondered what all the other people would do with their money. He was fairly certain his parents would pay bills and then save the rest. His mother was very conservative when it came to money. He was sure his two sisters would spend it as fast as they got it. They were both self proclaimed 'shop-a-holics.'

"Oh man, now I'll have to pay tithe on the money. There's no way out of it," Jay realized as he remembered the pastor and his wife had been at the bank meeting.

"I wonder if I should pay tithe on the whole amount I receive or only on the amount after taxes?"

In any case, Jay added nine thousand dollars to his list of bills. He just couldn't see any way around it. He did find humor in the thought of the offering counters for the next several Sundays trying to figure out where all the extra offering was coming from. It'd almost be worth staying late just to watch their reactions.

Jay pushed his chair back from the table. He stretched his arms out and back as far as he could reach. It felt good to let the stress of the day flow out of him. The phone caught his eye as he leaned back. Maybe Anna would feel like going out and celebrating. At least he could celebrate. He just couldn't tell her that he was celebrating.

This is going to be tough, he thought as he dialed the phone.

CHAPTER SIXTEEN

Jay rolled out of bed about ten the next morning. It felt odd to him to sleep in so long, since it was a Friday. He made coffee and turned on the T.V. Nothing much was on this time of day. He surfed around until he found the Northwest Cable News Channel and left it there until the weather came on. The forecast was for hot, hot, and more hot. Jay turned it off and enjoyed the silence.

He'd been thinking a lot about Anna. He really had wanted to tell her about the money last night at dinner, but knew she wouldn't want him to say anything if he wasn't supposed to. If she had been curious about his meeting since he'd made such a big deal about it for the past several weeks, she sure didn't show it.

Jay looked at the clock. It was almost lunch time. He decided to go to the bank and withdraw some more money. The thought of getting three thousand more dollars made him grin enthusiastically. "This is just unbelievable," he said as he headed to his bedroom to retrieve his wallet and sandals.

The thought brought a vision that threatened to dampen his happiness: his father sternly telling him, "If it sounds too good to be true, it is too good to be true. You can mark my word on that."

It suddenly dawned on Jay exactly how difficult the past month must have been for his dad. It was no wonder he'd been withdrawn and unresponsive. Jay wondered what his parents were doing now. He was sure his dad would still be suspicious of everything, not knowing what Milt was up to. But what could he do except trust that everything would work out the way his uncle had said it would?

Jay walked outside into the full sunlight. The weatherman had definitely gotten today's forecast right. Sweating already, he headed down the street toward the bank. Usually the long walk wouldn't matter to him, but usually it wasn't this hot.

I've got to get a car with air conditioning. The heat was radiating up off the pavement, making his legs feel like they were melting. His sandals offered almost no protection.

Jay walked along the rows of houses for several blocks before turning and heading for the main drag. Traffic was fairly heavy considering college was still out. Passing the lumber yard across the street, he tried to look in the window to see what was going on, but he couldn't really see anything. *Wouldn't they be surprised if they all knew I was heading to the bank to withdraw three grand?*

As Jay neared the bank, he noticed a car dealership. He stopped for a moment or two just so he could admire all the shiny new cars. There were so many of them that it was hard to look at any one model. His eye was eventually drawn to a sleek red car near the entryway of the building.

Walking over for a closer inspection, he saw it was a new Chevy Impala. Jay gulped as he read over the invoice: $29,422. That was a lot of money to spend on anything besides a house. *It would only take me ten days to pay for it,* he argued with himself. He had mistakenly figured it would only cost around fifteen thousand or so to buy a new car.

"How can people afford to buy these things," he said as he walked up and down the rows of new Suburbans.

"An amazing thing we call financing," a salesman said as he walked up behind Jay.

Jay nearly jumped out of his skin. He had no idea anyone was around, let alone had heard what he said.

"Are you looking for a new rig?"

"Not yet, I'm just getting some ideas for later," Jay said awkwardly.

"What'd you have in mind?" the salesman asked as he sized up Jay.

"I really don't have any idea. But nothing this expensive, though." Jay motioned toward the Suburbans.

"What kind of car do you have right now?"

"I, um, don't really have a car."

"Really, that's unusual. Do you have a driver's license?"

"Oh yeah, I'm licensed and all, I've just never seen the need to own a car."

The salesman paused, not sure if this individual was worth the time he was spending on him. It wasn't as if they were busy, though. It was a typical Friday midday during the summer. He decided it wouldn't hurt anything to keep talking, even if it was scorching hot.

"Are you from Pullman?" the salesman asked.

"Yeah, I live here," Jay answered, feeling somewhat uncomfortable being asked so many questions.

"Are you a student?"

"No, I don't go to school," Jay replied, not offering any other information.

"You must be on vacation or something," the salesman said, not wanting to come right out and ask Jay if he was employed.

"Yeah, I have a few days off."

"Do you work around here?"

"I work as counter salesman for the lumberyard."

The salesman was heartened to hear that. It was nearly impossible to sell a car to someone without a job. Emboldened, he became even more aggressive.

"So you know Bob and Nancy," he said, using first names to infer he had a personal relationship them. "I sold them a new Tahoe a few months ago."

"Oh, I've driven that rig," Jay said, becoming a little more comfortable with all the questions.

"I could fix you up with one just like theirs," he promised.

Remembering how much Bob had spent on his truck, Jay politely declined.

"Actually, I kind of like that red Impala over there." Jay pointed up to the front of the parking lot.

"Let's go take a look at it, I'll get the key," the salesman said, deciding to go for the sale.

Jay waited at the car, admiring it while the salesman went inside to retrieve the keys. He could picture himself driving around in this. He was sure Anna would like it too.

The salesman quickly reappeared with the keys. He unlocked the doors and had Jay sit behind the wheel. The gray leather seats felt smooth against his skin. The salesman handed him the keys and told him to start it up.

Jay didn't have to be told twice. He turned the key in the ignition and stepped lightly on the gas. It roared to life. The dash lights were red on a white background. Everything was digital. Jay was in love already.

"Do you want to take it for a spin?"

Jay hesitated. He really would like to drive the car, but he knew he wouldn't be able to purchase it today.

"No, I think I'll wait a few days."

"Are you sure? This baby has your name on it," he said, trying to keep Jay on the hook.

Jay sat there, tempted. He really wanted this car. "No, I'll come back after I have my money."

The salesman perked up when Jay mentioned money.

"Oh, you're not going to finance? We have zero down, zero percent financing for another week or so," he offered.

It was tempting to Jay, but he declined. The salesman's elation slowly subsided as he realized he wouldn't be making a sale that day. He handed Jay a business card and told him to call him or stop in whenever he was ready to buy the car.

Jay walked directly to the bank and took the wallet out of his shorts. He struggled to get the debit card out from the little compartment he'd placed it in. The air in the bank was cool and refreshing.

I have to get that car, if for no other reason than for the air conditioning, he thought to himself as he got in line to withdraw some money. He looked over at the help desk and noticed only one of the girls from the previous day was there. It was Mary, the young lady who had helped him fill out his initial paper work.

She looked up at Jay and smiled. "How are you today, Mr. Bilston?"

Jay blushed, realizing Mary had caught him looking at her. "Hi, fine I mean," he answered awkwardly as he moved up toward the open teller.

"If there's anything I can help you with, just let me know," she said with a big smile.

Jay nodded his head toward her, feeling like a fool as the teller asked him, "May I help you?"

Jay thrust the debit card to the lady behind the counter. "I'd like to withdraw three thousand dollars please."

The lady took the card and punched some numbers on her keyboard. She looked at her computer screen for a moment and asked him for some picture I.D.

"Oh, sorry." Jay quickly took out his driver's license.

"How would you like that, sir?"

"Um, half twenties and half hundreds," he said just to be different than the previous day.

The teller disappeared for a moment before returning and counting out three thousand dollars worth of bills in front of Jay.

"Will there be anything else, sir?" she pleasantly asked him.

"No, that'll be all," he answered as he gathered the cash up off the granite countertop and stuffed it awkwardly into his now bulging wallet.

Jay turned, nodded to Mary and walked back out the door into the sweltering heat.

The trip back home went without a hitch. Jay stopped at his favorite burger place and purchased a double bacon burger with onion rings. He resisted the temptation to buy a milkshake and purchased an iced tea instead.

Someday these things will kill me, he thought as he wolfed down his ketchup-drowned greasy burger and extra oily onion rings. *Oh well, I might as well enjoy life a little.*

Jay reached his house in short order. He headed right in and turned on the air conditioner. After excitedly counting his money, he placed it in his freezer on top of the stash from the previous day. "If this keeps up, I'll have to get a larger freezer," he said to himself as he chuckled at his own joke.

Then, for the joy of it, Jay grabbed his notepad and added three thousand dollars to the asset side of the list he'd made previously. He looked it over for a minute until he added twenty-nine thousand to the bill side of his list. "Might as well admit it, I'll be buying that car in no time."

CHAPTER SEVENTEEN

Anna called Jay at 6:45, just as he was finishing up his post-nap shower. "I'll pick you up in five minutes."

"Pick me up in what?"

"I borrowed Bob's Tahoe, it's too hot to walk tonight, at least for me anyway," she explained.

"I'll be waiting with bells on."

Jay was in a very cheerful mood. Money was coming in, he almost bought a car, and he was spending a lot of time with Anna. "It doesn't get much better than this," he shared with his furnishings.

"You sure look nice this evening," Jay said when she arrived precisely on time, noticing her nice summer dress as he got into the car.

"Why thank you," Anna replied, glancing over at Jay. He was dressed in shorts, tank top, and flip-flops which made it impossible for Anna to return the compliment in kind.

"You sure look, um, cool," she countered.

"Well, just knowing Bill, I'm sure this thing will be pretty casual," Jay explained as they headed down the street toward the church.

When Bill first started hosting his outreach Bible studies at the church, several people complained to the pastor, concerned the wrong kind of element was hanging around the church. "We just don't want to portray the wrong kind of image to the community, you know," their spokesperson said.

Much to his credit, the pastor staunchly defended Bill's program and even attended most of the events. "This is exactly the kind of image the Lord wants us to portray," was his point-blank answer.

They pulled up in front of the church five minutes early. There was already a bevy of cars and motorcycles in the parking lot. Anna leading the way, Jay got out and headed for the church. He had been to some of Bill's meetings before and felt somewhat uncomfortable. It wasn't that he didn't like the people who attended. They were just different than Jay, so he mostly kept to himself.

Bill, Susan, and Beth were in the foyer to greet them. Hugs were exchanged all around as they made their way toward the fellowship hall.

"Yo dog, what'd Anna have to do to drag you out tonight?" Bill teased, obviously pleased that Jay had tagged along.

"I had to promise him some ice cream."

"What? You know me, I wouldn't miss one of these things," Jay sarcastically replied.

"Ooh ow, a shot right to the heart, dude," Bill said as he grabbed his chest and spun around against the wall, feigning a mortal injury.

They reached the fellowship hall and walked into a gathering of society's outcasts and misfits. There were fourteen people in all, not counting Jay, Anna, and Bill. Six men and eight women. Jay knew Susan and Beth, but beyond that everyone was pretty much a stranger to him.

Bill walked right to the center of the makeshift circle and introduced Anna and Jay to the group. "These here pilgrims are part of my posse. They go by the handles of Miss Anna and Jittery Jay," he said, obviously enjoying being the center of attention.

The group gave them a collective hello before Bill opened the service up with prayer. He kept it short and simple before starting the class. The session was pretty much a free for all, with a little guidance every now and then from Bill. Everyone was encouraged to go around the room and tell of their struggles with their addictions during the past week. True to gender, the men pretty much stuck to one or two sentences while the women gave a much more detailed and emotional report. A couple of the women broke down emotionally and had to be supported by their peers.

Jay pretty much disengaged himself from the goings on while Anna jumped in and offered emotional nurturing coupled with scriptural support and promises. Jay watched, somewhat curious, but mainly out of amazement and admiration for Anna. As she had been with the children during vacation Bible school, she was genuine, sincere, and loving, and these people that society had written off embraced her and accepted her as one of their own. *That's why she's so effective, I guess,* Jay thought to himself.

The meeting lasted a good hour and a half, and the end didn't come a minute too soon for Jay. He'd been fighting drowsiness almost since the beginning.

"Yo dog, you're in another zone," Bill said as he walked up behind Jay and gave him a bear hug.

"Sorry man, for some reason I'm tired tonight," Jay responded as he struggled to break Bill's hold.

"It's all cool," Bill said, releasing his friend. "Work been grueling lately?"

"No, I've actually had a few days off."

"Ah, the ole boredom bug."

"I guess so. I don't know why, though. I've been busy."

They both walked into the kitchen, and Bill poured them both hot cups of coffee. "Sugar?" he asked Jay before handing him his cup.

"No, just black, thanks."

"Just like me, you're already all the sweetness you need," Bill said as he took a sip of the hot coffee.

They both stood there watching Anna interact with the remaining few people. She was a natural with them. *She is one of them,* Jay thought.

"Remember me when you're conversing with the Man tonight. Monday is a huge day for me," Bill said as he turned toward Jay.

"What's up?"

"I don't want to say anything 'til after Monday, let's just say it'll be life changing."

"Alright," Jay said, both curious and annoyed at the same time.

Anna was migrating toward the kitchen with Beth and Susan. The rest of the group had finally cut and run.

"Coffee? It's late," Anna protested when she saw Bill and Jay each with a cup.

"Girlfriend, we need this just to keep up with you!" Bill said between gulps.

"Well, I thought it was ice cream time!"

"You don't have to tell me twice," Jay said as he dumped his remaining coffee down the sink.

They all filed out of the church, Bill stopping to lock up behind them as the rest of the group headed for their cars. Jay rolled his window down and yelled at Bill, "Blizzard time."

"Enough said, we'll meet you there," Bill yelled back as he jogged to his waiting car. Beth and Susan were riding with him.

"That was a good meeting tonight, didn't you think?" Anna said as she pulled out onto the main drag.

"It wasn't that bad, I guess."

"What do you mean by that?"

"I don't know. I just feel uncomfortable around that type of person," Jay replied.

"They're just people, like you and me."

Jay didn't respond. He knew Anna was right, but there wasn't any way to change the way he felt. *Right?*

CHAPTER EIGHTEEN

Saturday came around just as quickly as Friday had ended for Jay. He got up and headed out for the bank a little earlier since it was only open until noon. It was mid-morning and already hot out. He kept thinking about that new car and air conditioning as the sun beat down on him.

Jay crossed the street as he approached the car dealership. He wanted to avoid contact with the car, and more importantly the salesman, at all costs. Still, he looked all over the lot for any sign of the red Impala. It wasn't there.

He started to grow anxious as he walked past. *What if they sold it already?*

"There's a whole lot full of cars, idiot," he said, irritated with himself for worrying about it.

Retrieving his cash was almost routine now, and the rest of his Saturday was spent lounging around. He felt like calling his parents to see how they were doing, but resisted the urge, fearful he'd say something about the money to them.

❧

On Sunday, Jay noticed Lisa and her family were absent from church, along with several of the others who had received money from his uncle Milt. *They probably don't want to chance talking to anyone,* he surmised. The pastor and his wife were there and seemed to be in a super mood. *They should be,* Jay thought to himself with a smile.

For once, church was over before Jay knew it. He received several offers for lunch, including one from Anna, but he declined them all. He was anxious to get home so he could try to pay off one of his credit cards. Promising Anna he'd be back for evening church, he got into Bill's car and drove off. Bill dropped him off in front of his home. "Catch ya on the flip side," he said as he started pulling away.

"Thanks for the ride," Jay answered without turning around.

Jay went into his house and headed straight toward his pile of bills. He sorted through them until he found one of his credit card statements. There was a balance owing of $2,719 even. Jay looked the statement over until he found a pay by phone number and directions. He quickly dialed the number on the statement and waited for someone to answer. Instead, an automated voice came on the line and gave him several options to choose from. After going through a whole litany of steps, a real live operator came on the line.

"May I help you sir?" the voice with an indistinguishable accent asked on the other end of the line.

"I'd like to pay off the balance on this card," he replied.

"The balance due now?" the voice asked.

"No, the entire balance owing, every cent of it."

"Would you like to pay with a phone check, sir?"

Jay had never heard of a phone check before. He wasn't quite sure how to respond to that question.

"Sir?" the voice asked on the other end of the line.

"Um, I'd like to pay with my debit card please," Jay finally answered.

"That'd be fine, sir, I'll just have to get some information from you first."

The operator asked a number of questions, took Jay's debit

card numbers along with his driver's license number, and asked him to please hold. After less than thirty seconds the voice came back on the line, gave him a reference number, and thanked him for the payment. Jay asked the voice if he'd receive a receipt or some sort of verification, momentarily forgetting that he received a statement every month in the mail that would show any and all activity on the account. The voice assured him that he would receive a confirmation in seven to ten working days, thanked him again, and hung up.

"Wow, that was really easy," Jay said aloud as he hung up the phone and looked his statement over again.

The rest of the day was pretty uneventful for Jay. He took his cash out of the freezer a few times and just held it. He had never handled so much money at once before. It was exhilarating.

<hr />

At the evening service, the pastor announced to the church that Anna would be meeting with the District Superintendent sometime the next week. He wanted everyone to pray for her and for the soon upcoming mission. It annoyed Jay somewhat, but he shoved his feelings aside without thinking about them.

After church, he visited for a little bit before hugging Anna goodnight and heading for home. He turned in early, knowing he had to work the next day. It was normal for him to be somewhat bummed out when Monday came around after a long weekend, but now he had extra incentive for it to get there—three thousand reasons, to be precise.

<hr />

Despite their ribbing about his absence from work, Jay cheerfully greeted all of his co-workers as he entered the store. It turned out to be a really busy Monday, just as most Mondays were. When lunch came around, he borrowed one of the work trucks and swung by his apartment. He took two zip lock bags of cold cash out of his freezer and headed to the bank to withdraw more.

After dropping by the bank to withdraw another $3,281—what was left of Sunday's deposit plus today's usual three thousand—Jay drove to the rental agency that handled his lease. He went inside and told the girl behind the desk he'd like to pay one whole year's rent.

She looked his account up and told him he could only pay ten months worth since that was all the time he had left on his lease. He counted the cash out for her and gladly took the receipt. With half an hour left in his lunch break, he rushed back to his home and put the remaining money in his freezer. Twenty minutes to relax.

The following day, Jay had enough time to actually get a burger after going to the bank, since he didn't have any other stops to make. On Wednesday and Thursday he drove through the parking lot of the car dealership to look for the red Impala. Sure enough, it was still there, shiny and new, waiting for him. "You'll soon be mine," he said to the car as he drove out.

Jay had to work until two on Saturday. He took an early lunch to make sure he got to the bank before it closed. The car dealership had the shiny red Impala sitting right out front with a sign on the windshield that said, "BUY THIS CAR!!!" Jay looked it over slowly as he drove past.

A couple was walking around the car looking in the windows. Jay could see the same salesman he had been talking to hand the couple a set of keys. *He's probably trying to get them to take it for a ride,* Jay worried.

He couldn't stop thinking about the car after returning to work. He couldn't stand the idea of someone else driving around Pullman in it. As soon as his shift was over, he'd go down there to see what the status of the car was.

The clock seemed to drag on forever. There were very few customers and literally nothing for him to do. It seemed like he looked at the clock every four or five minutes. With agonizing slowness, two o'clock rolled around.

Jay headed out for the car dealership at a half jog. It was a hot and sunny afternoon; the sun was blazing down directly on him. Jay didn't mind though, he was on a mission.

He reached the car dealership in record time. The red Impala was gone. He didn't see it anywhere. Anxiety that had been building inside of him all week reached a new peak as he crossed the parking lot and entered the dealership. Jay looked around the floor. There were several shiny new rigs inside that looked very appealing, but the red Impala already had his heart.

A salesman approached from one of the small offices just off the showroom floor. "Can I help you with something?" the young man inquired.

"The red Impala. I, um, am interested in the red Impala."

The salesman looked out the large plate glass windows onto the lot. He turned back to Jay, confusion on his face. "Sorry, I don't see a red Impala."

Realizing he wasn't making any sense, Jay started again. "I was in a while back, and you had a red Impala for sale. I've been looking at it for the past several days now, and I'd like to purchase it."

"Oh, you mean our featured car?"

"Yeah, the one with the sign that said 'Buy this car,'" Jay answered eagerly.

"I think someone has it out for a test drive right now. Maybe you could try out a different car," the salesman offered.

"No, I'll wait for the red Impala. I really like that car."

"We have several Impalas with the same package, just different colors."

Jay declined. "I'd like to wait for the red one, if that's all right."

"Suit yourself," the young salesman said as he turned and walked away.

Jay went back outside. The heat felt as if it were physically pushing him down onto the pavement. He walked around, looking for some shade to stand in while he waited. He found a small sliver on the northwest side of the building and promptly sat on the front-most corner of the building where he had a good view of the parking lot. On more than one occasion, a different salesman would approach, asking if Jay would like to look at a car. Each time he politely declined. Jay's fears continued to grow as the time slipped past. Before he knew it, he had been sitting there for over forty minutes.

Where in the world did they go? Clear to Spokane? he asked himself, growing frustrated in the length of time. *I'm not going to wait much longer,* he vowed.

Nor did he have too. Less than five minutes later the shiny red Impala turned onto the lot and pulled to the front of the store. A young couple got out of the car along with the salesman. They stood there looking at the car for a moment. Jay's heart was going to jump out of his chest. *What if they buy my car?* he asked himself in near panic.

The young couple walked slowly around the car again, salesman in tow jabbering away the whole time. *Shut up!* Jay yelled in his head at the obnoxious salesman. *Just shut up!*

The young man stopped and engaged the salesman in conversation for a few more moments before turning and rejoining his wife, who appeared to be looking at a new black Tahoe. They slowly moved off, got into a car that must have been their own, and drove away.

Jay was completely elated. He jumped up and headed over toward the dejected salesman, who was making his way back toward the front door, intent on getting out of the heat as quickly as possible. Jay approached him eagerly.

"Hello there, I'm ready to try out that red Impala now," he said as he extended his hand toward the salesman.

For a moment, the salesman just stood there rewinding his memory, trying to recall who this young man was. After several seconds, a look of recognition crossed his face, and he accepted Jay's outstretched hand.

"Jay, isn't it?" he asked as he pumped Jay's hand.

"Yeah," Jay answered, not quite sure what else to say.

"So, you've decided you might like to buy the Impala, huh?" the salesman asked as his enthusiasm returned.

"Well, I'd at least like to try it out." Jay tried not to act too eager.

"Sure, sure, I already have the keys."

The salesman retraced his steps back to the red Impala with Jay right behind. He opened the driver's side door and handed Jay the keys. "I'll have to ride with you, store policy," the salesman explained as he walked around the car and got in the passenger seat.

Jay placed the key in the ignition and turned it over. The car started immediately. It was quiet running, but it still sounded good to Jay. He quickly put his seatbelt on, stepped on the brake, and put the car in reverse, backing up far enough to clear the other cars before driving out onto Bishop Boulevard.

Jay drove down to the main highway and headed south toward Lewiston. The car handled better than anything he'd ever driven before. He picked up speed as they reached the outskirts of town, finally setting the cruise at sixty miles per hour. The salesman never stopped yapping, first telling him about one feature and then another, hoping to entice Jay into buying the car. Jay didn't have to be sold though. He already knew he was going to buy the car.

By the time Jay turned around in a farmer's driveway a few miles out of Pullman and headed back toward town, the salesman had found out Jay's age, job status, and even the size of his family.

They pulled back in front of the building and got out of the car. "What d'ya think?" the salesman eagerly asked Jay.

Jay didn't respond for a second. He walked slowly around the car, checking it over for any blemish that may exist.

"I like it," Jay replied, not making eye contact with the salesman. "How much is it again?"

The salesman read him the sales price and then, fearful of losing a sale, told Jay about an incentive package the factory had for first-time buyers, if he qualified.

They walked into the building and sat at the salesman's desk. He pulled out a large stack of papers and started to fill them out. He finished filling out his part and quickly handed Jay the paperwork. "I'll have you fill in the purchaser information yourself while I get some of these other forms filled out."

Jay bent to his task, finishing it very quickly. He waited patiently as the salesman finished his paperwork.

"Now for the moment of truth," the salesman said as he pulled out a finance form. He asked Jay where he worked, for how long, and how much he made per month. He scribbled down some numbers and turned the form around, handing it to Jay. It showed the sale price less the discounts and incentives before adding the sales tax and licensing. The grand total came to $28,439.44. Jay swallowed, his throat was dry. That was a lot of money. He decided he could afford it though and handed the paperwork back to the salesman.

"How much do you want to put down? Sometimes it helps banks loan money to first-time buyers," the salesman explained.

"Oh, no, I don't want to put anything down," Jay exclaimed. He could see the disappointment on the salesman's face.

"I want to pay cash for the car," he added quickly.

This caused the salesman to perk up instantly. He wasn't used to anyone paying cash for a new car.

"Well, that makes this a very easy transaction then," he said.

Jay calculated how much cash he actually had. He had withdrawn thirty thousand dollars so far and had spent six thousand for rent and almost three thousand toward a credit card. That left him with about twenty one thousand dollars, far short of what he needed to purchase the car. He hesitated for a minute.

"Could I um, look at the dollar figure again?" he asked nervously.

The salesman handed the form back to Jay. There it was in black and white, right in front of him. A little over twenty eight thousand dollars; he would have enough by Tuesday to pay the whole thing off. *Do I actually want to wait until Tuesday and take a chance that no one else will buy the car?*

"Is there something wrong?" the salesman asked, starting to get a little concerned.

Jay paused as he weighed whether or not he should tell the salesman anything. He decided it'd be alright to tell him a little. "Well, I don't quite have all of the money yet," Jay explained.

"Well, we could try financing then," the salesman offered.

"No, I almost have enough right now, and I will have enough by Tuesday afternoon. I have this kind of trust fund from my uncle and, well it's kind of hard to explain without going into a lot of detail, but to keep things simple, I have access to three thousand dollars a day. Right now I have twenty one thousand, and by Tuesday I'll have thirty."

The salesman sat there looking at Jay, not quite sure what to think. He'd heard a ton of stories over the years, but mainly stories about why someone's credit report was bad.

"So you have twenty one thousand dollars right now?' he slowly asked Jay.

"Yes, well no, not on me. It's at home. I could get it real fast though," Jay offered.

The salesman sat there pondering the situation for a moment before responding. He wrote a few notes down on a pad and told Jay he'd be right back, he had to run everything by his boss.

Jay waited nervously while one minute soon became five and eventually ten. Jay was beginning to wonder if the salesman would ever come back. After about fifteen minutes he emerged with his note pad.

"Would you mind telling my boss what you just told me a moment ago?" he asked Jay.

This made Jay a little nervous. He didn't want to tell any more people than absolutely necessary about the money. On the other hand, he didn't want to leave the car for three more days, available for anyone that wanted to purchase it. He made his mind up quickly.

"Sure, no problem."

Jay followed the salesman up a short set of stairs and into a plush office. A fat bald man sat behind a large cherry wood desk. Two empty chairs sat in front of the desk.

"Have a seat, have a seat," the fat man said.

Jay took his hand while introductions were made all around, noticing several awards hanging on the walls amidst framed photographs of the fat man and former Washington State University Cougar football players and coaches.

"Well now, Jack here tells me we're in some sort of dilemma," the manager said as he motioned toward the salesman. He picked the sales form up from the desk in front of him. "I guess I'd like to hear your offer with my own two ears," he said without looking up from the paper.

Jay repeated what he'd told the salesman just a few minutes before.

"Well, I think we could work something out. We wouldn't want to send you out of here without a car, now would we?"

Jay felt relieved. The fat man glanced back at the paperwork. "You wouldn't happen to be related to Milton Bilston would you?"

Jay's heart sank.

"Yes, he's my uncle all right," Jay answered quietly.

"Well, I don't see any problem at all then. I've sold ole Milt at least a dozen rigs over the last few years. He's a good egg."

Jay nodded.

"You don't mind if we call him, you know, for a reference?"

Panic gripped Jay by the throat, ready to fling him to the ground. He couldn't have anyone contact Milt or anyone else in his family for that matter. Not without risking the rest of the money. Milt had been very adamant about that.

"Well, I actually have most of the money. I don't see any reason for a reference," Jay told them sternly. "I'll pay you the twenty-one thousand today and the balance on Tuesday. If that's not acceptable, then I'll go elsewhere."

The fat man sat there for a moment looking at Jay. He didn't want to lose this sale, so he broke out in a huge grin. "There's no reason to go to that length, we trust you," he said, backpedaling the way only a salesman could.

They finally agreed that Jay and the salesman would go to Jay's house and retrieve his cash, come back, and finish the paperwork. Jay would sign a promissory note that would come due on Tuesday. In the mean time, he could take the car home with him.

Jay was grinning ear to ear. He couldn't believe he'd just made a deal for his first car. They jumped in the red Impala and headed for Jay's apartment. Once they arrived, Jay jumped out of the car, leaving it running and told the salesman he'd be right back. He unlocked his door and ran to the freezer, retrieving his zip lock bags of cash.

Back at the dealership, they both went inside the small office, where Jay slowly counted out twenty-one thousand dollars for the wide-eyed salesman. In the meantime, the secretary had typed up a promissory note for Jay to sign and date. He did so gladly, and handed the paper back to the salesman. "Here you go. That should be everything," Jay said with a smile on his face.

The salesman looked it over, took the cash and the promissory note out of his office and disappeared. Jay speculated the salesman was counting the money out to the fat man. He wished he could see the reaction on his face.

Apparently satisfied, the salesman reappeared with a photocopy of the promissory note and shook Jay's hand. He walked Jay out of the dealership and back to the waiting car, where he produced two sets of keys and a packet of information that was to be kept in the car at all times. After taping a temporary license into the back window, he gave Jay a gas card worth fifty dollars and told him to enjoy himself.

"Oh I will," Jay said as he pulled away from the building and out onto Bishop Boulevard, a proud owner of a brand-new red Impala.

CHAPTER NINETEEN

Jay drove around town, luxuriating in his new purchase. He was on cloud nine as he drove up and down the streets. He wondered how Anna would react. Hopefully she'd be excited for him.

Guilt at spending so much money tickled the back of his mind; he still hadn't paid any to the church and made a mental note to write "tithe" at the top of his "to pay" list. Somehow getting a new car made it easier for him to pay the tithe; kind of a trade off of sorts he guessed. A new car for him and nine thousand bucks for God.

"Not bad, not bad at all."

Jay looked at his odometer: fifty-nine miles and counting. He chuckled to himself. A month or so ago he'd have never thought he'd be driving a new rig, and now, here he was. He looked at himself in the rearview mirror just to make sure it all wasn't a dream. The seats were so comfortable, but they couldn't compete with the cool air blowing out of his vents.

Jay pulled up in front of his house and parked the car. He got out and walked around it several times. *It's a thing of beauty*, he thought as he got down on the pavement and looked under the car. Even the undercarriage was clean. He stood up and headed inside, locking the car door with his keyless remote. He chuckled when the car honked at him, indicating it was locked indeed.

The light on the answering machine was blinking balefully

when he walked in. He pushed the play button and grabbed a coke out of the fridge. The message started to play. It was Anna reminding him of the single's Bible study later that evening. In the excitement over his new car, he had forgotten all about it. He grabbed the phone and called Anna, promising to be by in twenty minutes to get her.

Jay hung up the phone, grabbed a towel, and quickly showered. He dressed in some clean clothes, slipped on his flip flops, grabbed his keys and wallet, and headed out the door. He smiled when he saw his new car sitting right where he left it, waiting patiently for him.

In just a few minutes, Jay pulled into the driveway and parked right behind Bob's Tahoe. He got out and proudly walked to the door and rang the doorbell. Anna answered with a confused look on her face. "I saw you drive up but didn't recognize you in that car. Whose is it?"

Jay beamed proudly. "It's mine, I bought it today."

Anna was stunned. She didn't know what to say. "Are you kidding me?" she asked with excitement as she walked over toward the car.

"No, I'm not kidding you!" Jay exclaimed, happy that Anna was excited. "Do you want to drive it?"

"You bet I do!" Anna laughed as she reached the driver's side door.

With a gentlemanly flourish, Jay opened the car door for her. Anna got in and searched for the seat adjustments. Her feet could hardly reach the pedals the way the seat was at the moment. Jay ran around and got in the passenger side. He didn't like it near as well on that side, but he wanted Anna to try the car out. She finally found the seat adjustments and moved the seat forward a little.

"This is cool," she said as she started the engine and carefully backed out of the driveway and onto the road. She placed the car in drive and away they went.

There were already several cars parked around their host's

apartment building that Jay recognized, including Bill's. They got out of the car and headed for the apartment. They could hear people laughing and joking inside as they approached the building. Jay knocked on the door and waited.

"Yo dog, what's up?" Bill asked as he opened the door.

Jay pounded fists with Bill. "Not too much, how're you doing?"

They walked into the crowded apartment and sat on the floor next to the couch. Jay leaned on the couch and Anna leaned on Jay.

The Bible study went by quickly. Even so, Jay absolutely couldn't concentrate. His thoughts kept wandering to his car. He couldn't wait to get out of there so he and Anna could cruise around town for awhile. *Man, I love that car!* he thought as Joy was saying the final prayer.

Everyone started visiting and making plans for ice cream or dessert. Jay grabbed Anna and headed out the door. "Let's go for a ride," he said enthusiastically. She followed along out the door without saying a word.

"Yo dog, where's the fire?" Bill yelled out the door toward them.

"We're just gonna go cruising," Jay said as he turned around. "In my new ride!" he exclaimed to Bill as he pointed toward his new car.

"No way, that's one bad ride!" Bill exclaimed as he ran past Jay and Anna over to the new car. "Coo-ool," he said as he slowly circled the car.

Jay was as proud as a new parent. He was hoping for just this response from everyone. Bill's reaction validated Jay's decision to buy the car almost as much as Anna's did. He was walking on clouds, indeed.

Before long, a whole group of people had gathered around Jay's car to admire it. Everyone gave it great compliments, and several people asked if they could have a ride in it. Jay was basking in glory.

"Let's go have coffee and dessert," he said to everyone.

Away they went, with Jay leading the way. Bill, Beth, and Susan crowded into the back seat of Jay's car. Eight people in two other cars followed Jay through town. He made sure to take the longest route he could think of just so he could spend more time driving.

They ended up at a local family restaurant on the south end of town that was open twenty-four hours a day. It wasn't very busy due to the late hour and the fact that college kids were gone for the summer. Their waitress, who was a young girl and new at her job, seated them at two large round tables near the back of the restaurant away from the few patrons who were there. Most of the group was hyperactive, but polite.

"Hey Jay, how much are your payments?" Bill asked as they picked their seats at the table.

Jay hadn't anticipated anyone asking him that question, and he started to become a little nervous.

"Um, they're not that bad," he mumbled quietly.

"I'll bet they're a pretty penny," Beth added.

Jay wanted the subject changed and now. There was no way he could tell them it was almost paid off. They'd want to know where he got the money from, and he had no answer to that question. He quickly scanned around the tables. It seemed as if all eyes were on him, waiting for a reply.

"I'll have it paid off in no time," was all he could come up with. Technically it was the truth, but it didn't satisfy everyone's curiosity.

"Really, how much are your payments?" Susan asked.

"That's for me to know, and you to never find out," Jay answered with a smile.

"Aw," and "Come on," were heard around the two tables, but Jay wouldn't reveal anything else. The waitress came back to take their orders.

"Hot fudge sundae cake all around," Bill told the young girl as she busily wrote the order down. She headed off to the kitchen to start making the desserts and to fill their beverage orders.

Everyone seemed to forget about Jay's new car, which made him very happy. He liked the attention but not the scrutiny that came along with it.

The waitress returned with their sodas and coffees and quickly passed them around the tables. Everyone was visiting with their neighbor, resulting in five or six individual conversations going on all at once. This created a small roar with each individual trying to talk over the person next to them just so they could be heard.

Then Bill stood up with his water glass in one hand and a spoon in the other. "People, people, the Billster has an announcement to make!"

He tapped his spoon on his water glass, and everyone stopped their conversations and diverted their attention to Bill.

"I'd like you all to be the first to know, you're looking at the proud new owner of an old but elegant eight-plex in central Pullman. This building, with help from all of you and more, will become, Lord willing, the new home for my Turning Leaf Foundation."

No one knew what Bill was talking about. Furthermore, no one knew what to say to Bill.

"What is your Turning Leaf Foundation?" Anna finally asked as Bill sat back down.

"That is a new foundation I'm forming to help people fight drug and alcohol addiction. The eight-plex will be an alternative to jail for addicts or alcoholics that meet certain criteria. The best part is it's all private, so God can be the focal point," Bill answered proudly.

Everyone congratulated Bill and told him what a neat and wonderful idea he had.

"I've known for awhile that God has called me to do this, and now the time is right."

"That's great, but it has to be real expensive isn't it?" Jay asked, halfway hoping to put a damper on things. He didn't know why, but for some reason Bill's announcement was making him a little jealous. He just wished that for once, he could be the story of the day. He knew he was being unreasonable and tried to shove his jealousy aside, but it gnawed at him nonetheless

"You don't even know, dog," Bill answered him with a wink.

"I mean, real estate in Pullman has gone through the roof, and it's not like you have a six figure salary or anything." Jay's pragmatic assault continued. "How can you ever afford the mortgage payments?"

"Faith, brother, faith," Bill answered, palms outstretched toward the heavens.

Everyone chuckled at Bill's theatrics, everyone except Jay.

"For real, you were worried about my car payment. I know your mortgage payment has to be way more. How do you figure on paying for it?"

"Jay," Anna exclaimed quietly as she nudged his arm.

The waitress came back with the hot fudge sundae cakes. Everyone was thankful for the distraction. They were all starting to feel uncomfortable with Jay's constant questioning of Bill. It didn't deter Jay though. He was nearly mad at Bill and couldn't give it a rest. He wanted to prove his point, especially in front of all these people.

"Seriously dude, have you thought about how expensive everything is going to be? The building upkeep, property taxes, other unforeseen expenses?"

Bill set his fork down and took a drink of coffee. "Well if you must know, I put thirty-eight thousand down, and the owners are going to carry the contract for three years at eight percent interest. At that time I'll have a large balloon payment of five hundred and twelve thousand and some change due. In the mean time, I have enough money in the bank for nine months of mortgage payments. I hope to drum up some corporate and private support to get this thing off the ground. I guess you could just call it a step of faith, dude."

Everyone but Jay clapped at Bill's proclamation. They were

all genuinely enthused and supportive of their friend, and many of them offered their help any time he needed it.

Jay still fumed. He wanted Bill to think about what he was getting into, and he was relishing the role of devil's advocate. He took a bite of his hot fudge sundae cake and waited for everyone to calm down a little.

"That seems like a huge *leap* of faith to me. I really think you need to put pencil to paper just to see what you've gotten yourself into." He added the last suggestion with satisfaction, feeling he'd definitely put Bill in his place.

"Why you bustin' my chops, man? You have been doggin' me the whole time about this. You're one person I thought'd have my back. Instead you sound just like my folks, man," Bill said as he pointed his finger at Jay.

Jay could feel his neck and head start to flush. Everyone was looking at him, waiting to see what he'd say next.

"I'm just trying to get you to think about what you're doing before you make a huge mistake with your life is all. I mean, it sounds great, but what if you can't swing it and your ministry fails?"

"Faith, man, faith. If the good Lord leads you to water, you better drink."

"How do you really know the Lord is leading you to water, so to speak? Maybe you're just acting on emotion."

"Man, when the Lord speaks you know it, if you're on the same channel anyway."

Jay was at a loss for words. He could see this conversation was no longer going where he wanted it to. Everyone else was nervously eating their dessert, avoiding eye contact with them. He wished somebody, anybody, would join him in his argument, but there were no takers. Dejected, Jay started eating his dessert too, keeping to himself.

Bill excitedly outlined his plans for the new rehab center. He told them a lot of work needed to be done to the building before they could occupy it.

"The biggest hurdle will be getting a conditional use permit from the city so we can operate in the community. It requires a public hearing, which knowing Pullman, could be difficult at best," he explained to everyone.

"We'll all chip in and help any way we can!" Anna exclaimed, causing Jay's sulking to become even more pronounced.

"Noted and accepted," Bill stated enthusiastically. "We'll succeed 'cause nobody can defeat the Lord!"

༄༅

Jay jumped out of bed and looked at the clock. It was already nine thirty in the morning and he was supposed to pick Anna up at nine forty-five for Sunday school. He quickly jumped in the shower and washed his hair. It was still hot, so he dressed in some nice shorts and a new cotton shirt he'd picked up a few days earlier. His mother lectured him on the kind of clothes he wore to church, but he figured the Lord was happy he was there no matter what he wore. At least that was the argument he always used.

He went to his kitchen and decided he didn't have enough time for coffee, so he gulped down a Red Bull energy drink instead. "This'll have to do for now," he said as he crumpled the can up and tossed it in his garbage can. "I hope someone brings cookies or snacks." He grabbed his keys and wallet, slipped on his sandals, and headed out the door.

Anna was waiting out near the street when Jay drove up. She quickly jumped in the car and closed the door behind her. "You're almost late," she said matter-of-factly as she fastened her seatbelt.

"I know, I almost slept in," Jay replied as he pulled away from the curb.

They drove the remaining distance without speaking, listening instead to music on the local Christian station. Jay carefully pulled up into the church parking lot and scanned around for a safe parking place so no one would ding their car door into his. He found an isolated spot near the little storage shop the church kept their van in. Pulling up near the front of the church, he let Anna out.

"I'll let you out here so you don't have to walk so far," he explained as he came to a stop.

"Where are you going to park?"

"Over by the shop, garage, or whatever you call that building," he said as she got out and closed the door.

Jay drove back around to his little parking spot and parked the car. He made a mental note to invest in one of those dash covers as soon as possible as he headed across the parking lot toward the church. Jay reached the sidewalk and slowly turned around toward the parking lot. He looked back out over the cars and slowly shook his head.

No less than six sparkling brand new vehicles sat in the church parking lot, not counting his own. He couldn't believe it. They had to belong to some of the people who had received money from his uncle Milt.

"This is unbelievable," he said as he placed his hand on top of his head. "Unbelievable, just unbelievable!"

People were going to figure out something was going on. They had to. It was too coincidental for that many new rigs to have been purchased about the same time at the same church. Questions were sure to follow, and he had no explanation.

After class, Jay walked out into the hallway and found Bill. "Sorry about last night and all. I really am happy for you," Jay awkwardly said as he approached Bill.

Bill held out his fist in greeting. Jay responded by banging it with his own fist.

"It's all good, brother," Bill said with a smile on his face. "I knew you'd come around. Ain't no one can oppose the Billster."

Jay still had jealous feelings toward Bill, and he wasn't sure why. In all honesty, Bill was his only true friend, and he didn't want to chance messing that up.

They waited out in the hallway for Anna and Beth to finish visiting with some of the other people before heading to the sanctuary. The organ music started playing, indicating the beginning of the service, as they took their seats near the front of the church. Jay looked around but didn't see any of his relatives, including his Uncle Milt. *Everyone's still avoiding each other,* he thought to himself as the worship leader started singing.

Jay just went through the motions during worship and then settled down for a good rest as the pastor started to preach. The sanctuary was a little warm, which made him feel sleepy despite waking up late. *If I'm ever a pastor, I'll keep the air turned to about sixty. That'll keep everyone awake,* he thought as he struggled to stifle a yawn.

The pastor was preaching on obedience again, one of his favorite subjects. Jay tried to listen, but he started wondering about the new cars in the parking lot. He glanced around again to see who was present, but there were too many people there to tell. He finally decided he'd linger around outside long enough to see exactly who the vehicles belonged to. *Anna's usually busy visiting with everyone, anyway,* he thought happily, pleased with the plan he'd come up with.

He settled down in the pew, trying to get comfortable for the last ten minutes or so of the sermon. *The pastor's really going at it today,* he noted to himself, not sure where the sermon was headed.

Watching Anna out of the corner of his eye, he started daydreaming about the reaction she'd have when he told her about the money. He could imagine her getting misty-eyed at the realization that money would never be an obstacle. They could do whatever they wanted. *She has to be happy. How could she be anything less?*

As the closing prayer ended a few minutes later, Jay anxiously turned toward Anna. "I'll wait for you outside," he said as he stepped from the pew to the aisle.

"Remember, I have a quick meeting with the pastor," Anna reminded him. "It shouldn't take more than five or ten minutes, though."

"That's all right, I'll be out by the parking lot," Jay told her as he turned and headed down the aisle.

Jay made his way into the foyer, where he had to shake hands with several people before heading outside onto the lawn. He quickly crossed the lawn and stopped where it met the edge of the sidewalk leading out to the parking lot. People were already heading out across the lot to find their cars.

From his vantage point, Jay could see the entire parking lot. Slowly, the people started to get in their cars and drive out, until all but a handful remained. Only one new car besides his was still left. True to his suspicion, all the other new cars were driven off by recipients of his uncle's money.

Wondering who the last mystery car belonged to, he sat down on the grass and continued to watch and wait for Anna. *She should be getting out of that meeting before long,* he thought.

Jay wondered if anyone had talked about their meeting with his uncle. He was almost positive his sisters would have talked. *They wouldn't be able to not gossip about it to their friends.*

"Yo, what's up?" Bill came up behind Jay, startling him.

"Not much, I'm just waiting for Anna to get out of her meeting."

"Dog, you were looking for someone, least from my vantage point," Bill continued.

"No, I was just looking out at all the new cars. Guess I started something."

"Word is, some folks inherited some money or sumpin' from your uncle Milt," Bill said, causing Jay to chill to the bone.

Bill didn't say any more, and Jay didn't offer any information.

He was shocked to have Bill, of all people, say something to him about the money. That meant practically everyone had to know.

Jay looked back at the church just in time to see Anna emerge with the pastor and his wife. Beth was right behind them, and they were all visiting as they headed out toward Jay and Bill. He was practically praying that Bill wouldn't say anything else about the money.

Now there were only three cars remaining in the parking lot: his, Bill's, and a brand new Buick Riviera. He couldn't believe it. His mouth dropped open as he realized the new Buick belonged to the pastor.

He stood up as the group approached.

"That wasn't too long, was it?" Anna asked hopefully.

"No, it didn't seem long at all," Jay replied as they headed across the blacktop toward his car.

"See you tonight!" Anna called to the others as she opened her door and got in.

Jay started the car. It was extremely hot inside, so he blasted the air conditioning on high.

"Did you see that Pastor got a new car?" Anna asked. "I'm so happy for them."

"Yeah, pretty cool," was all Jay could reply. He didn't really know what else to say.

"Everyone knows pastors don't make all that much money, so I'm glad they finally could afford something new and reliable," Anna continued.

Jay didn't reply. He didn't know if Anna was trying to go someplace else with this conversation, and he didn't want to find out. It would only be a matter of time before she heard the rumors that were going around. He wondered if she would put two and two together. If Bill had heard something, practically everyone had to have heard something. That meant more than one person must have talked.

Suddenly, Jay wished he hadn't bought the car so soon.

"That was quick," Anna said as Jay placed her salad and lemonade down in front of her.

Jay sat down and poured ranch dressing over his salad. He was ready to take a bite when Anna asked him to bless the food. Jay sheepishly put down his fork, surreptitiously looked around the room to see if anyone was watching him, and said a quick prayer thanking God for their food. Satisfied that no one had been watching, he began to eat.

"That was a real good service today, don't you think?"

"Yeah, I thought it was okay," he said as he stuffed another fork full of salad into his mouth.

Anna started to slowly eat her salad. Jay could tell by the expression on her face that she wanted to say something more, but he wasn't sure what. He didn't feel like discussing the sermon or the Sunday school lesson, though. The truth was, he couldn't even remember what they were about.

"Do you know what my meeting with Pastor was about?" she asked before taking another bite.

"Um, I guess I don't." Jay frantically tried to recall if Anna had told him anything about her meeting.

"Well, I have a meeting coming up with the District Superintendent in a little over a week, remember? Anyway the pastor talked to the D.S., and they want to ordain me as a missionary in front of the church the weekend the D.S. is here."

Jay continued to eat, unsure what he could say. The good news he'd promised to give Anna had been put on hold for a whole month. He was sure if he could tell her about the money, she'd stop this missionary foolishness. He couldn't tell her though, so he'd have to go along for a few weeks more. *Better to go along than to rock the boat,* he thought to himself before answering Anna.

"That's great, what's it mean?" Jay finally asked her.

"It means I'll be a full-fledged missionary in the eyes of our church, contingent upon completion of my schooling at Colorado Springs, of course." Anna's face lit up as she discussed her future.

The only thing Jay knew for sure was that he wanted to be with Anna, and he didn't want to be a missionary. Nevertheless, he pretended to be interested.

"What does that do for you? Will you get discounts at restaurants and stores, or something?" he asked teasingly.

"No, silly, it means that the church officially recognizes my commitment to the Lord and to mission work."

Jay had to bite his tongue not to say anything. He really didn't want to have this conversation right now, and knew if it continued, he'd probably say something he shouldn't and really upset Anna. He took a long drink of his lemonade and tried to think of a safe subject.

"What'd you think of Bill's announcement last night?" he finally asked, not sure he wanted to go there either.

"I think it's absolutely wonderful!" Anna exclaimed.

Jay wasn't surprised at her answer. He expected no less from her, as a matter of fact. The problem was that he didn't know what else to say about the venture.

"He's sure got his work cut out for him," was the only thing he could think of.

"That's all right, Bill's up to the challenge. He's really committed to the Lord's work and feels that anything is possible through God. Besides, we'll all be there to help him."

They both went back to their lunch. Jay was grateful to eat in silence. He didn't want to talk about either subject any more than absolutely necessary. Anna mentioned she hadn't seen his folks for the past couple weeks and wondered if everything was okay with them. Jay told her he hadn't heard anything, so they must be fine. They finished their lunch with nothing more than small talk, which suited Jay just fine.

"Jay, is there something wrong? You seem to be preoccupied or something."

"Nope, everything is just fine," he responded. "I'm just tired out." The concerned look on Anna's face told him his weak response was less than convincing.

He cleared the table when they were finished and drove Anna home and dropped her off.

"See ya tonight?" she asked as she got out of the car.

"Yeah, I'll pick you up around 6:45."

※

Jay tried to keep to himself at the evening service. He didn't want to hear anything, and he didn't want to say anything. Whenever anyone tried to visit or ask him a question, he simply kept his answers to one or two words. Before long, everyone pretty much left him alone.

A familiar voice caught up with them as they walked across the parking lot. "Yo, what's up?"

They turned and waited as Bill and Beth hurried over toward them.

"What's the hurry? Offering's already been taken, man," Bill said as he reached the two of them.

They all laughed at Bill's joke, but Jay wished he'd gotten out of there before Bill spotted them. He didn't want to hear about Bill's big plans, and he didn't want Bill asking anything about Milt either.

"We're just heading home, no hurry though," he finally answered Bill.

"Ya'll up for din or something?"

"I don't know. I'm kind of tired," Jay said as he looked at Anna.

"I think it'd be great. Doesn't Chinese food sound good?" she said enthusiastically.

Jay turned away from the rest of them and rolled his eyes. He was kind of hungry, but this scenario was not appealing.

"Chinese it is then," Bill said without waiting for an answer from Jay.

They arrived at the restaurant at about the same time. It wasn't overly busy, and they were seated right away. When they decided to eat family style, Jay politely deferred his choice to Anna. It only took a few minutes for their food to arrive, and after Bill quickly blessed the food, they all dug in. Jay was much hungrier than he thought, and he quickly cleaned his plate and dished up seconds. Anna, Bill, and Beth were busy discussing Bill's new venture; consequently they were eating much slower.

"What's your next step?" Anna asked Bill.

"I have to do a bunch of paper work, so the gov recognizes me as a non-profit. After that, I have a public hearing in a little less than two weeks."

"What's the public meeting for?"

"You know, the people have a right to protest, or be heard. Something like that."

"Then do you get your permit?"

"I don't know. If all the neighbors are up in arms and create a big enough fuss, the city council can table their decision a month or more. My goal is to have all my ducks in a row so I can answer any question they might throw at me half-way intelligently. What I need is someone to charm them, someone like you maybe," Bill tried to enlist Anna.

Jay continued to eat and keep to himself. He didn't want to be part of the conversation at all. Beth didn't say too much either. Unlike Jay, however, she was usually enthusiastic about everything, so her attitude seemed a bit out of place.

As they finished their dinners, the conversation shifted from Bill to Anna. She told them of her upcoming ordination, and they congratulated her wholeheartedly. It seemed to Jay that Bill had a hundred or more questions about mission fields. He just kept going on and on.

Jay could hardly wait for this night to end. He was extremely happy when their waitress brought the check for them to pay. He snatched it up. "I'll get this," he announced as he got up.

The others put up a mild protest, but Jay was already heading toward the cash register. He pulled out his wallet and paid the cashier, telling her to give the change to the waitress for a tip. The other three slowly got up and followed Jay to the front of the restaurant.

"Boy, when you're done, you're really done, dog!" Bill exclaimed as he clapped Jay on the shoulder. "Thanks for din; we sure didn't expect a poor working stiff like you to buy."

Jay was taken aback. He wasn't sure exactly what Bill meant by his remark. He thought it was laced with sarcasm, but who could tell when it came to Bill. Jay held the door open as the other three filed out and headed for their cars. It was still light out, even though it was a little after nine. They said their good-byes, and Jay pulled away from the restaurant and headed toward Anna's house.

"Is anything wrong?" Anna asked. "You've been acting funny for a couple days now and I'm beginning to worry."

Jay pulled up to a red stoplight and fidgeted with his turn signal. A group of young people were crossing the road in front of his car. There wasn't much traffic, and Jay accelerated quickly through the intersection as soon as the light turned green.

"No, I'm just kind of tired," he told her, unable to think of anything else to say.

"Are you sure? You hardly said a single word tonight," Anna continued, unwilling to just let the subject drop.

Jay pulled up in front of the house and placed the gear shift in park before turning to Anna. "I'm sure. I was just listening to you guys talk." Jay looked down at the floorboards near Anna's feet.

Anna waited patiently to give him a chance to talk about what was going on between them and what might happen when she was ordained. It seemed as if the closer they grew, the stranger Jay acted. It was almost as if he was becoming a complete stranger right before her eyes, and that worried her. She decided against pushing the subject any further that night.

"Well, I sure hope if something's bothering you, you'll tell me," Anna said quietly.

"I will, I'm just tired is all," Jay meekly offered.

Anna gave him a hug and told him good-bye as she got out of the car.

"Call me tomorrow," Anna said as Jay started to pull away from the sidewalk.

He waved to her indicating he would, and drove off down the street toward home.

"Another week down, another week closer," he said to the image in the rearview mirror.

༄

Jay sped to work. Somehow his alarm hadn't gone off and he'd overslept. He wasn't exactly late, but he was rushed. He hated the feeling of being rushed worse than anything.

He parked on the side street next to the lumberyard and got out. It wasn't quite a residential neighborhood, but it wasn't commercial either. Jay felt it would be the safest place for his new car. He locked the doors and jogged to the lumberyard. Once inside, he logged in and looked at the clock: a minute to spare.

Jay walked up to the front counter and grabbed a donut and a large cup of coffee. The lumberyard was already bristling with activity. Most of the time Jay liked it this busy, but not today. Not when he overslept and hadn't quite shaken all the cobwebs out of his head.

He walked to the counter, coffee in one hand and notepad with precariously balanced donut in the other. The hot coffee scalded his tongue as he took a quick drink, but he didn't have time to think about it as he started helping his first customer.

Two hours later his donut still wasn't eaten and his cup was full of cold coffee. He finished up with the customer he was helping and slipped into the back office/break room with his mug. Sitting down with a fresh cup, he took his first bite out of the donut just when Bob came in.

"Well good morning, youngster," his boss said, placing his hand on Jay's shoulder.

"Morning," Jay answered between bites.

"I heard you got a new ride."

"Yeah, I guess I did."

"Did you get a good deal?"

"I don't know, I guess so."

"Not that it's any of my business, but did you remember to have insurance put on the car, seeing as how you haven't had any before?"

Jay gulped. He hadn't even thought of insurance for the car. It seemed that the salesman had mentioned something about insurance, but he couldn't remember for sure. He had been so excited he'd kind of spaced it off.

"Well, I'm kind of embarrassed to admit it, but I completely forgot about insurance."

"That's all right, but you better go down the road here at noon and get some. If you don't, the bank will be after you in no time."

Bob asked a few more friendly questions about the car before heading out to the counter to wait on more customers. Jay was relieved that he hadn't asked about car payments nor mentioned anything about Jay's uncle Milt. He didn't know what he'd say to Bob if either subject came up. Not that he expected it to. Bob usually minded his own business and absolutely didn't have time for gossip.

Jay finished his coffee and donut and headed back out to the front counter. He felt a lot better now that he finally had some coffee in him. There were far fewer customers now, so Jay returned several phone messages that had piled up on his desk while the clock raced toward his lunch hour.

Jay made the quick walk to the insurance company in less than five minutes. He walked in and introduced himself to the agent as he sat down.

"How can I help you today," the agent asked as he peered out over the top of his glasses.

"I need some kind of car insurance, I guess," Jay answered nervously.

The agent handed him some forms to fill out and proceeded to ask him seemingly trivial personal questions. He used this technique to measure whether the potential customer had a job, how stable he was, and even if he was a savvy insurance shopper. It didn't take long to discover that Jay was stable, had a job, and even better, was completely naive about insurance.

Jay finished filling out the forms and handed them back to the waiting agent, who scoured them for any additional information that might be beneficial. Jay had marked 'none' on the box that asked if he currently had insurance.

"This must be a mistake," the agent said as he pointed to the box. "Surely you've had insurance before."

"Nope, I've never owned a car before."

The agent raised his eyebrows at this good news. His assessment of Jay had been accurate. The young man really didn't know anything about insurance. The agent finished looking over the forms and started scribbling on a notepad. He wrote down the rates for the most expensive coverage with least possible deductible and handed the figure over to Jay.

"This would be your premium for six months coverage," he said as Jay tried to decipher the writing.

Jay had no idea what he was looking at, but if it was the best, then it was for him. "I'll take it," he said to the surprised agent.

The agent wrote up the coverage on official forms and asked Jay which payment plan he'd like to use; the monthly plan or the semi annual plan. "The monthly plan will be $309 a month or the semi-annual payment will be $1840 up front, saving you twenty-eight dollars a year."

Jay gulped. That was a lot of money he hadn't planned on. *Oh well, it costs money to have things,* he thought.

"I'll take the semi-annual payment option," Jay told the excited agent.

They finished up the paperwork, and Jay signed on the dotted line. He took out his checkbook and wrote a check for the full amount of the insurance while the agent readied a copy for Jay's personal records. He handed Jay a brochure on life insurance and asked him to read it over.

"Come back in a week or so, and I'll fix you up with life insurance too," the agent said as Jay got up to leave.

"I sure will," Jay replied, embarrassed that he'd never thought of life insurance before.

The agent stopped Jay as he walked out the door. "Do me a favor, if you have any family or friends that have insurance, don't tell them the rates I gave you for your insurance. It was a special rate for first time buyers. There's absolutely no way I could give everyone the same rate," he nervously explained.

"No problem," Jay said as he shook the man's hand and headed out the door. *I'm sure glad I picked an agent who treated me so well.*

☙❧

Jay's afternoon went almost as rapidly as his morning. He grabbed his paycheck from the office and ran to his car. Dealing with his insurance agent had taken up his entire lunch break, and he had no idea what time the Bank of Whitman closed. It was a little after five, and he was in a near panic as he jumped in his car and headed down the road. The streets were busy, adding to Jay's agitation.

"Hurry up!" he yelled at both the cars in front of him and the red light.

Slowly the traffic started to move, and before long Jay pulled up to the bank. He was extremely relieved to see the bank didn't close until six. He'd made it with over thirty minutes to spare.

Jay went in and immediately withdrew six thousand dollars: three thousand for Sunday and three thousand for Monday. It was almost enough to pay his car off.

"One day to go," he said proudly as he pulled out of the parking lot and drove to his old bank, where he deposited his paycheck. This check, along with his current balance, would barely cover the check he'd written earlier for his insurance premium.

"Good thing I have a little cash on hand," he said with a little laugh as he pulled out and headed for home. "Yes sir, things are definitely looking good for me."

Jay drove home for the evening, counting his money in his head.

☙❧

Tuesday went a lot better for Jay. He arrived at work early and cruised through the day without a hitch. After work, Jay drove to the car dealership and paid his promissory note on the car in full. Ecstatic, he could hardly believe he was the proud owner of a brand new car.

"No payments, nothing due!" he said to himself as he drove from the dealership. Jay drove home and showered before calling Anna. He invited her out for dinner to celebrate, though once again he couldn't tell her he was celebrating.

His date with Anna went without a hitch. She was amazed Jay was in such a good mood—not that she was complaining. They had pizza before driving to an ice cream store for dessert. Jay ordered a banana split to share, and they visited for more than an hour. He even asked her a few questions about her upcoming ordination.

Maybe he is coming around, she thought to herself as he drove her home. But all the while she had an uneasy feeling that she couldn't explain, deep down inside of her. *I'm just being paranoid,* she decided as she gave him a hug and got out of the car.

"I'll call you tomorrow," Jay promised right before she closed the door.

"I can't help but love that boy," Anna said as she watched Jay drive down the block and turn the corner.

"Man, I love that girl," Jay said as he watched Anna growing smaller and smaller in his rearview mirror, turning the corner for home.

CHAPTER TWENTY

The rest of Jay's week went exceptionally well. He even found time on Friday to make another visit to his new insurance agent friend, who gave Jay another special rate on a term life insurance policy valued at five hundred thousand dollars. It seemed like kind of high coverage to Jay, but he was going to be worth over a million dollars very soon, so Jay could see the merits of having a policy that valuable.

He wasn't sure who to make the beneficiary of the policy, but he finally settled on Bill. At first he was going to list Anna, but he wasn't sure how she would feel about that. Jay paid the agent up front for a year's policy and once again promised not to divulge the special pricing structure he was getting to his family and friends.

The agent walked Jay to the door and shook his hand before Jay turned and headed back to the lumberyard. He stood and waved at Jay until the young man was more than half a block away, amazed at the good fortune the week had brought him. With a broad smile, he took a small pad out of his pocket and made a note to put Jay on his Christmas card list.

Jay finished work and drove to the bank to withdraw his daily cash before heading back home. After a stop at the local car wash to quickly wash and dry his vehicle, he stood and admired his shiny new car for a few moments before heading home for the weekend. He decided he'd pay the nine thousand dollar tithe this Sunday, just to get it over and done with. The idea didn't make him very happy, but he knew he didn't really have a choice.

"The pastor will know if I don't, and besides, I'll have a lot more in a couple weeks anyway," he finally said in an attempt to comfort himself.

He just couldn't see what the church would do with all the money. It wasn't as if they could just go out and spend it any way they wanted. He finally decided it'd probably go to some good, one way or another.

Saturday started off well for Jay, but quickly changed for the worse at the weekly Bible study. He and Anna arrived a few minutes early, and it was already a packed house. They had barely walked in the door when Jay heard some of the others talking about his uncle, Milt Bilston. As the story went, some of the people in the church had received a small fortune from Jay's uncle. A few of the singles shot Jay side glances to try and gauge his reaction, but turned away when they saw Jay look at them. He felt like the center of attention and could feel the perspiration start to bead up on his forehead.

The lesson started, and none too soon for Jay. He didn't want to hear any more about the money, and he definitely didn't want to be anywhere nearby when people were talking about it. It would be disastrous if he were accused of saying anything, and the best way to prevent a misunderstanding was to avoid the whole conversation, and people too, if necessary.

The Bible study proceeded without delay, and Jay didn't hear any more rumors. Even so, he felt as if people were looking at him and talking about him. *I'm just being paranoid,* he told himself over and over, trying to ease his fears.

Once the final prayer was said, Jay was pestering Anna to leave. They had several offers of dessert or coffee, and Jay declined them all without comment.

"What's the matter with you?" Anna asked as she buckled her seatbelt. "Are you sick or something?"

"I don't feel overly well," Jay said and left it at that.

If Anna had heard the rumors or suspected anything, she didn't indicate so to Jay. She talked about the lesson a little bit and about how excited she was to see more new faces almost every week.

"Before long we'll have to have two Bible studies. Everyone won't be able to fit in one house."

Jay could remember when they first started holding these Bible studies a few years earlier. Only a handful of people would attend every weekend. At the time it was almost depressing. Most of the new people were a direct result of Anna's incessant witnessing. She told practically everyone she met of her relationship with God and how they could have one too.

Jay drove up in front of Anna's and stopped the car. "Sorry. I'm not feeling all that well," he sheepishly told her.

"That's alright, just go home and get some rest. Hopefully you'll feel better tomorrow."

Anna got out of the car and closed the door. Jay pressed the button to roll down the passenger side window. "I'll call you in the morning if I don't feel better," he told her, instantly feeling guilty for lying to her. He wished he could tell her everything, but he didn't dare risk it.

"Okay, get some rest," Anna repeated, then smiled brightly at Jay.

He waved meekly and drove off down the street and turned

toward home. After only a few blocks, his stomach reminded him that he hadn't eaten. Detouring back to the main section of town, Jay drove straight to the double golden arches and ordered a super value meal and a milkshake. He saw some of the people from the Bible study inside and slid down as far as he could in his seat. He didn't want anyone to see him and say something to Anna the next day.

The young girl in the drive-thru handed him his order, and Jay drove straight to his house, went inside, and locked the door. He sat down on his couch and proceeded to eat his meal alone while he watched an old movie on television.

Jay didn't know what he was going to do. He still had almost two weeks until his next meeting at the bank, and everyone was already talking about it. He wondered who had talked. It had to have been more than one person, it seemed to him.

He decided he'd go to church the next day to gauge everyone's reaction. If it was too bad, he'd ask Nancy for his vacation time and just lay low until August sixth. He had almost three weeks worth coming to him, but Nancy usually wanted a month or more notice. Summer was always the worst time of the year for vacation time because it was the busy building season coupled with the fact that most of the married help wanted time off when their kids were home from school.

Jay hoped Nancy would be sympathetic to him without the need for him to go into any detail about why he needed the time off. He didn't want to make up some sort of lie to her, but he couldn't risk telling her anything either. He decided he'd tell her she just needed to trust him, it was for a personal reason.

Who knows, maybe I'm just being paranoid about the whole thing anyway, he thought as he surfed through the channels, wishing away the time.

For once, Jay picked Anna up fifteen minutes early. He decided it would be good to get there early so he could hear if anyone was talking about Milt. The parking lot was over half-full already, with people waiting to turn into the lot. Jay let Anna off at the sidewalk and drove to the back of the lot. He started to park next to a brand new Cadillac Escalade just in time to see his sister Lisa get out.

"What in the world? I can't believe it!" Jay said as his sister waved at him. "Nothing like being obvious, Lisa," he muttered as he straightened his wheels and turned the car off.

Lisa waited outside the car for Jay. "Hey little brother, nice car," she said with a bright smile.

"Same to you," Jay said, none to happy to be talking to her.

He was afraid she'd say something about the money or Milt, but she didn't. She just asked how Anna was and told him they'd have to come over to dinner one of these nights.

They walked over to where Anna was waiting, and Lisa gave her a big hug. They chatted for a minute and then headed for the church. Jay looked around at all the cars and noticed several more new ones.

This is becoming a nightmare, he thought as he held the large double doors open for the two girls.

By the time Sunday school was over Jay was a nervous wreck, desperately listening for mention of the money and Milt. He and Anna made their way back to the foyer through the throng of people and slowly worked their way toward the sanctuary. Everyone was talking at once, creating a small continuous roar.

Jay felt lightheaded and dizzy as he tried to avoid eye contact with everyone. He thought he heard his uncle's name a couple of times, but couldn't be sure of it. They finally broke through the wall of visiting people and entered the much quieter sanctuary. Jay followed Anna down the aisle to their regular seat up near the front. She sat down on the cushioned seat and slid over, making room for Jay next to the aisle. He leaned up against the high curved arm of the pew and closed his eyes. His nerves were completely frayed.

"What's the matter? Do you feel sick?" Anna asked, a concerned look on her face.

"I really don't feel well at all," Jay told her without making eye contact.

It wasn't that he was feeling ill, he was just ultra-jumpy. He'd heard that high stress could make people sick, and now he believed it.

The organ music began, followed quickly by the worship music. The worship leader bounded up onto the platform and started to sing while clapping his hands in time with the music. "Everyone stand up and make some noise to the Lord," he said loudly over his mic to the crowd. "Show some life people. Raise those hands to the Lord!"

Jay really wasn't in the mood for vigorous worship. He just wished the service would end so he could go home and hide from everyone. He glanced around the sanctuary, trying to see if his parents were there. They hadn't been around since the bank meeting.

They're the only smart ones, he concluded as he focused his attention back on the worship leader.

The worship service ran a little longer than usual. By the end of the singing, Jay was feeling a little better about things. The pastor came up on the platform, called the ushers, and said his worship prayer before the offering.

Jay took out his wallet and removed the tithe check he'd written the night before. He grabbed an envelope and pencil from the back of the seat in front of him and filled it out. Name, address, date, what the offering was for. He paused at the section that said amount. He looked at Anna out of the corner of his eyes. She wasn't paying any attention to him. Jay quickly wrote down nine thousand dollars and slipped the folded check inside the envelope, licked the flap and sealed the envelope. Once he was satisfied it was sealed he folded the envelope in half, information side in, and waited for an offering plate.

The usher was an elderly fellow who had been an usher for as long as Jay could remember. He was extremely friendly and always had a funny story to tell, with his Missouri twang only making the stories more enjoyable to listen to. He handed Jay the offering plate and winked at him. Jay placed the folded envelope under some loose currency and handed the plate to Anna, who passed it on down the line.

For some reason, paying the tithe made Jay feel a lot better about everything; he even smiled at the thought of the offering counters unfolding his check. *That ought to set them wondering*, he thought to himself with a smile.

Jay sat through the rest of the service trying to decide what he was going to do the following week. He hadn't come up with any concrete plans by the time the pastor asked them all to rise for the Benediction. When the congregation was dismissed, Jay sat back down and told Anna he was going to wait until the crowd thinned out a little before he tried to get out of the sanctuary. She sat down next to him and visited with some of the people in the pew directly behind them.

Jay turned when someone with a firm grip grabbed him by the shoulder. "Yo dog, you lounging out on the stink?" Bill's code word for pew.

"Yeah, we're just waiting for the crowd to thin down a bit," he explained.

"Well, Beth and I are gonna lounge with ya," Bill told Jay as he sat facing backwards directly in front of Jay.

Jay didn't feel much like talking, but Bill had a way of dragging everyone into a conversation. Before he knew it they were talking about different types of sheetrock and what it would take to tape and finish it.

"Since you know so much about it, I'll make you in charge of sheetrock in the eight-plex," Bill said with a laugh.

"Not so fast," Jay started to protest.

"Sorry brother, it's too late for you to back out now."

The crowd was thinning out, so the four of them got up and headed into the foyer and then out the door into the bright sunlight. Jay could see Lisa in the parking lot talking to another couple, gesticulating wildly with her arms. Jay really didn't want to get close to whatever conversation she was having, but he didn't have much of a choice since he'd parked right next to her. He took his time, holding the other three back, but a person can only take so long when covering less than a hundred yards.

Jay found himself straining to hear Lisa, curious to what she might be saying. Her conversation sounded like nothing more than a garbled mess until he was within fifteen or so yards. The sun was beating off the blacktop and reflecting back onto Jay and the others at almost full strength. The heat, coupled with the fear of being drawn into whatever conversation his sister was having, made him start to sweat profusely. He decided he'd avoid eye contact at all expenses and hopefully Lisa wouldn't say anything at all to him. He concentrated his eyes on the rear tire of his car and started to speed up. Now he wanted to go as fast as possible until he was safely inside his car.

He barely knew the couple Lisa was talking to. They were a fairly new couple in the church, and since they were married, Jay didn't socialize with them. The group was close enough now that they could all hear Lisa plainly. Jay tried to not eavesdrop, but he plainly heard her say, "I'm not sure. Most of us figure he must be sick or something."

Jay felt sick to his stomach. The world lurched around him. He was sure Lisa was talking about Uncle Milton. He kept walking, head down, eyes focused on his tire. Lisa continued, "Well, here's my little brother Jay. He's in the group too."

Jay was horrified. Now he knew Lisa was talking about the money, and she had just included him in her conversation! He wanted to scream at her to shut her mouth, but he just kept on walking. Unlocking his car with his remote, he practically lunged the final eight feet or so to the driver's door. He opened it and slid in as quickly as possible without saying a word.

Anna stood outside the car with her mouth half open. She couldn't believe how Jay was acting, let alone the fact that he hadn't opened the car door for her. She opened the door and got in. "What in the world is wrong?" she asked Jay as she fastened her seatbelt. "You didn't even tell Bill and Beth good-bye."

Jay was caught. He couldn't tell her abut the money, but he was sure she'd heard Lisa's conversation. Hopefully she wouldn't be able to make sense of it. Lisa hadn't actually said a word about money, at least not when they were within earshot of her. If he was lucky, it'd all pass over without much thought.

"Sorry, I didn't want to talk to Lisa."

"Well, that's no reason to be rude."

"I just didn't think about it."

It was a lame excuse, but there was nothing else he could say. He'd have to leave it at that and hope Anna wouldn't stay upset with him.

Unfortunately, Anna wasn't satisfied to just let matters drop. Not this time. "I can't figure out what's going on with you."

"Nothing's going on with me. I told you, I'm sorry about Bill."

"That's not it. One day you're up on top of the world, and the next you're withdrawn, and, well, nervous acting."

"I just haven't been feeling overly well is all."

Jay turned onto Anna's street. By now he was feeling really uncomfortable. Anna was right; he had been acting odd lately. But it would all make sense to her in a couple of weeks. As much as he wanted to tell her why he was acting weird, it would have to wait.

He pulled up in front of the house and stopped. The two of them usually went out to eat on Sundays after church, but all Jay wanted to do right now was get home, away from everyone. "I think I'll go home to bed," he said as he gave her a sheepish sideways glance before looking down at the floorboard.

Anna hesitated for a moment. She wanted to continue their earlier conversation but either felt it was useless or would lead to a disagreement. Instead, she turned to Jay and told him, "Well, I hope you get to feeling better soon, or I'll start thinking I'm the reason you're feeling so ill lately."

Jay just sat there and didn't say a word. He wanted to tell her so badly that it was driving him absolutely crazy. Finally, he told her the only thing he could think of. "It's not you at all, Anna, it's me. It'll be alright in a couple of weeks. You'll see."

Anna opened the door and started to get out. It was obvious she wasn't happy with his response. She leaned back down to speak to him through the open door. "Well, see you later then. Let me know if you're planning on going to church later or not."

She closed the door and walked through the plush grass up to the front porch. Jay waited for her to turn around so he could at least wave to her, but she didn't. She gingerly climbed the concrete stairs up to the porch, walked across the decking, and retired to the house without so much as a backwards glance.

Jay drove home completely frustrated. "What am I supposed to do?" he asked no one in particular.

"Lisa is ruining my life!" he added as he emphatically slammed his right fist against the seat next to him.

He couldn't believe she was right out there in the parking lot in plain sight, waving her arms around excitedly, telling everyone and God about the money they were getting. "How stupid can you get?" he continued his one-sided conversation.

His biggest fear was that he would somehow be found guilty by association, even though he hadn't taken part in any of his sister's conversations. He knew he was just being paranoid, but the mind has a funny way of making people imagine the very worst.

By the time he parked his car, he had made up his mind; he was taking vacation time whether Bob and Nancy liked it or not. He couldn't take the chance of someone saying something to him about the money. Not emotionally, and definitely not fiscally.

Jay entered his house and headed straight for the phone. He wanted to call before he lost his nerve, so he dialed up Nancy and Bob's number and waited for someone to answer. It rang several times before the answering machine kicked on.

"Bob, Nancy, this is Jay. Um, I'd like to take my vacation time starting um, tomorrow. I know it's less than short notice, but something personal has come up, and I really need the time. I hope you'll understand and not be too mad at me. Well, um thanks," and he hung up.

His heart was pounding wildly now. He fully expected Nancy to call him to see what was going on, if for no more reason than motherly concern. He couldn't tell her anything either, and he knew she'd be more persistent than Anna was. He'd just have to hold her off too, at least for another two weeks.

Jay walked into his living room, plopped down on the couch, and placed his head in his hands. "I can't take this much longer," he whined to himself. After a few minutes of indulgent sulking he broke out in a huge grin.

"For a million five, I can go through fire," he said chuckling.

CHAPTER TWENTY-ONE

Jay did hear from Nancy, and more than once. At first she was upset with him, but after a few conversations, she was only concerned with his well-being and told him that she and Bob would be praying for him. Jay thanked her and assured her that everything would be alright in three weeks time.

"You'll just have to trust me," was his pat answer every time she questioned him.

Nancy did seek answers elsewhere, namely with Anna, who uncomfortably told her that Jay had been acting very peculiar for the past six weeks or so. Anna didn't like talking about anyone, so she was very vague to Nancy. She was just as concerned, but it was private as far as she was concerned.

Jay didn't go to church Sunday evening and avoided contact with everyone, including Anna. He was worried that she was mad at him, so he just avoided her, not considering that it was probably compounding her troubled feelings. He couldn't afford to think of that. His entire concentration was on his upcoming meeting and the money.

The first week of vacation was successfully spent in near isolation, surfing the television and running out for fast-food only once a day—at the same time that he made his daily trip to the bank. By the end of the week, his freezer was starting to look like a mini vault of cash on ice.

He found himself drawn to it several times a day. He'd just open the door to the freezer, stare and laugh without restraint, like a little child mesmerized by the colorfully wrapped gifts under a Christmas tree.

Sometimes he'd take it out and stack it up and try to gauge how tall the pile of money would be by the time he had the meeting with his uncle. It dominated his thoughts night and day. Without anything else to distract him, he had an almost uncontrollable desire to tell anyone and everyone he knew about the money.

By Friday, Jay was going stir-crazy. He was restless and bored out of his wits and decided he had to do something before he went completely insane. He'd purchased a newspaper the day before and noticed several sales ads for Macy's. Jay had been a Wal-Mart and Shop-ko type of customer his whole life, but he'd always wanted to go into the Macy's store at the mall, just to see what it was like. He knew it was high-priced merchandise, so he'd never given in to temptation. Now he decided the time was right. Grabbing a couple hundred dollars out of his freezer, he headed out the door for the mall.

The drive to Moscow took about ten minutes, and Jay loved every minute of it. He pulled into the mall, which was no more than a half mile from the Washington border, and parked in front of Macy's. For some reason he felt like a school kid making his annual outing to purchase clothes and supplies for the school year.

The store wasn't all that busy as Jay walked around looking for the men's clothing section. There was a large variety of clothing that he quickly learned was very expensive too. He picked out some shirts he liked, all in the fifty dollar range, before heading toward the pant section. Slacks weren't really his style, so he bypassed them in favor of jeans. He was shocked to find most of the jeans were in the ninety dollar and up range. He'd seen people wear them all the time, and he wondered how they could afford it.

A young lady, very pretty, came up behind him and asked if

she could help him with anything. Jay was embarrassed and shyly avoided eye contact with her.

"I'm just looking for some new jeans is all," he mumbled to the girl.

She quickly took charge of the situation. "You look like you're about a thirty-two waist with a thirty-four inch inseam," she said as she sized him up.

"You're right on," Jay replied in amazement.

"I'm Wanda," the pretty girl said as she pulled several different pairs of jeans off various racks.

"Try these on, they'll look hot on you," she said to Jay as he turned red from embarrassment.

Jay obediently took the jeans and headed for the dressing room. He tried them all on and more. Before he knew it, the young sales lady had talked him into five pairs of jeans to go with five different shirts. She even convinced him to purchase a sleek black leather coat that was just under a thousand bucks.

"You'll be the talk of the town when you go out in this," she told him as he admired himself in the full-length mirrors.

He was shocked when the young lady rang up the merchandise for him. It came to a little over eighteen hundred dollars. His hand shaking a little, he sheepishly took out his wallet and handed the lady a credit card he'd only recently paid off. He was embarrassed he'd spent so much, but justified it by telling himself he was a millionaire now, so he needed to dress like one.

Jay signed the sales receipt in an untidy scrawl, thanking the girl when she handed him his bags. He headed out to his car and put his new merchandise in the trunk. The sun was hot, and he started to sweat as he got into the driver's seat and turned the car on.

He just sat there in the parking lot, not wanting to head for home already. With his air conditioner on high, he drove out of the parking lot, turned onto the main road, and headed deeper into Moscow. He didn't have any destination in mind, so he just drove, scanning every business along the way. At the other end of town, he turned the car around and headed slowly back toward Pullman.

An appliance store not too far from the mall caught his attention. Its front windows were painted in several colors announcing a huge closeout on all big screens. Even though he'd never really desired a big screen TV, he decided to stop in to see what they had.

"I'll only go in for five minutes," he promised himself.

More than an hour later, he emerged from the store, new owner of a sixty-five inch, flat-screen, top-of-the-line television set. The total cost including tax was a little over $6,800. Jay didn't even know if it would fit in his little home. He guessed he'd find out when the delivery men brought it the next day and set it up for him.

In just over two hours, he'd spent almost nine thousand dollars. He looked at himself in the rear view mirror and shook his head. *What was I thinking?* Then he smiled and headed toward home.

༺༻

Saturday rolled around, and Jay pulled himself out of bed. It was already 11:30, and he hadn't been to the bank yet. He quickly threw on some clothes, ran out the door to his car, and dashed across town to the bank. With a sigh of relief, he withdrew his money and headed to the grocery store to re-stock on essentials, like Coke and ice cream.

As he was getting back into his car, he heard someone call his name a couple times. He looked around and spotted Bill jogging over toward him.

"Oh great, this is just what I need," he said under his breath, setting his groceries on the passenger seat.

"Yo dog, what's up," Bill said as he extended his fist toward Jay.

Jay banged fists with him before answering. "Just getting a few groceries is all."

"Yo, Anna told me you were feeling a little yuckers lately."

"Yeah, a little under the weather, I guess."

"Well, I was wanting to tell you how my hearing went man, but I didn't want to bother you any."

Jay had forgotten all about the conditional use hearing Bill had on Thursday. For a minute he wasn't sure what his friend was talking about, but it quickly dawned on him.

"Oh yeah, how'd it go?"

"Yo dog, it was amazing. Me and a bunch of supporters, including Anna, were on one side, and it seemed like the whole city of Pullman on the other. The hearing went on for over three hours of live testimony, most of it opposed to the plan. Then they shelved it for another month."

"That doesn't sound so good."

"Ah, we expected it, bro."

"Where do you go from here?"

"More planning, more statistics, more expert testimony, and then we'll see how it goes," Bill explained. "Man you should've heard this one lady. I won't name any names, but we've both seen her in church plenty of times. She gets up in front of the crowd, gets all teary-eyed, and asks 'What's happening to my beautiful little town of Pullman?' Not only that, but she went on to tell everyone this would ruin her property values, and who would compensate her for that? Then she really rubbed salt in the wounds. You know what the chick said next?"

Jay didn't have time to answer before Bill started again.

"She stood up there crying her eyes out in front of God and everybody, fine Christian lady that she is, and told everyone, 'This is as bad, if not worse than Wal-Mart coming to my lovely little town.' Can you believe that dog? All these people that need saving, and all she's worried about is Wal-Mart coming to town."

They talked for a little while longer before saying their good-byes.

"Catch ya tomorrow."

"Yeah, I'll be at church for sure. Tomorrow Anna will be ordained."

They banged fists again, and Jay got in his car and drove home, back to his solitary confines to wait out another day.

※

Sunday brought a fresh set of emotions for Jay. He was excited to see Anna, but nervous to see everyone else. Dressing in some of his new clothes, he wished the weather was cooler so he could wear the leather coat. He decided to not go to Sunday school to minimize contact with anyone. Instead he drank some coffee and ate some pop tarts for breakfast and waited impatiently for 10:45 to get there.

At 10:30, unable to wait any longer, he drove to the church and sat in the parking lot listening to music for ten minutes or so before heading into the church.

The organ was already playing when he entered the foyer. Jay could feel his heart beating rapidly as he approached the sanctuary. He opened the door right as the worship leader walked up on the platform and started to sing. He scanned the room nervously, looking for Anna. She wasn't in her usual seat, and it took Jay a few moments to find her. She was sitting up in the front row next to Beth and Bill.

Jay frowned. He didn't want to walk up in front of everyone, but had no choice if he wanted to sit next to Anna. With a deep breath, he headed up the aisle in front of everyone and sat down. Anna looked up at him in surprise but smiled brightly when their eyes made contact. She hadn't been sure he was going to show up.

Jay could feel butterflies when he looked at Anna. She always dressed up nicely for church, but she looked as if she'd worn her nicest dress today. She'd also pulled her dark hair back into a French braid, which really showed off her pretty face. She didn't wear any makeup, and she didn't need any either. Her natural beauty was more than enough, and today she appeared to glow.

Anna gripped Jay's upper arm and squeezed in excitement. "You look nice," she whispered to him, referring to his new clothes.

"Thanks, you look nice too," Jay whispered awkwardly.

When it was time for the sermon, the pastor got up and introduced the district superintendent, who quickly called Anna up onto the platform. Anna went up on stage as the D.S. went through his ordination service, explaining what it meant to Anna and to the church. He continued to talk about her upcoming mission at length, which made Jay really uncomfortable, even to the point of being upset.

We'll see about that in a few days, he thought to himself as the D.S. went on and on. After fifteen or twenty minutes, he presented Anna with a new leather bound Bible and a framed certificate before presenting her to the church. Everyone in the congregation stood and clapped for Anna as she blushed deeply from embarrassment. Everyone seemed genuinely happy for her.

Everyone but Jay.

After the service, there was a potluck dinner in Anna's honor. She tried to talk Jay into staying, but he insistently declined. "This is your day, go enjoy it," he told her as he started to leave the foyer.

Anna was reluctant, but finally relented. "Okay, but call me tonight, please," she said to him before he turned away. Jay told her that he would and then walked out the door and drove home.

Anna watched him go as conflicted emotions filled her heart. Part of her was extremely happy. The happiest she had ever been. Today was a culmination of a life's work to realize her goal of becoming a missionary.

Tears of joy and relief welled up in her eyes every time she realized that she had finally accomplished one of her main goals in life. The other part of her emotions were a jumbled mess of anger, resentment, hurt, confusion, and sadness. Each emotional state was directly related to Jay.

She was angry at him for leaving her at such an important and significant time of her life. She wanted to share her experience of accomplishment with him, the one she loved, yet he seemed to want nothing to do with her achievement. She resented him for being so selfish and thoughtless. The ease with which he blew her off was simply unbelievable to her. He knew how much this meant to her.

He seemed lost in his own world, unaware of anyone or anything around him. The matter-of-fact way he told her to go enjoy her day, with not a hint of remorse, was nearly too much for her. The pain in her heart was almost unbearable. More than ever, she was confused about their relationship.

She was sure he knew she loved him and would do almost anything for him. What she wasn't sure of was whether he loved her or not. He told her he did, repeatedly, but failed to show it so much of the time. She didn't know what to think or feel anymore. Maybe her affection was for naught.

The sadness of this realization was overwhelming. She began to admit, deep down in her soul, that this relationship, the one she felt God intended for her, was not going to last. An ache filled her heart and threatened to overtake her other emotions on this happiest of days.

All of these emotions bundled together caused the tears to flow constantly. She took a deep breath and quickly asked God to help her, to lift her up emotionally. Then she wiped the tears from her eyes, put on the best smile she could muster, and entered the busy fellowship room, alone.

❧❧

Jay thought about the service all afternoon, with more and more agitation. He wanted Anna to slow down and wait with all this missionary talk until he had a chance to show her she was being foolish, that she could do just as much for God here as she could in some strange and remote country. Events were spiraling out of his control.

After he got his money, they'd be able to make a wonderful life together. Anna would be free to minister to everyone in Pullman to her heart's content. He would even help her any time she wanted him to. He'd already seen first hand the great job she'd done with the people in the community. Everyone responded so positively to her. They absolutely loved her. He didn't know what he'd do if she didn't come around. He was too afraid to think about it.

Later that evening, he gave in and called Anna. He congratulated her and told her he missed her. She thanked him in kind. They talked a little longer, but Jay felt awkward and finally told her he was tired and that he'd talk to her Monday sometime. After hanging up, Jay stood by the phone for a moment or two, contemplating calling her back, but he resisted the temptation. He didn't feel like talking about missions anymore.

❧❧

The next week brought a wild spectrum of emotions to Jay. One minute he was elated, but before he knew it, his elation had changed to anxiety. Monday through Thursday were a blur as he went from high to low and back again more times than he could keep track of. He hardly slept at all and talked only to Anna for a brief minute or two every day. It seemed as if she was withdrawing from him. He thought he was going insane and figured everyone else must think likewise.

The only other contact he had with the world was when he

made his daily journey to the bank to withdraw his daily allowance, as he'd started calling it. By Thursday afternoon, he was nearly exhausted. The thoughts of the money and his upcoming meeting were the only thing on his mind all week. He had spent most of the agonizing time trying to remember if he'd told anyone about the money.

He was fairly confident he hadn't, but his mind continued to go back to his conversation with the car dealers. There didn't seem to be any way his uncle could have found out about his conversation, but he had to admit to himself that it was a possibility, and the admission terrified him.

The memory of his sister and her gesticulations tormented him the most. Even when he tried to get some sleep, he could think of nothing but her statement, "Jay's in the group too," over and over and over in his mind.

When the daylight thankfully faded into darkness, he looked at himself in his mirror. *Twelve hours to go to the moment of truth. Twelve long hours.*

He retired to his bedroom a little after midnight, setting his clock early. *There's no way I'm going to take a chance on sleeping in and missing this meeting.*

On his computer desk he spotted the letter his uncle had written him. He picked it up and read it through again for the first time in weeks. "You're the cause of this crazy journey," he said accusingly to the letter before setting it back down on his desk.

He shook his head and smiled slightly before walking over and shutting off his light. "Ready or not, here comes tomorrow," he said as he snuggled down into his bed and tried futilely to get some sleep. The last time he could remember looking at the clock, as he tossed over again in the tangled sheets, it was past three. *Eight hours until the moment of truth.*

CHAPTER TWENTY-TWO

Jay was up, showered, and dressed two hours before his alarm went off. He'd made himself a breakfast of two eggs over easy, toast, and one cup of coffee and was wishing now that he'd passed on breakfast altogether. His stomach was tied up in knots of anticipation. Sitting in his living room in the dark, looking at his reflection in his new big screen television set, the past month seemed like a dream to him.

He looked at his clock, noting that it had only been five minutes since the last time he checked. It was 9:00 a.m. sharp. He decided he'd head for the bank about five minutes after ten to assure he arrived on time. That gave him sixty-five more agonizing minutes to kill. It seemed like an eternity.

He'd already received almost ninety thousand dollars for the month, with today's deposit rounding out the total. To pass the time, he counted his cash and was shocked to realize that he'd spent over half of the money already. At first he didn't think it was possible, so he frantically searched his freezer for some misplaced baggies of money that weren't there. When there wasn't any he sat down at the kitchen table with a pen and paper and listed everything he'd spent money on for the month.

Sure enough, everything added up to well over half of the ninety thousand. Buyer's remorse began to set in. He'd never been a consumer driven by emotion before, and he vowed he would never be again. In thirty short days he'd spent more than a year's salary. Granted, much of what he'd spent the money on was good, but much was unnecessary too.

His thoughts turned inevitably to Anna. She'd tried to call him earlier, but he'd let the answering machine answer. She sounded a little upset that he hadn't answered and asked him to call her if he had time. Jay thought her voice was tinged with sarcasm, so he played the message over and over to determine if he was right.

He finally decided he was being paranoid. Even if Anna was upset, he couldn't blame her. He'd been totally unpredictable for the past two months. Although he couldn't understand what she saw in him, he was glad she loved him nonetheless, and he was going to make it up to her.

All of his plans for the two of them hinged on the money he was supposed to receive. He had to think positively that he was right, that Anna would choose him and the security and possibilities that the million and a half bucks would bring them. Even so, all this recent talk about missions and missionaries was making him doubt his logic. The timing of her ordination ceremony couldn't have come at a worse time for him.

"Why couldn't Milt have just given us the money a month ago?" he asked his reflection out loud. At least he didn't get a response—that had to be a good sign for his sanity.

"Oh well, the day is finally here, the moment of truth," he declared as he stood up and walked into the kitchen. He looked at the digital read-out on the microwave. It was twenty after nine.

"Ugh!" he said in frustration. He turned on the tap and poured himself a small glass of water. "Better not drink too much before my meeting. I don't want to be squirming in there."

He drank the water and went back into the living room, raising the blinds just long enough to look outside. The sun was shining brightly, causing Jay to squint. He looked at his car, which appeared to be just fine, and let the blinds fall back into place.

Jay sat back down on the couch. He placed his head in his hands. The anticipation was unbearable.

He went over all the rules his uncle had laid out for everyone during the last meeting. Jay had followed all of them except one. He had let it slip to the manager at the car dealership that he was receiving a kind of trust from his uncle Milt Bilston. With a fresh stab of fear, he could remember how the manager's eyes had lit up at the mention of Milt's name.

We know Milt really well, repeated in his mind, haunting him incessantly.

"Ugh, why did I say anything?" He wished once again that he hadn't bought the car. If he'd only been content to walk, as he had been for years, he wouldn't have one thing to worry about.

He thought about his sister, Lisa, and wondered how many people had talked about the money. From the amount of people in church who were talking about it, other people had to have slipped up too. He couldn't imagine the reaction he nor anyone else would have if his uncle dismissed them for talking. The mere thought was devastating, so he turned to the television for a distraction.

The screen lit up the whole room. He had to sit back as far as humanly possible to see the screen without distortion. It was too big for his living room, and he really wished he hadn't bought it. He flipped through the channels, one at a time, pausing no more than five minutes on any one station. It was impossible to focus on any one particular thing.

This must be the way defendants feel when they're waiting for the jury to come back with a verdict, he thought as he gave up and turned off the TV. He looked at the clock again. It was three minutes before ten.

Making a pit stop in the bathroom before leaving, he looked at his reflection in the mirror and was shocked. His eyes seemed sunken with large, dark circles around them. His skin was pale and unhealthy.

"Must be from lack of sleep and stress," he said as he ran cold water over his head in an attempt to shock himself back to normalcy. A few minutes later he re-emerged from the bathroom, grabbed his keys, and headed out the door to his car.

Jay pulled away from the curb and started his drive across town to the bank.

"Well old boy, you'll either be a millionaire in an hour, or you'll be busted," he said as he pulled up to a stoplight. Traffic wasn't heavy, and there didn't seem to be many pedestrians out. He didn't hit another red light the rest of the way and pulled up in the bank parking lot at twelve minutes after ten.

At least ten brand new vehicles, including his sister's Escalade, sat scattered across the parking lot. He spotted his parents' old car, indicating they hadn't purchased a new one. A smile creased his face as he thought of all the times his father had told him and his siblings not to count their chickens before they hatched.

"I guess he's taking his own advice," Jay said as he opened the doors to the bank and went in.

He was eighteen minutes early, which allowed him plenty of time to withdraw his final three thousand dollars. As he placed the envelope in the right front pocket of his jeans, he turned and headed toward the same room he'd been in one long month earlier. There wasn't any sign of Milt as he approached the open door.

Jay reached the doorway and walked in. The room was laid out identically to how it had been one month earlier, except that now there was an overhead projector on a cart right next to the dark brown podium. Next to the projector and cart stood an eight foot by three foot table with fold-up legs, similar to the type the church used for potlucks. Jay figured they must be left over from a previous meeting as he scanned the room. Almost everyone was already present and in their assigned seats.

Nodding to some of his family as he walked up to his seat near the front, he could see his parents sitting over to the left of his seat. The stress on their faces was obvious, which was understandable, all things considered. They both looked over at Jay and nodded. He went over and gave them a big, long hug, suddenly realizing he missed them very much. He hadn't seen them for a month, and it seemed to him that they had aged.

Jay walked back to his assigned seat and sat down. He looked up at the clock: 10:24. He wondered if Milt would be late again, and watched the second hand make its slow trip around the clock.

Anxiety forced him to finally look away. He sighed deeply as he glanced back at the door through which he had just entered. From his angle, all he could see was the opposite door jamb, so he turned back toward the front. He couldn't believe how nervous he was. This made the first meeting feel like a lazy walk in the park.

Three minutes had passed. None of the others were talking. Jay could hear someone cough every now and then, but other than that it was silent. He wondered what Anna was doing.

I sure wish she was here with me right about now, he thought. His heart was pounding in his chest in anticipation of what was to come. The palms of his hands were wet with sweat. He took a deep breath to try to calm down. It didn't work.

"Oh why bother," he said to himself under his breath. Jay looked at the clock again. It was ten thirty straight up. At exactly ten thirty and twenty three seconds his heart nearly exploded, for that's when the door at the rear of the room opened and Milt Bilston entered, followed closely behind by the banker, George Gillis.

Milton looked like a man on a mission as he strolled across the room, head up, shoulders back, toward the podium in the front of the room. He was wearing a double-breasted charcoal-colored suit, white silk shirt, a red power tie, and patent leather shoes. His head was clean shaven, and his eyebrows were furrowed in deep concentration over his steely blue grey eyes, which gave the appearance he was glaring. That particular aspect of his appearance was legendary in the business world. It had helped him during business negotiations on more than one occasion.

The banker, a large portly man, slouched across the room behind Milt like an obedient dog following his master. It looked like he was wearing the same suit he'd worn in the previous meeting. He stopped a step or two short of the podium and waited for Milt to turn around and engage him in conversation.

Jay strained to hear what was being said but was too far away to make out any discernable words. He watched them in nervous anticipation, not knowing quite what to expect. The banker appeared to be nodding his head in agreement with something Milt was saying, before walking past him to his familiar spot on the opposite wall.

Milt appeared to be vigorously studying some notes he'd removed from the inside pocket of his suit only moments before. Apparently satisfied after only a minute or so, he placed the notes back into his pocket and looked out at the group, scanning over each and every person present. Jay felt small and self-conscious when Milt's gaze paused on him. His eyes didn't appear to be either mad or friendly. He cleared his throat, checked the mike on the podium, and began his speech.

"Once again I'd like to thank all of you for being patient with me over this past month."

Jay could hear murmurs throughout the crowd as Milton paused.

"I'd also like to thank you for coming out today, and on time," he added emphatically.

He scanned the room again before continuing.

"I'm going to trust that none of you had trouble with your debit cards this past month."

He paused to see if there was any indication of the opposite being true, and there wasn't.

"Well, we all know why we're here today. I gave you all a few simple rules to follow for a month before you could receive the entire amount of money that has been placed in your accounts, all one million, five-hundred-sixty-two thousand and five-hundred dollars."

Jay could hear several people murmur in anticipation. He was getting all jacked up even though he already knew the dollar amount he'd be receiving. It was just something about hearing someone else stating it aloud that got his juices flowing.

Milton waited a moment for all the excitement to die down.

"The rules I set were simple and reasonable. They didn't place any undue hardship on anyone. As a matter-of-fact, all a person really had to do was keep their mouth shut for one month."

The room was quiet as everyone gave Milton their full attention. Jay found his heart pounding even faster at the thought of what Milton would say next.

"That brings me to this simple question. Did any of you talk amongst yourselves or to others about the gift or money?"

No one moved or said a word. Jay tried to avoid all eye contact with Milt by focusing on the second hand of the clock on the wall almost directly behind him. He could feel the temperature in his face rising. He felt like yelling out, "I didn't do it!" but refrained.

Milt looked around the group, back and forth, back and forth. His gaze stopped on each one of them for only a moment or so, but it seemed like an eternity.

He raised his voice as he asked the question again. "I asked if any of you spoke amongst yourselves or to any other person about the gift."

Still no one moved a finger. Milt continued to look out over them, waiting for someone, anyone to respond. Jay looked around quickly. It appeared that everyone was returning Milt's gaze intently. He knew nobody would voluntarily raise their hand; not with what was at stake.

"So, no one will admit to talking about the money?" Milt asked the group.

Nobody said a word or moved a muscle. Jay felt like jumping up and pointing his finger at Lisa while yelling, "she talked, she talked," but again, he refrained.

Milt paced back and forth behind the podium. He had placed

his hands together, palm to palm, almost as if he was praying. He placed his two thumbs under his chin with his index fingers running across his mouth and touching the end of his nose. He held them there as he continued to pace back and forth. It appeared as if he was deep in thought, contemplating what he would say next. He turned back to the podium and faced the group again.

"All right people," he paused. "I know some of you talked."

Another pause, only longer than the previous one. Jay started squirming a little, as did some of the others.

"I'm going to ask you one last time, did any of you talk about the gift to anyone else?"

Still no one responded. Milt appeared to be agitated with them. His hands gripped both sides of the podium as he waited for a response. No one moved an inch. *No one's going to admit to anything*, Jay thought to himself. The silence, along with his uncle's constant gaze, was making him feel extremely uncomfortable.

"Nobody at all will come forward?" he asked in a defeated tone, as he shook his head back and forth in disbelief. "People, I've been approached by no less than eight people, including a reporter from the local paper, asking me about the money. 'Am I dying?' 'Why am I giving away my fortune?' etc., etc., etc. All in the last two weeks. Could anyone here explain to me how these people got their information if none of you spoke?"

Jay looked around the room. Milt's questioning was beginning to get very uncomfortable, and it showed on the faces of nearly everyone present. Jay turned back to the front of the room. His stress had reached a new pinnacle, making the room feel like an oven. Even though he'd told the car salesman of the money, he had no intention of owning up at this point, ruining whatever slim chance he might have that Milt didn't know about his slip. The only satisfaction he had right now was the thought of Lisa squirming in her seat. She had to be feeling extremely guilty right about now.

Jay wondered what Milt's next move would be. He didn't

have to wait long. Milt abruptly stood up straight, turned and walked out the door he'd come through several minutes previous. Jay heard several people make remarks, "Where's he going?" "What's he doing?" "What's going on?" He wondered all of those things himself.

Everyone remained in their seats, facing forward, not knowing what to expect next. When there was no sign of Milt after several more minutes, Barbara spoke up to the banker.

"Excuse me, Mr. Gillis, are we having a break or something?"

All eyes were on the banker. He shifted his weight, obviously uncomfortable. "Um, I don't think so. Milton never said anything about a break to me."

"Well this is stupid," somebody said from the back of the room. The voice sounded like Lisa's, but Jay couldn't be sure.

After nearly ten minutes, Jay was wondering whether or not he should go looking for Uncle Milt. A glance around the room again showed that everyone was restless.

"Maybe someone should go look for Milton," Jay's mother said.

"Well this is just ridiculous!" Jay's dad no more than got the words out of his mouth when a large thump made everyone collectively jump and turn toward the door.

The source of the noise was a hand cart bumping against the door jamb as it was being maneuvered through the doorway. On the handcart was a large cardboard storage box, the type often used to store files. On top of the storage box was a smaller box, a little larger in width and length than a standard piece of typing paper. It was about six inches in height. On top of the smaller box was a large padded legal size envelope, obviously full of something.

Milt was half pushing, half steering the handcart through the doorway. With some difficulty, he jockeyed the handcart through the door and emerged in the room. He then wheeled the cart up to the front and parked it next to the card table, making sure to balance his load before he walked back to the podium. He looked out over the group again without saying a word. After what seemed like a minute or more, he checked to make sure the microphone was on.

"I'm sorry it took me so long," he paused.

Jay wondered what could be in the two boxes and the envelope. He had no idea, but he figured it couldn't be good, whatever it was.

"Again, I'm going to ask all of you, does anyone want to voluntarily admit that they talked to someone about the money?"

Milt's voice wasn't overly loud this time. As a matter-of-fact it seemed almost weary to Jay. Still no one moved a finger.

Jay could almost feel the tension in the room. It seemed to be rising. Something had to give soon. He looked back at Milt, who was leaning on the podium, looking out over the group.

"No one?" he almost pleaded with them.

Still no one moved.

"All right then."

Milt walked passed the overhead projector, passed the card table, and stopped at the hand cart. He reached down and picked up the large stuffed envelope and held it out in front of himself, moving it back and forth slowly for everyone to see before throwing it onto the table. Everyone watched it arc up into the air, and they jumped when it hit the with a large whack and slid across the table toward the overhead projector, coming to a stop right on the edge of the table.

"Bank and financial statements. Loan documents and promissory notes," was his simple explanation.

Jay's heart practically quit beating when Milt said promissory notes. He just knew his promissory note, or a copy of it, must be in the envelope. His dreams shattered around him in the eerily silent room.

Milt looked out over the group as he walked back to the podium. "Now does anyone want to confess to talking about the money?"

"How many times is he going to ask that?" Jay heard his sister Lisa whispering to someone in the back.

Milt either didn't hear her or chose to ignore her. He picked up the smaller of the two boxes and held it up for everyone to see before he turned and tossed the box on the table, just as he had with the envelope. Again, all eyes watched the box rise up into the air and then everyone jumped as the box slammed down on the table.

"Sworn statements from individuals documenting to whom, where at, and the date and time that they were told about the money, and by whom they were told." He let that point sink home a little longer than the last point as he practically glared out at the group.

Milt gripped both sides of the podium, head down, eyes fixed on the top of it as if it had the answer to his relentless questions. Slowly he raised his head, his eyes were red and looked tired.

"Now does anyone want to admit they talked to someone?" he asked in an almost dejected voice. He looked around the room, waiting for a response, waiting, waiting.

Jay felt absolutely sick. His heart was beating erratically, uncontrollably. He felt as if he was at a revival meeting at the church and the minister was pleading with sinners to come to the altar to have their sins washed away. An almost uncontrollable urge to raise up his hands and wail his guilt to the heavens, freeing the burden from his soul, consumed him.

Still he resisted all temptation to confess, holding onto hope that somehow his guilt would miraculously be overlooked by Milt. *Maybe no one talked to the car dealers,* he thought desperately. He wished that someone, anyone, would come forward and admit they talked, hopefully taking all the heat for the rest of them. Somehow, he didn't think he'd get off that easily.

No one came forward. Milt looked out at everyone and shook his head before walking back to the end of the table, and with considerable effort, picked up the last box. It by far was the largest of the three packages, and by Milt's expression, was fairly heavy.

He turned and presented it to the group, pausing several seconds before plopping it down emphatically on the table and sliding it across the top until it was touching the other box.

Jay was a complete wreck by now. He could feel his chance at the money slipping away, and fast. He felt like running, like doing something, but there was nothing he could do and nowhere for him to go. His hands were wet with perspiration. His face felt flushed. He wanted to die.

How could I have been so stupid? he asked himself as he remembered his conversation with the car salesman. *I really messed up.*

"Actual transcripts from recorded phone and cell phone conversations between you and other people," he indicated to all of them as he moved his hand back and forth, gesturing to include the whole group.

"Transcripts from recordings made from actual person to person conversations from you to, once again, other people."

Again he gestured to all of them in an indictment of guilt. He stood there watching, hands once again palm to palm, both thumbs under his chin, index fingers bisecting his mouth, and barely touching his nose. After a few moments he walked back over to the podium, gripped the sides, and once again asked everyone.

"Is *anyone* going to admit talking now?" he queried.

Despite the huge burden of evidence they had been confronted with, again no one moved a finger. Milt continued to watch them. Several people were literally squirming in discomfort.

"Come on people; look at all of the evidence."

Everyone seemed to be clinging to the hope that Milt wouldn't have any evidence on them.

"Let me ask you this, would those of you that are guilty rather I embarrass you in public, right here, right now?"

For a moment there was nothing but silence in the room. Milt's incessant questioning and presentation of the evidence finally broke Jay's sister Lisa. She jumped up in the back of the room.

"Milton Bilston, you're an evil, evil man," she screeched venomously at him before storming from the room in a torrent of tears. Her husband jumped up and started to follow her for a step or two, thought better of it, and returned to his seat and sat down.

Milt didn't say a word. He simply continued to watch and wait.

"Okay, have it your way," he relented as he turned and started toward the envelope and boxes on the table.

"It's not fair," a subdued Barbara said, stopping Milt in his tracks.

"Excuse me?" he said as he returned to the podium.

"I said it's not fair!" Barbara exclaimed, gaining some confidence.

Jay watched with interest. For once he was rooting for his sister to keep going. Maybe she could convince Milt that they all had tried their best, therefore they should receive the money.

"What's not fair?" Milt asked politely, showing genuine interest.

"This, this whole thing; you send us all this mysterious letter telling us to not tell anyone, then you meet with us, give us some of the money and make us wait for another month, all the while we haven't been allowed to tell a single soul of our sudden good fortune. There's no good reason that I can see for it other than for some perverted satisfaction you get from manipulating our lives."

Milt stood there in silence, looking out at Barbara. No one knew what to expect from him, but they all feared he would blow a gasket. Instead he surprised them all by keeping his cool. After a few moments he answered Barbara.

"Go on," he simply said.

"Go on with what?"

"Convince me why I should just give you the money. Let's say maybe I'm intrigued by what you're saying."

Jay felt hope springing anew. He couldn't believe what Milt was saying. Maybe he would just give them all the money. He waited for his sister to continue her argument.

"I don't really know what you want to hear from me." She

paused. "I mean you have to understand that nothing this unbelievably good has ever happened to probably any of us before. It was one thing to not say anything before you gave us some money, but once we started getting the three thousand dollars daily, well, how could a person be quiet about it. It was impossible to not say something to someone."

"Yeah, that's right!" someone called out.

"Exactly!" several other people exclaimed at the end of Barbara's statement.

Milt stood there nodding his head, seemingly in agreement with everything being said.

"I can kind of see your point, I guess." He pondered for a moment. "Your joy was too great to not tell the world."

He rubbed his chin in contemplation.

"Basically what you're saying, if I understand you correctly, anyway, is that in no way should I have held you to such high expectations, on my part anyway?"

"That's right, your rules were impossible to keep! You enticed us by giving us a very generous sum of money every day, seemingly by design. In other words, you set us up to fail."

It seemed to Jay that Milt was starting to waiver. Oh, how he hoped Milt would realize that Barbara was right. He watched him with tenacious enthusiasm.

"I can see the merits of your point. It would have been very difficult to remain silent for that long under those circumstances."

Jay's heart leapt with joy. It seemed as if Milt was wavering in their favor. He crossed his fingers under his desk in hopes Milt would cede. He didn't have to wait long to find out the answer.

Milt walked back and forth behind the podium, apparently in deep thought. Almost everyone sat on the edge of their seat in anticipation, waiting for his response, most of them realizing that their financial future hinged on what he said next.

"You've made an excellent point; a most compelling argument that under most circumstances I would be forced to agree with." He paused and looked slowly around the room before continuing.

"Unfortunately, I can't agree with you today."

A murmur of disagreement could be heard around the room as Milt let his statement sink home.

"I can't agree because all of you have had a much better gift given to you than the one I offered you, and most of you, if not all, have done a remarkable job of keeping it a secret."

A general mumbling of disagreement could be heard throughout the room.

That's ludicrous! I've never received more than a million and a half dollars before, Jay thought as his uncle looked out at them.

Finally some brave soul in the back of the room spoke up. "How do you figure, Milt?"

Jay wasn't sure who posed the question, but he was glad someone did.

"Take a moment and take a look around you, all of you," Milt commanded.

Jay, along with the rest of the people, timidly looked around the room at each other. He still couldn't see what Milt was talking about.

"Some of you have more than one thing in common, but all of you have one thing that connects all of you, one to the other."

"Yeah, like we're all alive at the same time, and we're all here at the same time," Barbara said sarcastically.

This time, Milt didn't react to her statement at all. He watched out over them like a teacher, waiting for the correct answer during a chapter review, his agitation with the group seeming to grow every moment the correct answer was not given. To him the answer was simple and logical. An answer that each of them should know right off.

"Many of you are related to me. That's one common factor for some of you. All of you however are professed active Christians and good friends of mine. That's the common link I'm talking about today."

Once again Milt paused, waiting for the correlation between the gift and the common thread linking all of them to sink in.

Sink in it did for some, but Jay didn't connect the two. *So... I'm lucky enough to be his relative.*

"The gift I'm talking about, for those of you for whom it hasn't sunk in, is the gift of eternal life."

He paused dramatically.

"Each one of you has done a remarkable job of keeping that a secret for a long, long time, it seems to me."

An uproar erupted instantly from many in the crowd.

"How dare you!" the pastor said as he stood and stepped toward Milt in anger.

He was quickly joined by others in protest. Phrases like, "Who do you think you are to judge us?" could be heard throughout the room.

Jay sat there listening and watching all of the protests and anger unfold around him without joining in. He knew to his core that Milt was right, but it still made him angry to be called out in that manner.

"Now hold on a minute, hold on, hold on," Milt said, extending his palms out toward the pastor and the others. "I'm not trying to make you mad, and I'm not trying to be arrogant, so just hear me out." He waited as the group slowly calmed down and returned to their seats.

"I want all of you to sit there and seriously think about when was the last time you actually told someone about your personal relationship with Christ. I'm not talking about sitting in Sunday school and church talking about God. I'm talking about spontaneously telling someone—a friend, a neighbor, an enemy, a stranger, or even a salesman—about the greatest gift anyone could and did give you, the gift of salvation and eternal life."

He took a deep breath and continued. "You sure didn't have

any difficulty telling people about the money you were receiving, and the large amount that was sure to follow. When was the last time you had as much excitement and hope about your Christianity as you've had about the money these past two months?"

"I don't think it's your place to question or judge us when it concerns our spirituality," the pastor answered.

"Then whose place is it to question all of you? Whose is it?"

"I think that's a personal issue between each of us and God," the pastor retorted.

"You know what? I think God has asked, and asked, and asked. I think he's tired of asking when all we do is ignore him. People, someone has to wake you up. You all have placed more hope in money than you have in Christ. I'm here to tell you, no amount of money in the world can replace your eternal life. It won't bring you happiness, and it won't sustain your joy. I'm speaking from firsthand experience."

The room was silent once more. Jay decided this whole thing must have been a charade just so Milt could stand up in front of them and hear himself talk. He didn't like it, and it didn't help any knowing that his uncle was right. Worse, it made him feel guilty. He didn't like it one bit.

"So, is all this an elaborate church service or something? Are you bored with life, so you schemed up this, this elaborate deception?" Jay's father asked, visibly upset with his brother, his voice shaking as he spoke.

"No, and yes. I wanted to somehow get all of your attention, and what better way is there than with money? Believe me though—I'm not doing this to get some kind of satisfaction out of manipulating you or your emotions. I wanted all of you to realize the false hope and excitement you placed in money, or other things in your lives." Milt spoke passionately now, desperately.

"It has saddened me more than I can tell you to sit through church service after church service, always seeing basically the same people week after week attending those services. Don't get me wrong, I think it's important for all of us to attend church and to have fellowship with our fellow Christians, but I think too many of us have turned church into some sort of entertainment or affirmation of our own Christianity. We go there, listen to the pastor preach, visit, and go home to start our busy weeks without spreading the Word to a single soul. I'm here to tell you, people, there's more to Christianity than sitting in our nice pews behind those stained glass windows feeling good about ourselves when the whole world is out there crying for something to believe in."

Everyone was stunned into silence. They all knew that Milt was essentially correct in everything he had said. It didn't mean they had to like it.

"Why us? Why now?" Barbara asked quietly.

"People, we're running out of time here. I firmly believe we're in the eleventh hour. Jesus could return any moment, and we're not ready. The fields are full and ripe, and there are no workers. People are dying on the vine, waiting, searching for salvation, but no one is there to show them the way."

Barbara still wasn't convinced. "People have been saying that for decades, and Jesus hasn't returned."

"Take a look at the world around us. There's turmoil in the Middle East, rumors of war around the world, and Christianity is under attack right here in our own country. The same country that was founded on freedom of religion now has Christianity dead in its sights."

When no one responded, Milt spoke up again, elaborating, "Prayer has been removed from our schools, and the high court has heard an argument and is considering, as we speak, whether to remove God from the pledge of allegiance. Several cities in the state of Colorado have removed Christ from Christmas. It is now called simply the 'Midwinter Holiday.' Can you believe that? No more Christmas right here in our own country. Who would have believed that?" Milton asked incredulously. He paused for only a moment before continuing, his voice thick with conviction.

"A winning football coach somewhere in the Midwest has been removed from his job for simply praying to God for the safety of his and the other team's players. None of his players even voiced an objection to the prayers, but his school board still terminated his employment for the fear that someone would sue them for religious discrimination.

"Right now an effort is underway in the courts of California to remove a large white cross that was dedicated to the veterans after World War Two. The group that is petitioning its removal is doing so because several of the churches from the San Diego area hold their Easter sunrise services there. The group is claiming separation of church and state, and will most likely be successful in their attempts.

"The list goes on and on, people, and this is only the beginning. The attack on Christianity will only intensify in the coming months and years. The world wants us to believe that sin really isn't sin, and the Bible is just a guideline. Death is legally doled out to millions in the name of convenience and 'privacy,' and so many who live suffer from the choice.

"In the meantime, we sit back, listening to our pastor's sermons, while telling ourselves we know the truth, so it doesn't really matter. Maybe it doesn't for us, but it does for a lot of other people that don't know any better."

When Milt finished, nobody said a word for a long time. Finally Jay's brother Todd spoke up.

"All of these things you talk about, though maybe true, are the workings of only a few fringe people. They don't represent the rest of America."

"That's right! They are only a handful of people, and that's what should scare you into action if nothing else does."

Surprisingly there were a few 'Amens' at the end of Milt's speech. Jay thought it was good, but he'd heard it all before. He didn't really see what this had to do with the money. Another voice at the back spoke up, uncertain.

"What you say is fine and dandy, but there are a lot more people in our church than just us. What can the few of us do?"

"Surely you've heard the saying, it only takes a spark? I was hoping that you all would help provide that spark. I want to remind you, Jesus told us all to go out into the world to spread the word to all humanity. To emulate him in all we do. I doubt that he would be sitting in church week in and week out, listening to the pastor and to an evangelist twice a year, without telling one single person about God.

"To better answer your question, look what only a few dedicated people can and have done for the other side."

No one spoke a word. Some were mad, some in agreement with Milt, and a couple of them had completely tuned him out.

Milt waited a few moments in silence before beginning again. "Well, I guess I'll get down off my soap box and back to business at hand if no one has any other questions."

Jay looked around at the group, wishing someone would talk Milt into forgetting about the evidence next to him.

Again, Barbara couldn't hold her tongue. "Don't you think you kind of went to extremes to make your point? I mean fifty million bucks to make someone listen seems pretty extreme to me."

Milt shook his head in sadness.

"You just don't get it. The times are extreme. People are dying and will continue to die every single day without ever knowing Jesus Christ as their personal savior. What could be more extreme than that?"

"Yeah, but fifty million bucks! Come on!" Barbara exclaimed.

"Obviously what I'm saying to you isn't sinking in. Let me try posing it to you in the form of a question. How much is a person's life worth?"

"How much is a life worth?"

"That's right, what is the value of a human life?" Milt asked all of them.

Finally Jay spoke up. "I saw a program on *Sixty Minutes* about this very subject. After the twin towers collapsed, the government decided for some reason to compensate the survivors of the victims in the collapse. They appointed an individual to calculate a person's value, and thus compensated his family for that particular amount. The official had some sort of equation that took the victim's age into account, his job, and estimated earnings for the rest of his life, coupled with the number of dependants that were left. The equation worked for him, but not without some controversy."

"Wrong!" his uncle exclaimed loudly. "I saw that program, and it was completely flawed."

He paused for reaction. No one else responded.

"I'll tell you right now, I know personally the individual that came up with the correct formula to figure out a person's value. Not only did he come up with the formula, he proved it!" Excitement laced Milt's voice again.

"Do you know how he proved it?" he asked, and then continued without waiting for an answer. "He proved it by dying on the cross for each and every one of us. The person I'm talking about is none other than Jesus Christ, Himself." Milt stressed the last three words, as if he could force them to understand.

"His decision to take the whole world's sin upon Himself just so we could all have access to Him and His Father up in heaven tells me that every single person, from the lowliest poor person to the wealthiest king in the world, is *priceless* in His eyes. Not one single person, more valuable than the other. Therefore, from a business standpoint alone, if I can spend fifty million dollars and just one of you wakes up and leads one single soul to Christ, I come out way ahead.

"Fifty million dollars is a cheap investment for a priceless return," Milt finished emphatically.

He walked around behind the podium, pacing back and forth. Finally he headed toward the boxes and the envelope on the table, seemed to have second thoughts, and walked back to the microphone. "Jay could you come up here and give me a hand please?"

Slowly, Jay got up and walked up to the front next to Milt and waited for further instructions.

"Would you please walk over to the largest box and open the lid?" Milt asked. Jay reluctantly took the few steps over to the table. He was shaking out of fear of what was in the box.

"Now, would you take the top off the box, reach into the box and take one of the pages out of the center of the pile."

Jay did as he was asked, pulling a piece of normal typing paper out of the box. Everyone in the room watched in nervous anticipation, nervous that their name may be on the paper.

"Now read to everyone whatever is on the paper," Milt instructed.

Jay looked at the paper and then looked over at Milt. "Excuse me, sir, but the paper's blank."

"Then pick another piece out of the box," an agitated Milt exclaimed.

Jay pulled another piece of paper out of the box and again looked to Milt. "This one's blank too," he explained with a nervous chuckle.

"Let me see that!" Milt demanded.

Jay obediently handed him the blank piece of paper and backed away, returning to the opened box.

"Pull some more papers out of that box and bring them to me," Milt demanded loudly.

Jay grabbed a handful of papers out of the box and handed them to his uncle. They were all blank.

"What in the world?" Milt asked in astonishment as his eyes squinted down into a frown.

The whole room sat in stunned silence. It appeared as if something was wrong. They watched in amazement, waiting to see what would unfold next.

"Open the other box and take a piece of paper out."

Jay did as he was told.

"Read it!" Milt again demanded.

This page was blank too. Jay showed it to Milt, who stormed over and angrily dumped all the pages out on the table. They were all blank. Several of the people sitting in the room laughed nervously as Milt grabbed the envelope and dumped its contents out.

More blank papers.

Jay looked at his uncle in amazement, wondering what in the world was going on. It appeared as if someone had destroyed or replaced Milt's evidence.

Milt looked out at the crowd and then returned to the podium. His face was contorted with anger. "There is no evidence. I have no phone records, no statements from individuals, and no financial records on any of you. I didn't keep track of a single person these past two months, and I never intended too. You all get the money."

Several people clapped, but some of the group was mad—mad that Milt had put them through such a rollercoaster of emotional highs and lows. A rumbling murmur could be heard building throughout the room.

"I want you to do one thing for me," Milt said as the crowd calmed down. "Remember the joy and anticipation, the excitements and hope that you all had over the money. Remember it and think about what your salvation is worth. Ask yourselves this, what's more important to you: eternal life or one point five million dollars. Then try and remember when your relationship with Jesus was ever this exciting.

"I'll tell you one thing, if your answer is never, then you had better re-evaluate your relationship with Christ. I also want some of you to realize that you were prepared to lie to receive this money, despite the cost paid for your salvation.

"I hope that some of you, if not all of you, will take something valuable away from this experience. I hope that a little light will come on and we can start changing Pullman, Whitman County, even the state of Washington."

He paused a moment before continuing.

"I hope that my attempts at awakening your Christian spirit will not have been a failure. That's all I have to say. Mr. Gillis will have more paperwork for you to fill out along with some financial and tax advice. I'd like to thank all of you, and ask you to please forgive me if I made you upset with me. Remember, I love all of you."

With that Milton Bilston turned and walked across the floor and out the door. Jay sat there wide-mouthed and watched him go, as did the rest of the group. Someone started to clap. Pretty soon, everyone joined in.

Jay didn't know whether they were clapping for Milt or for the fact they were all receiving the money.

They all quieted down as the banker got up and addressed the crowd.

Well, that's that! Now I'm a millionaire, Jay thought, feeling none of the euphoria he thought he'd feel. He sat and listened as the banker went on and on for more than twenty minutes, wondering where Milt was going now.

CHAPTER TWENTY-THREE

Jay walked out of the bank with his parents. They were extremely happy with the outcome of the meeting and informed Jay that his father would be retiring immediately. They had made plans to travel with a Work and Witness group to rural areas of the U.S. to perform much needed maintenance on old churches.

"Most of the churches are in depressed areas where the congregation can't afford the upkeep. It's a good ministry for us, and your father will be very useful with his construction background and all," his mother explained as he walked them to their car. Jay hugged them both and told them he'd come visit soon as they got in their car and drove away.

He walked to his car and got in. The temperature was in triple digits outside and about twenty degrees warmer inside the car. He started it up and blasted on the air as he pulled out of the parking lot and onto the main road.

Jay was surprised at the way he was feeling. He thought he'd feel elation when he became a millionaire, but instead he was subdued. He drove across town and pulled up in front of a large, new office building. It was his uncle Milt's. A quick scan of the parking lot revealed Milt's Silverado.

After a few minutes he mustered enough courage to get out of his car and go into the building. A receptionist greeted him as he walked into the building. "May I help you?"

"Yes, I'm here to see Milt Bilston, please," he answered.

"Do you have an appointment?" the young lady asked as she studied her day timer, obviously confused.

"No, I don't have an appointment," Jay assured her.

"I'll have to check to see if he's available. Could I have your name?"

"I'm Milt's nephew, Jay."

The receptionist warmed up considerably with that bit of news. She immediately called through to Milt's office to see if he had time to see his nephew. Milt practically made it up to the front before the receptionist had a chance to set the phone down.

"Jay, my boy, come in. Come in," Milt motioned to him as he held open the door.

Jay walked through the doorway and into Milt's office with his uncle close behind.

"Sit down, sit down. Make yourself comfortable," Milt said as he walked back and sat down behind his large cherry wood desk.

Jay did as he was told and sat in a large leather chair with high, curving wooden arms. He was surprised how comfortable the chair was. He looked around his uncle's large office. The wall directly behind Milt's desk had floor to ceiling windows. It was an excellent view of the northern part of Pullman. The only decorations on the walls were pictures of his cousins and a family portrait, including his deceased aunt. He was surprised the office wasn't more lavish.

"What a fine surprise. I sure wasn't expecting you here today."

Jay fidgeted nervously before beginning. "Well, um, I never got a chance to thank you at the bank, so I came out to thank you in person."

Milt sat smiling for several seconds. His eyes looked really weary. "Well thank you, Son," Milt said, obviously pleased that Jay had taken the effort to come all this way just to thank him. "I was hoping I hadn't ostracized myself after my passionate speech."

Jay was suddenly very self-conscious. "No, sir, I think everyone took it really well."

Milt seemed larger than life to Jay. He had always been very kind, but at the same time very intimidating. It made it very difficult for Jay to have a normal conversation with his uncle. He always felt like a little child whenever he was around him.

"Well, good. You have to understand it's just something I'm very passionate about. I felt as if the Lord had placed a burden on me to do something to rekindle people's spirits, so I did something. Granted, it was very unorthodox, but that's what I felt He was leading me to do. I only hope and pray it works."

"I think it will," Jay replied, unsure what else to say.

"Well, you stick close with those friends of yours. You know, that young lady Anna and that character Bill you are always chumming around with."

Milt sat forward in his chair, as if eager to explain a point. "That Anna, she personifies Jesus in everything she does. She doesn't preach to the people, she loves the people. She doesn't just tell them about Jesus, she lives Jesus to them. Her whole life is dedicated to Jesus, and consequently to others. You can learn a lot from her.

"And that Bill, every tattooed and pierced bit of him, he's the same way. As goofy as he is, as strange as he talks and looks, when he sees people, he loves them first and never asks questions. Every day, he's down there in the gutter with the most desperate and depraved members of society, showing them there's hope and love in Jesus Christ. He's showing them where to find strength to kick their addictions and habits when all else has failed. He and Anna are making a huge impact on our community through Jesus Christ. You, young man, need to be more like Bill."

"Yeah, I love him, but I don't know if I want to be like him. He's a bit of a freak."

Milt slammed his fist down on his desk, causing Jay to jump in his seat. "That's what I'm talking about! You have to be a freak! A

Jesus freak! You have to be willing to go out in the world, shining like a beacon from a lighthouse, personifying Jesus in everything you do. You have to go to the people and love them on their level no matter where they're at or what they're doing. At first people will shun you and mock you every step of the way, and all you can do is love them. Eventually, you'll start to make a difference in their lives, and people will start to pour their hearts out to you; that, my son, is when you will start making a difference in this old world.

"You see, everyone is searching for something they can believe in, a purpose for their lives, if you will. By standing firm on your convictions, and loving them along the way, you can be the one to show them the truth. Live the life Jay, live the life.

"Make no mistake about it, the road won't be easy, but it'll be worth it. Trust me on that. Remember, no matter how hard it gets, the Lord will be there every step of the way! *That's* something you can bank on!" Milt sat back in his chair and folded his arms behind his head. He had a "what are you going to do now?" look on his face.

Jay had come over to tell his uncle thanks, not to get another sermon; but that's exactly what he'd gotten. He really hadn't meant anything bad by his remark, referring to Bill as a freak. After all, he loved Bill like a brother. He just couldn't think of any other way to describe him on the spur of the moment. Jay sat there, unsure of what to say. Obviously Milton was waiting for some sort of response from him.

"I understand what you're saying, and I agree with you about Bill and Anna, but I don't feel like direct ministry is necessarily for me. I mean, I have no problem taking a stand for what I believe in, but getting down and talking to the people on their level the way Anna and Bill do comes naturally for them. I, on the other hand, have a hard time talking to strangers at all," Jay offered in a feeble attempt at an excuse.

"Those natural qualities you're talking about are what I call the Holy Spirit at work. Don't underestimate Him either. He can work through anyone," Milt said calmly.

Jay had braced himself for another explosion and was relieved when Milt didn't erupt. *Maybe he understands where I'm at,* Jay thought.

Milt sat up in his chair and pointed his finger emphatically at Jay as he spoke. "We're running out of time until the good Lord returns. You need to get off the fence and start working for the Lord!"

Jay felt his ire raise a little. He didn't like the implication made with Milt's last remark. Sure he didn't get overly involved with church and all, but he didn't feel that meant he wasn't a Christian. He didn't feel as if he was on any fence. As far as he was concerned, he was totally committed to the Lord. But he decided not to start an argument. It would put a bit of a damper on his "thank you."

"I will," Jay responded as he started to fidget in his chair.

Neither of them spoke for the next several seconds, until Jay decided it was time to leave. "Well, I'd better get going so you can get back to work," he said awkwardly as he stood up and inched toward the door.

"Of course you must," Milt said as he rose out of his chair.

Jay walked to the door and started to open it when Milt's voice stopped him.

"Jay, remember my door is always open if you want or need to talk to someone."

"Okay, I appreciate that," Jay replied.

"Remember, I love you and God loves you!" Milt called out as the door to the waiting area closed.

☙❧

Jay headed home with a dark cloud hanging over his head. This was supposed to be a happy day for him, but it was turning out gloomy. His mood darkened as he thought about Anna and the things Milt had said to him. *Why can't everyone just mind their own business?*

As usual these days, the light on his answering machine was blinking, so he pushed the play button as he took an ice cold Coke out of the refrigerator. He smiled as he listened to the message. When it was finished he pushed the play button again.

"Hi Jay, this is Sandy Calbot. I'm calling to welcome you to the Bank of Whitman and to inform you that I'm your personal banker. You'll be receiving a letter from me in the mail in the next day or so with your personal portfolio and my office and cell phone numbers. You can call me anytime you want, day or night, and I'll help you in any way I can. I'm looking forward to meeting with you in two weeks when we set up a financial plan. Feel free to stop by the bank for a face to face if you'd like to meet sooner. Thank you. Oh, by the way, welcome to the Millionaire Club."

Jay's mood lifted considerably after listening to the message a second and then a third time before saving it. One single call had restored the expected joy to his day.

There was another phone call that could brighten his day even more, a call he'd been looking forward to all week. He decided not to tell Anna about the money until he saw her in person, and since she was leaving for a teen retreat over the weekend, the good news would have to wait just a little longer. Still, it would be good to hear her voice, and to be able to talk without worrying about losing a million dollars.

He dialed her number and waited for an answer. All he got was her answering machine, so he left her a message and told her he'd try her on Nancy's phone. No one answered there either, and he didn't leave a message.

Anna must have already left for the weekend. He felt a tinge of jealousy at the thought of her doing things without him. Not that he blamed her for not trying to get hold of him though. Not with the way he'd been acting lately. He decided to look at the bright side—at least he didn't have to help with the teens.

Jay spent the rest of the afternoon watching TV and eating chips. As dinner time approached, he decided to go out to eat and celebrate, but didn't really feel like going anywhere by himself. He tried Bill's number, but only got his answering machine.

Wow, everyone's gone, he said to himself as he hung up the phone. He grabbed his keys and wallet and headed out to the local steakhouse anyway.

The restaurant wasn't very busy, which surprised him since it was a Friday night. The hostess immediately seated him and handed him a menu. Jay looked it over and decided on the most expensive steak. He wasn't really used to eating steak, and didn't know that much about cuts, but it must be good if it cost so much.

The waitress came and took his drink order. She asked him if he wanted an appetizer, and on an impulse he decided to order onion rings. He was surprised at how quickly she returned with his Coke and a glass of water.

Jay took a drink of his Coke and looked around the restaurant. Most of the tables were empty, but there were several people sitting at the bar. A pretty young lady with long blond hair was sitting at the end of the bar closest to Jay. She nodded and smiled at Jay. He smiled back and then blushed and turned away, disgusted with himself. *Great, now she'll think I was staring at her.*

His waitress returned with his onion rings and several different kinds of dipping sauce. She set them down in the middle of the table along with a little plate for him to place the sauces on. Jay tried a few of them, but settled on just plain ketchup.

Hungrier than he had realized, he attacked the onion rings ravenously. He had just bit his fourth onion ring in half and started chewing when a female voice startled him.

"You should try some nacho cheddar sauce on your onion rings sometime," the voice said as Jay looked up.

He was shocked to find it belonged to the pretty blond who

had been sitting at the bar. Jay was embarrassed and awkwardly said, "Uh-huh," as he swallowed his mouthful of food.

The girl smiled again and held out her hand. "Hi, I'm Sandy."

Jay wiped the grease on his pants and shook her hand. "Um, hi, I'm Jay."

"Oh, I know who you are," she said coyly.

Jay was shocked. *How does this pretty young lady know me? I don't know anyone, at least not any young ladies.*

Sandy must have seen the confused look on Jay's face, for she quickly added, "Sandy, Sandy Callbot."

The name sounded familiar, but it took Jay a moment to place it. "Oh, Sandy Callbot, my banker," he stated.

"The one and only," she said as she executed a dramatic curtsy.

"Well, glad to meet you," Jay said, still self-conscious and unsure. His food was completely forgotten.

Sandy stood there with a drink in her hand, waiting for Jay to invite her to sit down. After a few moments she evidently grew tired of waiting and invited herself. "Do you mind if I join you?" she asked as she sat down without waiting for Jay to answer.

Jay wasn't sure how to react to this new development. He was very uncomfortable, and he looked around nervously.

"Don't worry, I don't bite," Sandy said with a smile. "I was just surprised to see you out alone. I figured you'd be out celebrating with someone tonight over your good fortune. I'm not intruding am I?"

"Um, no, I guess not."

"You're not a recluse or something, are you?" Sandy inquired in a teasing tone.

"No, everyone I called was gone, but I still have to eat," Jay nervously answered in his own defense.

"You are right about that, everyone needs to eat."

They were interrupted by the arrival of Jay's steak. Self-consciously, Jay asked Sandy if she'd like to eat too. At first she hesitated, but it only took a moment for her to change her mind and order a salmon dinner. It arrived shortly, and they ate their dinners and visited for over an hour.

Their waitress returned several times with more beverages for the two of them. Jay continued to drink Coke while Sandy had some sort of alcoholic concoction with little umbrellas in the glass. She was getting more and more giggly as the night wore on, which added to Jay's continuing discomfort. Sandy definitely wasn't shy, and no subject was off limits. He really didn't know how to talk to her and didn't say much, which didn't seem to bother her at all. She talked and flirted enough for the two of them. Growing weary, Jay finally told her he needed to get home.

"Would you mind giving me a ride?" she asked.

After a moment's hesitation, Jay decided it wouldn't hurt anything if he gave her a ride. "Sure, I'll take you home," he said as he put several bills into the waitress's little folder. Usually he tried to calculate a tip, but this time he left her twenty dollars.

I am a millionaire, after all, he thought as he got up and waited for Sandy at the edge of the table.

"Oh dear, I think I've had a little too much to drink," she laughed as she held out her hand to Jay. He helped her out of her seat and then offered her his arm as they walked out of the restaurant. Sandy leaned on him as they walked to his car. He wasn't sure if it was an effect of the alcohol or if she was doing it on purpose. After settling in the passenger seat, she gave him directions and he headed off across town.

Sandy's house was small, with a very tidy yard. Two flower gardens flanked the sidewalk up to her house, and they were full of several kinds of flowering plants in full bloom.

Jay got out of the car and hurried around to the passenger side to open the door. He helped her out of the car and onto the sidewalk. "Well, I'll see you later sometime," he said as he pointed her toward her house.

"Won't you walk me to my door?" she pleaded. "I don't think I can make it by myself."

Jay didn't want to help her, but he decided it was probably for the best. She took his arm and they walked up the sidewalk to her little blue house, still laughing and leaning. Jay helped her up the steps and across the porch to the front door. Sandy struggled with her keys, trying to get the front door unlocked. She finally handed the keys to Jay.

"Would you be a gentleman and unlock my door for me please," she said with an intoxicated giggle. There were several keys on her key chain, and Jay looked them over carefully until he found one that looked like it might open a deadbolt. He carefully slid it into the lock and was relieved to hear a little click indicating the deadbolt had opened. He tried the door, and it opened right up.

"There you go," he said as he handed the keys back to Sandy.

"You're going to come in aren't you?" she replied.

"Well, I wasn't planning on it," Jay answered, not wanting to be rude but well beyond his comfort zone.

Sandy grabbed at his arm and tried to pull him in the door. "Come in, come in. The night's still young and we could have some fun," she said playfully.

"No, no, I've got to get home."

"What's the matter, don't you like me?" she asked.

"Well, yes I like you, but I'm kind of engaged," he said, hoping to end the flirtation before it got out of hand.

"What do you mean, kind of engaged? There's no such thing as kind of engaged. You either are or you're not," she argued.

Jay stood there for a moment not knowing quite what to say. It was true he and Anna had really never talked about marriage, or engagement for that matter. He'd just always assumed they would become engaged when the time was right.

"Well, I haven't given her a ring yet, but we're kind of promised to each other," he finally offered weakly.

"If there's no ring, then you're on the open market as far as

I'm concerned, Jay Bilston," Sandy threatened. "Are you sure you won't come in?"

Jay resolutely declined. "No, I need to be going."

Sandy only smiled provocatively and ran her finger slowly up his arm and across his chest. "I'll let you off this time, but next time you won't be able to say no."

Jay flushed and turned away.

"Call me soon, Jay Bilston!" she called as he practically ran to his car.

Jay drove home in shock from the evening's events. He wasn't used to females paying that kind of attention to him. Other than Anna and Nancy, he hardly even talked to the opposite sex. He definitely wasn't prepared for an encounter like he'd just had. Now that he had some distance and a chance to look back over the evening, he surprised himself by admitting he had enjoyed the attention.

Maybe I will give her a call sometime, he thought as he got out of his car and went into the empty apartment.

Hopeful, Jay checked his answering machine for any messages, but there were no new ones. He pushed the play button anyway just so he could listen to the message from earlier in the day. *It's even better now that I have a face to place with the voice,* he thought as he smiled.

He was surprised how tired he was, and headed off to bed. *My first night as a millionaire,* he thought as he snuggled down under the covers.

Even though he was tired, sleep eluded him. He kept thinking about his encounter with Sandy earlier in the evening, smiling at the idea of an attractive young lady like her having a genuine interest in someone like him. "First day with money and I already have women chasing me. A guy could get used to this," he admitted as he drifted off to sleep.

CHAPTER TWENTY-FOUR

Jay woke up around ten the following morning. He smiled to himself as he realized the events of the past day were real. The truth of his good fortune was just beginning to sink in.

He hurried to the kitchen to see if he had any messages on his answering machine. To his disappointment, the light wasn't blinking.

"I thought maybe Anna would have called by now," he said out loud. In his mind he added, *Or maybe even Sandy.*

He thought about calling Sandy, but couldn't think of a single reason why he should. He didn't want to call her unless it was for a legitimate reason. "That way she won't get the wrong idea," he reasoned.

After a dull morning of trying to find something entertaining to watch and checking his answering machine needlessly, he had a brilliant idea. *I know what I'll do. I'll go to the mall in Moscow and buy two cell phones; one for Anna and one for me.* He'd almost forgotten the previous plans he'd made to purchase them.

Besides, it'll give me a reason to get out of the house, he thought as he headed off to take a shower. *I'll have to call Sandy and give her my cell number; after all she is my personal banker.*

Jay was happy to have a legitimate reason for calling Sandy. She was intriguing to him, though he didn't fully understand why. Even so, he vowed to himself to keep their relationship business, and business alone.

"I love Anna and no one else," he said as if trying to convince himself of something.

Traffic on the road between Moscow and Pullman was fairly light. A paved nature trail that linked Pullman and Moscow ran parallel to the highway on the south side of the road. Jay noticed that foot traffic, interspersed with an occasional bicycle and stroller, was rather heavy. Some sort of blue and purple wildflowers were in bloom next to the little creek that meandered back and forth under wide foot bridges constructed to accommodate the trail. There were literally millions of the flowers, which gave the illusion of a bright semi-colored carpet bisected by a black ribbon of blacktop. Jay thought it was absolutely beautiful, glancing over at the sight whenever traffic allowed. He decided he and Anna should go for a walk on the path to enjoy the beautiful colors when she returned from her retreat.

Entering the mall parking lot, Jay parked his car safely away from all the other cars. He quickly walked across the hot pavement and entered the air-conditioned mall. *I don't know how I survived without air conditioning all those years,* he thought as he paused beneath one of the overhead ducts that were blowing cold air.

The mall was fairly busy for the amount of cars that were in the parking lot. Jay navigated through the throng of people until he came to a kiosk in the middle of the mall manned by two young men in dark suits selling cell phones and signing people up for service. There were a couple customers in front of him, and they seemed in no hurry to finalize their deals.

Jay grabbed a brochure that showed him several different plan options and headed off toward a little restaurant that sold fruit smoothies, hot dogs, and hamburgers. He decided to eat lunch while he was waiting and ordered a chili dog with the works and a large orange smoothie.

His meal was ready in only a few minutes. Jay paid the young cashier and picked a booth that looked out into the mall hallway. He enjoyed watching people, and what better forum than a busy mall on a Saturday? He took a sip of his orange smoothie followed by a larger gulp.

This is absolutely my favorite meal, Jay thought as he savored another bite. The two people who had been in front of him at the kiosk both left with new phones and were quickly replaced by new customers. Jay looked over the brochure but had trouble making heads or tales of the colorful graph depicting peak, off peak, roaming, rollover minutes, along with other terms he wasn't familiar with.

He finished his chilidog and sipped his orange smoothie, enjoying the cold frothiness of the beverage. He watched all of the pedestrians for another fifteen or twenty minutes as he finished his drink before getting up and disposing of his garbage in the refuse bin up by the front counter.

Jay headed straight to the cell phone kiosk. He timed it almost perfectly. A customer was just finishing up so Jay only had to wait a little more than five minutes before being helped.

"May I help you sir?" the young salesman asked Jay.

"I, um, would like to purchase a couple of cell phones, one for me and one for my girlfriend," Jay announced.

"Have you ever had cell phone service?"

"Nope, never have."

The salesman handed Jay a clipboard with two pages of questions to fill out.

"Sorry, we'll have to do a credit check then," he explained apologetically.

Jay picked up a pen and looked around for somewhere to sit.

"There's a bench in the entryway," the salesman pointed to where Jay had come in earlier.

Jay walked over to the bench and sat down. He filled out the pages as quickly as possible but paused at the blank that asked for balance on hand.

He didn't want to put one and a half million dollars; they would never believe that. So he finally wrote down fifty thousand dollars. He listed several credit references, all with a zero balance, and put Nancy and Bob down as references. *All of this for a stupid phone?* he thought incredulously.

With the last of the paperwork filled out, he returned to the kiosk. There were two people ahead of him again, so Jay had to wait. After fifteen or twenty minutes of waiting, he was really starting to get annoyed and was on the verge of leaving.

"Sorry sir," the young man said in a less than convincing tone, taking the clipboard. "This looks real good," he said as he sent Jay's paperwork into the electronic world somewhere via fax.

Jay looked at the different options and styles of phones as he waited for a response on his application. He finally decided on the smallest, most stylish, and consequently most expensive phones available. The salesman talked Jay into hands free devices for the phones, along with real leather carrying cases.

The fax sputtered as it started to spit out some paper with writing on it. The salesman snatched it off the fax and read over the paper. He wadded it up and tossed it into the garbage as he turned to Jay.

"You've been approved, no problem," he announced to a relieved Jay.

Jay was annoyed that he'd become nervous. He knew he had good credit, not to mention all the money that was in his account. He couldn't help himself though and smiled widely as the salesman congratulated him.

He spent a good twenty minutes longer going over the different plans before finally settling on a nationwide plan with fifteen hundred minutes per phone and free phone to phone calling, with roll over minutes. It didn't occur to him that Anna was probably going to be the only person he would ever call with any frequency, so he'd never use up any of his minutes. Discovering to his surprise that he could purchase insurance for the phones, he immediately did so.

"You can never have too much insurance," he explained to the salesman.

All told, Jay spent over eight hundred dollars on the two cell phones, including payments for two months of service.

"Thank you very much sir," the young man said, realizing that his commission off this one transaction was more than he made most weekends.

Jay headed out of the mall and into the bright sunlight. He couldn't remember for sure where he'd parked, and the lot had many more cars in it than when he'd arrived. There seemed to be an unusual amount of red cars, so he wandered for a few minutes before finally remembering he'd parked out near the outer limit of the parking lot to avoid any door dings.

There were now cars on both sides of Jay's Impala. He was annoyed that someone had parked right next to him and made a circuit around his car to check for damage. A smudge about door height nearly panicked him as he rubbed his finger across it. The mark came off with considerable ease, satisfying Jay. He finally got in and headed for home, carefully backing out of his spot.

Fifteen minutes later, Jay walked into his apartment and tossed the phones onto the couch. He was hot, thirsty, and tired. In the kitchen he grabbed an ice-cold Coke out of the fridge. He cracked it open and guzzled over half the Coke in one drink.

"That never gets old," Jay said with a smile before finishing off the can.

He opened the fridge and grabbed another can as he headed back into the living room. There were a couple different direction books in the phone boxes that he promptly tossed on the floor without so much as reading a single word. He installed the battery and tried to turn on the phone. When it failed to turn on, he remembered the salesman telling him he would have to charge them first. Impatient, he took the other phone and charger out of its box and plugged them into the outlet next to the couch.

Sweeping everything else onto the floor, he stretched out on the couch to take a nap since it'd be awhile before the phones were charged. He fell asleep with the TV on and slept for a couple of hours.

Jay awoke to the ringing of his phone. He sat up quickly and checked both cell phones to see if they were ringing. Realizing that both phones were off, he rushed to the kitchen to pick up the receiver before it went to the answering machine. *Maybe it's Anna,* he thought with anticipation as he grabbed the receiver.

He picked up the phone and said hello to silence. He said hello again into the receiver and waited for a response for a moment or two, until a voice of foreign descent answered on the other end. Jay listened politely for a minute or more as the voice on the other end of the line tried to sell him a membership to some sort of travel club. He politely declined several times until the person on the other end of the line finally gave up and hung up.

"That was annoying," Jay said to himself with disappointment in his voice. He hung up the phone and returned to the living room to check on his cell phones again. They were still charging.

Jay was restless and decided to go out and wash his car. He raided the change jar he kept in his bedroom for quarters and headed out the door to give his most prized possession a much needed bath.

He spent more than an hour washing his car before heading for home. First, he stopped by a pizza place and grabbed a Hawaiian pizza for dinner and some cookie dough for dessert. *Who needs steak?*

Jay spent the evening eating his pizza and dessert while watching a couple old western movies, which he paused intermittently to check his cell phones to see if they were ready for use. After the movies he stood in the kitchen looking at his answering machine for a moment or two as if his mere observation could in some mysterious way suddenly produce a message from Anna, Bill, or even Sandy.

"I can't believe no one has called me," he said as he walked down the hall toward his waiting bed.

CHAPTER TWENTY-FIVE

Jay was up and around earlier than usual on Sunday morning. He immediately went to his living room to see if his cell phones had been activated. They hadn't been, which annoyed him to an irrational degree.

What's going on with these things? he asked as he tossed the phones onto his couch, where they bounced toward the far edge before coming to rest on top of each other.

Knowing Anna wouldn't be there, Jay decided to skip Sunday school. He figured she'd be back sometime before the evening service, since the teen group always held service after one of their retreats. It gave them a chance to thank the church for supporting them and to give a testimony to the work God was doing in their lives. Jay really enjoyed those services, since they almost always let out early. He'd hated them when he was a teenager however, never being one to stand up in front of a group and talk.

Seeing his checkbook sitting on the kitchen counter reminded him that he needed to tithe on his new-found wealth. He grudgingly wrote out a check for ten thousand dollars, recorded it in his check register and tore it out of his checkbook before stuffing it into his wallet.

"That's all they're going to get for right now whether they like it or not," he said defensively, referring to the church. "There's absolutely no way I'm going to give them ten percent of the total either. They'll have to settle for ten percent after taxes."

He got up from the table to make some breakfast, searching for something appetizing in the nearly bare refrigerator.

"Besides, they just got nine thousand dollars from me a few weeks ago. Nineteen thousand bucks in a single month is nothing to sneeze at. If they don't like it, they can go fly a kite!" he said with a bravado that surprised even himself. "Besides, what could they possibly do with so much money anyway? They'd probably just send it overseas to some stupid mission field or something."

Jay felt bad after his last statement, especially considering Anna's intentions of becoming a missionary. Even so, he grumbled all morning about having to pay that much money for tithe.

***

Despite his early start to the day, Jay arrived at the church a couple of minutes late. He noticed several spots were vacant in the parking lot as he wheeled in. Knowing the teens were using the church van, Jay parked his car in the parking space directly next to the vacant church van spot to avoid any car to car contact. At first he worried the teens would get back during the service, but dismissed the idea as a long shot.

"Besides, the bus doesn't have any doors that can open into my car anyway," he concluded with satisfaction.

The congregation was already singing a second praise song as Jay slipped into the back pew. He hadn't sat in the back pew since he and Anna had started seeing each other again. It was welcoming and felt extremely comfortable. He scanned around the room but failed to see any of his family. Even Bill and Beth were missing, which seemed odd to Jay for a moment or two before his mind began drifting away to other things in his life, namely money.

He couldn't help himself as he thought of the different ways he could enjoy some of his money. Judging by how fast he had gone through last month's money, he was beginning to realize that a million and a half bucks wasn't really that much—at least not if you intended to make it last the rest of your life.

Jay sat through the service without really hearing a single word. He placed the check he'd written into an envelope and printed out the word "tithe" directly below the space for his name. He left the little space for the amount empty, figuring the counters could fill it out themselves.

He placed the envelope on the nearly overflowing offering plate as it was handed to him by the smiling usher. No one was sitting near Jay, so he simply handed the plate back to the usher and watched as the usher, joined by another one, exited the Sanctuary to count the morning take.

What a racket, Jay thought with disdain as he turned back toward the front of the church.

Drowsiness was setting in, and Jay fought off the urge to close his eyes for a quick catnap. He was grateful when the pastor asked everyone to please stand for the Benediction. Jay was the first one out of the sanctuary, which prevented him from having to talk to anyone.

Now I remember why I love sitting in the back pew, Jay thought as he slipped out of the church and headed for his car without so much as a "hello" to or from any of his fellow churchgoers.

Traffic was light; so Jay was home in mere minutes. He parked his car and headed inside to see if the cell pones had been activated. He was pleasantly surprised to see that they had been. Eager to try them out, he flipped one open and dialed his home number, waiting anxiously for the phone to start ringing. After a moment or two, he could hear a ringing in the cell phone. His home phone came to life with a ring of its own just a second later.

"That's cool!" Jay said as he realized his home phone was a moment behind his cell phone.

He quickly hung up the cell phone and grabbed the other one

to repeat the process. It worked exactly as the first one had, much to Jay's delight.

"Way cool!" he said as he looked the phones over.

He grabbed the operator's manual off the floor and sat down on the couch with the two phones. Flipping to the section entitled "Selecting your ring," he started scanning the directions. After a few moments, Jay grabbed up one of the cell phones and started pushing buttons.

Much to Jay's delight, there was even a ring that resembled the clucking of a chicken. After a short deliberation, he finally selected the clucking chicken for his ring before turning his attention to Anna's phone. He ran through the choices again before settling on "Take Me Out to the Ballgame" for her ring.

"She'll probably change the ring anyway," he decided as he programmed her phone.

Jay picked his phone back up and dialed Anna's number. After several rings, he decided he wasn't going to get an answer so he hung up. He paused for a moment before trying Bill's number. The answering machine picked up after only two rings. Bill's voice came over the line in a long greeting instructing the caller to leave a message after the beep. When he was sure it was his turn, he started with his message.

"Hey man, it's just me. What'd you do, leave the country or something? Anyway, I'm just trying out my new cell phone, and it seems to work, so I'll call you again later, when I know you're home or something."

Without any better options, Jay reclined in his chair and began pushing different buttons to see what they'd do. Although it would be easier, he hated reading instructions and opted for the hands-on approach to learn how to operate his phone. It didn't take him long to find the electronic phone book and he proceeded to enter the name and number of everyone he could think of.

After several seconds of hesitation Jay succumbed to temptation and entered Sandy's name and number for both her cell phone and personal phone. As soon as he was finished, he turned his attention to Anna's phone and began programming the same numbers and names in it, omitting Sandy's, of course.

Jay got up and paced around his house several times. "I wonder when Anna'll be back," he said as he checked the clock for about the fortieth time.

It was ten after two in the afternoon, and he still hadn't heard from her, or from anyone else for that matter. He grabbed his cell phone and dialed Anna's number only to reach her answering machine. He left a short message asking her to call. He didn't have any more luck with Bill or his parents. *Wouldn't you know it; I finally have a cell phone and no one to call.*

Jay spent the rest of the afternoon watching a baseball game on television. He jumped up off the couch and nearly made it to the kitchen in one bound when his phone began ringing.

"Hello, hello."

"Hi, there!" said a familiar voice.

"Well, welcome home finally. You've sure been gone a long time," Jay said, surprised at the edge of irritation in his voice.

"Well I've been at the teen retreat. You knew I was going to that, silly," Anna said without as much as a hint of frustration in her tone. "You should have come too. You would have had a good time."

"I had some things to do. I doubt you had any air conditioning anyway."

"Just mother nature, it really wasn't all that bad. It cooled off real well every night."

Jay really didn't know what else to say. He wanted to see Anna, but he wasn't going to rush right over to her house. He was really hoping she'd invite him to the evening church service. They talked mainly about the retreat. Actually, Anna mostly talked and Jay listened. She was extremely excited about the retreat, especially at the large number of teens that committed their lives to the Lord for the first time.

Jay listened, somewhat irritated, as Anna went on and on about all the great events. He practically dropped the phone when Anna lauded the job Bill and Beth did with the teen group.

"They went too?" Jay asked incredulously.

"Yes they went. What's wrong with that?"

Jay felt a twinge of jealousy. Knowing full well that his feelings were irrational, he couldn't help himself. He sighed as he pushed his unwarranted feelings aside.

"Nothing, I guess. I was just surprised," he finally answered with a stiff voice.

Anna paused on the other end of the line. She wasn't sure what to make of Jay's response. It troubled her, but she'd decided a few weeks earlier to go forward with God's plan for her with or without Jay. She hoped and prayed it would be with.

"Well, I hate to cut this short, but I'm seriously in need of a long hot shower before church tonight. Are you going to be there?"

"Well, if you want me to be," Jay said in his best neglected voice.

"Sure I want you to be there. Are you picking me up, or should I meet you at the church?"

"I'll pick you up."

"Good, see you soon," Anna said as she hung up the phone.

Jay hung up his receiver and stood there for a moment, unhappy with the conversation he'd just had with Anna. He was upset, and he didn't know why.

I'm being stupid! I'm a millionaire now! he said to himself in an attempt to lighten his mood. It wasn't working very well.

"I can hardly wait to see Anna's reaction," he said in an attempt to psyche himself up. He was starting to get excited to see Anna and decided to take a shower and dress up somewhat for church. *Or for Anna,* he thought as he headed down the hall to the bathroom.

Jay pulled up in front of Anna's a few minutes early. Grinning like a boy with a shiny new toy, he pulled out his cell phone and dialed her number. The phone rang twice before Anna answered.

"Hello," she said tentatively into the receiver, unsure whose number it was on her caller I.D.

"Hi there!"

"Jay, is that you?"

"Who else would it be?"

"I don't know, I didn't recognize the number. Where are you?"

"I'm sitting in my car waiting for you. Right outside your door."

Anna looked out her upstairs window onto the street below. She smiled and waved when she saw him.

"Cool, you must have gotten a cell phone."

"What great deductive powers you have," Jay teased.

"I'll be down in just a few minutes."

She sounded very upbeat and happy, which made Jay smile. His anticipation of seeing her was growing, which surprised him a little. It wasn't as if he hadn't seen her for a long time. As a matter-of-fact, it had only been a few days. He'd had a lot of excitement the past several days, and finally decided that was probably why he was reacting this way. Whatever the reason, he felt good and that made him happy.

A few more minutes passed before Anna emerged from the house. She closed the front door and half ran to the car. "Hi there, I missed you," she said breathlessly as she got in and buckled her seatbelt.

Jay returned her smile with one of his own. "I missed you too."

He pulled away from the curb and headed toward the church, listening intently as Anna told him how excited she was about the teens in the church and the wonderful things God was doing in their lives. Jay smiled in amusement as Anna continued talking almost nonstop. He hadn't seen her this excited since the episode with the missionary a few years earlier.

This is exactly what she needed to help her realize she can make a difference right here and doesn't need to rush off to a missionary field somewhere, Jay thought with satisfaction.

"Look at me, I'm being rude doing all the talking," Anna said with a smile.

"I don't mind at all," Jay replied as he pulled into the church parking lot.

Anna turned her full attention on Jay. "Did you have a good weekend?"

"It was pretty good. I do have some really good news to tell you."

"You do? What is it?"

Jay parked his car and started to get out. "I'll tell you later."

"Come on, you can tell me now, can't you" Anna asked with genuine curiosity, which made Jay all the more determined to make her wait.

"I'll tell you when the time is right," he promised as he walked around the car and offered Anna his arm.

She slid her arm inside Jay's and smiled. "What a gentleman!"

Jay, feeling suddenly weak in the knees, smiled back at Anna. *She's the prettiest girl I've ever seen!* Jay thought as they walked arm in arm to the church.

Several people were already at the church and were busy visiting in the foyer when Jay and Anna walked in. A couple of teenage girls rushed over and started talking at the same time while completely ignoring Jay, which annoyed him immensely. Anna smiled and patiently listened to first one and then the other before stopping them and telling them she could only understand them if they talked one at a time.

They started again, one at a time, while pulling Anna toward the ladies restroom. Anna looked back at Jay, halfway smiled, and shrugged before disappearing around the corner. Jay stood there watching the hallway where Anna had disappeared.

Great, now what? he said to himself as he headed toward the sanctuary to pick a seat. He scanned the mostly empty sanctuary before picking a pew in the middle and sat next to the side aisle so he could lean on the side arm and make a hasty departure when the service was over. He was comfortably leaning against the arm of the pew, resting, when a familiar voice made his heart jump.

"Yo dog, what's up?" Bill said into his right ear.

Jay turned around with a surprised look on his face. "Hey man, I thought you must have fallen off the face of the earth or something."

"Nope, I was playing shepherd this weekend to a bunch of wild and crazy sheep."

"That's what I heard, no pun intended."

They both laughed and visited for awhile, Bill doing most of the talking. He went into great detail about the difficulties he was having getting his recovery and rehab program off the ground, but much to Jay's surprise, Bill wasn't one bit discouraged.

"It's all in the big Guy's hands. I'm just a little peon running errands."

They visited until Anna and the teen group came into the sanctuary to start the service. Jay watched as Anna walked up to the podium and waited patiently for the teens to be seated in the front two pews. A moment or two passed while everyone wrapped up their conversations and diverted their full attention to Anna. She started with a word of prayer followed by a praise chorus. When the song was finished, she thanked everyone for coming out and quickly explained to the congregation that the teen group would be performing the service from that point on. She continued by telling them about the teen retreat and the great fellowship everyone had experienced over the past couple of days.

"I'm most proud to tell you that eleven of our young people made a commitment to the Lord," she said, beaming to the congregation.

Everyone clapped at this bit of news as Anna turned the stage over to the teen group president. Jay watched Anna with admiration as she descended the stairs and came to sit next to him.

"Good job," he whispered to her as she sat down.

Anna just smiled and mouthed, "Thanks!"

The teens got up one by one and gave a little testimony and told a little about the retreat, but Jay didn't hear a single word they were saying. Instead he was daydreaming about Anna and the reaction she would have when he told her about the money. He could picture her jumping into his arms at the good news and could hardly wait to tell her. It had to be at the perfect place and the perfect time.

Several places came to mind. Finally, he decided he'd tell her the following day on the nature path that ran between Pullman and Moscow. He would take her to the little bench, surrounded by all of the little blue and purple wildflowers he'd seen earlier in the week.

Who knows—maybe I'll even propose to her, he thought with a smile. Jay kept imagining the scene over and over in his head, his mood getting brighter each time. Before he knew it, the service had come to an end.

"You want to get some dinner?" he quickly asked Anna before turning to Bill and Beth to repeat his question.

"Why sure I would!" Anna exclaimed with a huge smile, which made Jay all the giddier.

"We're in!" Bill added.

They visited a minute or two with some of the teens before driving to their favorite restaurant. Dinner and dessert lasted for a few hours before everyone headed home for the night.

Jay pulled up in front of Anna's house and put his car in park. They had spent so much time in the restaurant, it was already dark.

"I have some good news I think you'll like," he said as he turned to Anna.

"Really, I like good news!" She waited patiently for Jay to continue, but was met only with silence.

"Well, what's the good news?" she finally asked.

Pleased that she was curious, Jay took his time answering. "I've decided the time isn't right to tell you," he teased. "You'll have to wait another day—if you're available that is."

This time Anna paused without saying anything. She decided to turn the tables on Jay to show him two could play the suspense game. She waited until Jay couldn't stand it any longer.

"What's the matter? Is something wrong?" he asked, concern filling his voice.

Anna laughed. "Of course I'm available, silly. I just wanted to make you sweat a little."

Jay felt foolish as he laughed a little. "All right, you got me," he admitted. "Would you be available tomorrow sometime, or am I too low down on your totem pole for this short of a notice?"

"I guess I could squeeze you in sometime in the afternoon."

"Don't trouble yourself or anything," Jay said dejectedly.

"I'm sorry, I was just teasing. I can be available whenever you want me to be."

Jay sat there for a moment trying to figure out when would be the best time. "How about three in the afternoon?"

"Three in the afternoon it is!" Anna exclaimed.

They visited for a little while longer before Anna got out of the car and told Jay good night. Jay watched her as she walked up and into the house.

"Tomorrow it is, my Anna," he said as he pulled away from the curb and drove home.

CHAPTER TWENTY-SIX

As soon as he woke, Jay's mind started conjuring up images of Anna and her reaction to the upcoming revelation he would make. He needed to decide exactly how he was going to tell her about the money while somehow tying it in to their future together. It was important to make sure she understood the money was for both of them, for their future, and their children's future. He knew Anna wanted to have children someday, and he hoped by including them in his conversation she'd soften emotionally and eventually relent on her decision to become a missionary.

Who in their right mind would want to raise their children in some foreign, destitute third-world country? he asked himself in an attempt at a reasonable argument. *Besides, it wouldn't be right to keep them away from their grandparents, aunts, uncles, and cousins. They will need all the love they can get, and who better to give it than their own flesh and blood?*

He polished and sharpened his arguments in his head until he was absolutely certain Anna would have no choice but to see things his way. Then he sat back, proud of himself for being so clever. By making their future family the focus point of his conversation and the money secondary, Anna would fall right in line with his reasoning.

"How could she think any different?" he asked out loud as he stretched his arms out as wide as he could and yawned.

Jay spent nearly three hours getting ready for his upcoming date with Anna. He picked out some new shorts along with a new polo shirt from his first visit to Macy's. The shorts were gray and the shirt was purple, one of Anna's favorite colors.

Dressed to impress, he found himself getting more and more nervous as the three o'clock hour drew near. He even contemplated writing her a letter telling her of the money and how much he loved her, but finally decided he didn't have enough time to perfect it.

"Shoot, I barely passed English. What makes me think I could write some romantic letter?" he said as he wadded up the notebook paper containing his third attempt at just that.

He looked at the clock and realized he needed to get going. It was only five minutes to three, and Anna would be waiting for him. He knew she wouldn't forget. Anna said she'd be ready, and she always did what she said.

When Jay pulled up in front of her house, Anna emerged as if on cue. She was wearing a flowered blouse and summer skirt and looked more beautiful than ever. His stomach was full of butterflies. He was more nervous than he'd ever been before, even including the last meeting at the bank.

Here goes nothing, he thought as Anna opened the car door and got in.

"Hi there," Anna said with one of her enchanting smiles.

"Hi," Jay replied awkwardly, suddenly intoxicated with Anna's beauty.

Her nearly black hair was shiny and bright, and she smelled of flowers. Jay breathed in deeply, absorbing as much of Anna's fragrance as possible. She fastened her seat belt and adjusted her skirt before turning to Jay. "Ready," she said enthusiastically.

He smiled back as he put the car in drive and pulled away from the curb. He drove through town and headed toward Moscow, to the waiting field of wild flowers.

The weather was perfect. There were several fluffy white clouds dispersed around the deep blue sky. The clouds had depth, which gave them a life-like appearance. They were the kind of clouds Jay remembered from his childhood.

He had spent many summer days with his friends or nearest siblings, all lying on their backs in the grass, looking up as the clouds floated past; a rabbit here, a dragon there, a squirrel, or even a bear, always moving, combining, and changing as if God Himself were using the sky as His canvas and the clouds as paint.

Today, a slight breeze moved them from west to east ever so slowly, changing their shape as they moved along the sky. It was one of those picturesque days that the Palouse presented so often that most people simply took them for granted. It was a perfect day, Jay decided, for telling Anna of his good fortune and possibly even for a marriage proposal.

The Moscow-Pullman highway was under construction, so the traffic was moving along at a snail's pace, doing nothing to ease Jay's tension. He kept both hands on the steering wheel and his eyes focused on the road and the cars directly in front of him. Every so often he stole a quick glance over at Anna, who was sitting calmly in her seat, her hands folded in her lap. Jay's *Casting Crowns* CD was playing quietly over his stereo as he worked his way toward Moscow.

"How has your day been so far?" he asked awkwardly, breaking the silence between them.

"It's been pretty good. I used the time to write a little more on my doctoral thesis," she answered politely.

Jay absolutely loved Anna's voice. It was soft and comforting, no matter what she was saying. Never once had he heard a cross statement come out of her mouth. He often thought he could spend hours listening to her talk, no matter the subject.

Finally, Jay reached the pullout area near Moscow and pulled his car off the side of the road. "We're here," he said to a surprised Anna as he unbuckled his belt and opened his door.

"Wow, this is a surprise," Anna said without a bit of sarcasm in her voice.

The construction crew was busy across the highway building a new section of roadway. The heavy equipment was very loud and was kicking up a huge amount of dust. Luckily for Jay and Anna, the wind was blowing in the opposite direction, preventing the dust from reaching them.

"Come over this way, to the path," Jay said as he motioned for Anna to follow him across the little footbridge that spanned the nearly dry creek before it intersected the ten-foot-wide paved nature path.

Anna followed him without question and came up beside him when they reached the path. There were several other people using the path, either walking or rollerblading past the couple.

"I wanted to bring you here to see all the flowers," Jay said as he motioned out over the field of purple and blue wild flowers directly in front of them.

"They're absolutely beautiful!" Anna exclaimed as her eyes slowly scanned the colorful field of flowers.

Jay could see the little bench several hundred feet ahead as they continued to walk. It was extremely hot out, and the sun was beating down on them with full strength, making it very miserable for both of them. The heat hadn't entered his mind when he planned the outing. He looked over at Anna to see if she was sweating too. Her face was very flushed, but no moisture was visible.

"Man, it's hot today," he said as they reached the bench.

"It is very warm," Anna added without complaint.

Jay motioned for them to sit on the bench and Anna obliged. The steel seat was extremely hot and nearly burned them through their thin clothes. Little gnats were swarming over the stagnant water directly behind them.

"I guess this wasn't as good an idea as I thought it would be," Jay said apologetically.

"It's alright; just a little warm is all. Besides, the flowers are just beautiful," Anna said cheerfully.

He wondered if Anna was sincere or just being nice. He finally decided she was sincere. She saw the bright side of every situation, it seemed.

They sat there in the heat, looking out over the flowers, not saying a word to each other, occasionally waving their hands in a feeble attempt to chase the gnats away. Jay wanted to tell Anna about the money, but despite his careful planning, he was unsure of what to say, and he was a little scared.

Several people rolled past on bicycles causing a little breeze that felt extremely good to Jay, even though it was but a fleeting hint of relief. He took a deep breath and sighed. *Well, here goes nothing,* he thought as he took another deep breath.

"Well, this was a perfect setting in my mind for what I am about to tell you. Unfortunately, in reality it's unbearably hot, the machinery is noisy, and the gnats are unmerciful," he began.

Anna sat looking at him questioningly. She had been very curious about the surprise Jay had told her about the previous evening and wasn't sure what to expect next.

"I don't know if you remember the letter I received in the mail a couple months ago or not," he started quietly.

Anna tried to remember what Jay was talking about. Nothing came to mind, so she smiled and shrugged at Jay, who was intently watching her. "Sorry, I don't remember a letter," she finally answered.

A moment or two passed before Jay began again.

"It was when you helped me clean my apartment before the single's Bible study we held there. You found a couple bills and a letter that were buried underneath some old newspapers. You kept them out for me. Do you remember that?" he asked inquisitively.

Anna looked at Jay with a blank expression on her face. She was scanning her memory, trying to bring that particular day back to mind, but it was slow in coming.

A ram hoe started working on a basalt ledge nearly half a mile away. The noise was loud and unnerving despite the distance. Jay found himself flinching from the incessant noise the large machine was making. The heat, gnats, and noise, coupled with Anna's difficulty in recalling the events of the day in question were starting to annoy Jay.

"You know, the letter that was handwritten with no return address, the one I said was junk mail?" he half-asked, half-pleaded with a tinge of irritation in his voice.

Anna furrowed her brow in concentration.

Suddenly her eyes lit up, "Oh yeah, I can kind of remember that now. It seemed like the envelope was heavy, you know, really nice paper or something."

"Yes, that's the one!" Jay said with excitement in his voice.

"Okay, I remember it; you kind of shoved it in your pocket or something."

"Well, that's the surprise. At least, the letter inside that envelope is the surprise."

Anna's eyes were fixed on Jay as she waited patiently for him to explain. She wasn't sure how to respond or what to say, if anything.

Jay paused, unsure exactly how he should word the revelation he was about to make. Even though he had thought about this moment and what he would say to Anna many, many times, his nerves, along with all the other distractions, were causing him to draw a blank.

Finally, slowly and carefully, he started again.

"The letter was written by my uncle Milton, and the contents will, um, or have, changed our lives."

Jay paused, unhappy with himself, as Anna's confused eyes locked on his. He took a deep breath and started at the beginning. This time he calmly told her the whole story, front to back, without stopping until he'd told her every detail. He let out a deep breath when he'd finished and studied Anna.

Her face showed no expression, which deeply surprised and disappointed Jay, who had imagined so much more.

After a moment or two, Anna noticed Jay looking at her expectantly.

"Well, congratulations."

"Congratulations? That's all you have to say?"

"Well, I don't really know what else to say," Anna answered him slowly.

"How about 'Great! Super! Wonderful!' Or something like that?"

"Well, great! That's great for you, Jay. I don't know what else you want or expect me to say."

"No, Anna, it's not great for me. Don't you see? It's great for us!" Jay exclaimed, practically pleading with her to understand.

Anna was confused. Maybe she just hadn't thought it through yet.

"Look Anna, this money is for both of us. It gives us a chance for a good beginning of our lives together. We can get married, have kids, buy a new house, and live a comfortable life without having to worry about our financial future at all."

Anna looked at the ground without speaking. A look of sadness appeared on her face, and she didn't say anything for the longest time.

Jay waited impatiently, nervous to hear her response now that he had explained what the gift meant.

Finally, after several more moments, Anna began.

"I hope I've never led you to believe anything but the truth, Jay. I've tried to be up front with you about my plans—God's plan—for my life from the very beginning. I don't want you to misunderstand what I'm saying to you right now. I mean I'm very happy for you, but the money, house, everything, isn't what God intends for me. Not now anyway. I fully intend to become a missionary and go to the mission field just as God has called me to do. I have to be obedient to His will, Jay. I'm sorry if that hurts you."

Jay sat stunned for a moment, but refused to just let his future with Anna slip away.

"Anna, you can be a missionary right here in Pullman. I've seen the good works and deeds you've done with all the different people in the community. We can have our life and still serve God. People are people. It shouldn't matter where you're a missionary as long as you're leading people to God," Jay argued with confidence in his voice.

Now Anna looked truly upset and didn't say anything for awhile as she gathered her composure. She watched an approaching couple as they strolled by, hand in hand, until they passed.

Jay waited, certain he'd made a point Anna couldn't refute. He was positive she'd come around to his way of thinking, given the chance to think about it.

He was wrong.

"I'm sorry, Jay. You just don't understand I guess. Being in Pullman isn't what God has in store for me at all. He has a definite plan for me, and I'm going to be obedient to his wishes. I've made it known to you and everyone else I know, too. It's no secret nor has it ever been."

Jay was starting to get really annoyed with Anna. He had to fight the urge to strike out at her verbally for her stubbornness. He couldn't understand at all why she was being so rigid in her determination. Spreading God's Word was spreading God's Word regardless of one's whereabouts. He knew he was right and had to convince her of it.

Somehow he had to make her see the value of having the money. If he could make her see that, he just knew she'd come around to his way of thinking. He took a deep breath and started again.

"Look, I'm not asking you to make some earth-shattering decision right now. I'm just asking that you think about everything, consider everything I've said to you. You said you love me, and I do believe you. I love you too! Can't you see that? Everything I'm saying to you now is out of love and love alone. I want your future, our future, to be the very best it can be, and this money affords us exactly that opportunity. The money didn't just fall out of the sky or something. There has to be some reason my uncle gave me that money. Isn't it possible God led him to give it to me for us? What other explanation could there be?"

Anna looked absolutely miserable and she answered Jay almost immediately, determination in her voice.

"I can't consider any of what you said. The money doesn't mean a single thing to me. I come from a wealthy family and have already turned my back on wealth once in favor of God, and I'll do it again. I meant what I said. I love you, but that doesn't make it okay for me to disobey God. If I consider anything other than what God has planned and revealed to me for my life, it'll only give Satan a foothold in my life to start eroding the relationship I have with God. Nothing, not even you, is worth that, harsh as it may sound. But that's the truth," Anna said as tears ran down her cheeks.

Jay was bent over, elbows on his knees, his head resting in his hands with his eyes fixed on the ground as Anna's stern words sunk in. He couldn't believe what he was hearing. He'd lived this day, this moment, for the past two months over and over in his head, and now that it was here, not one part of it was as he'd imagined.

This moment was supposed to be his best moment, and Anna was completely denying him that. It wasn't fair, and he wasn't going to stand for it.

She just can't stand to have anyone else in the limelight but herself, he thought as the sweat dripped off his forehead. *Now that I'm the man of the hour, she thinks she has to put me in my place.*

He was mad, sad, and dejected all at the same time, and he wasn't sure how to respond to Anna's last statement. It took all of his effort to keep from lashing out, to tell her how unfair and unreasonable she was being. He waited several moments before abruptly standing and turning away.

"It's hot, I'm ready to go," he announced in a gruff voice, an emotional lump in his throat.

He was near tears, which only angered him all the more. With a deep sigh he began walking down the path, back the way they had come, without so much as turning around to see if Anna was following. To tell the truth, he didn't care if she was or not. The only thing he knew for certain was that he wanted to be as far from there, and from Anna, as quickly as possible.

Anna stood up and followed after Jay. She was upset and wanted to say more to Jay, but could think of nothing that would help. She followed a step or two behind him and quickly said a prayer asking God to give her guidance and wisdom with dealing with the situation she was in.

Almost instantly she felt God's reassuring, calming influence come over her. She gladly succumbed to his comfort and praised him for being there for her. Tears of sadness mixed with tears of joy ran down her cheeks and fell to the ground, where they evaporated immediately, as she struggled to keep up with Jay and the long strides he was taking. She'd had a premonition for several weeks that this day was coming, but that didn't make it any easier. She loved Jay so much and still felt God intended him for her, but she had to hold her ground.

Jay covered the distance back to his car in less than half the time it had taken them initially. He was sweating profusely and could feel his heart pounding raggedly in his chest. The heat was staggering, and, mixed with the constant noise of the heavy equipment, was causing a massive headache. He reached his car, unlocked the doors, and got in without checking to see how close Anna was. He turned the car on and blasted the air to max.

Anna was fifteen or twenty yards behind Jay and was struggling to keep up. She heard him start the car and half expected him to drive off without her. Out of breath, she approached the car and slowly got in. She had decided not to say any more unless Jay specifically asked her something. Before she buckled her seatbelt, Jay put the car in drive and sped off down the highway toward home. Neither one of them said a word. Jay's anger continued growing with every passing minute. He made a deliberate effort to concentrate on the roadway and the cars ahead of him instead of Anna and their doomed relationship.

I'll be better off without her, he thought without conviction.

The air conditioner was beginning to cool the air considerably, which helped to alleviate his headache. He entered Pullman and drove straight to Anna's house and pulled up to the curb right out front. Anna undid her seat belt, opened the door, and got out slowly. She held the door open, turned, and spoke back into the car.

"Jay, I'm sorry you're so upset," she said quietly. "But I have to follow God. I'll continue to pray for you."

Jay sat there, both hands gripping the steering wheel, eyes focused straight ahead. He didn't say a single word or even acknowledge whether he'd heard Anna's words or not. She waited a moment or two before slowly closing the door. She had just started up the sidewalk toward the house when Jay rolled down the passenger side window.

"I don't want to see you any more!" Jay said through the window, causing Anna to stop in her tracks.

Both of her shoulders hunched up as Jay's words reached her, almost as if someone had just punched her in the back. Anna stood motionless for a moment or two before taking one slow step after another up the sidewalk toward the house.

"Ever!" Jay added emphatically, surprising even himself with the hateful tone of his voice.

The finality of his last statement brought a small gasp and even more tears to Anna's red and swollen eyes, yet she trudged on up the sidewalk to the house. Jay watched her until the door closed behind her. He shook his head in anger as he rammed the gas pedal down to the floorboard. The front wheels of his car spun on the loose gravel on the street and launched little rock missiles out behind his car onto the parked car behind him, causing him to feel foolish.

His anger quickly took over, extinguishing any shame he felt for his actions or for the hateful words he'd just spoken to Anna. He sped home and parked his car haphazardly in front of his apartment building and sat there for a moment or two before turning off his ignition. He pounded on the steering wheel a couple times before getting out.

Once in the apartment, he paced back and forth like some sort of restless cat in a zoo. A lion or tiger full of restless energy, back and forth, back and forth, back and forth. After what seemed like several hours, but was more like ten minutes, Jay sat on his couch.

"I can't believe it! I can't believe it! What am I going to do?" he asked himself out loud, surprised at the hollowness of his voice.

His mind raced.

"What are people going to say? What am I going to say?" he asked with a hint of panic in his voice.

He sat rocking back and forth for several more minutes until an idea popped up in his mind. He got up, went into the kitchen, walked straight to the phone, and quickly dialed a number. The phone rang and rang until an answering machine picked up and instructed Jay to leave a message.

"Hello Sandy, this is Jay, Jay Bilston. Hey, I just wanted to let you know, if you're still interested, I'm on the open market now. Give me a call."

He left both his home and his cell phone number and hung up. Just in case, he tried her cell phone and left the same message when it went straight to voice mail.

"That'll teach her!" he exclaimed as he imagined Anna's reaction when she saw Jay and Sandy arm in arm.

Jay stood by the phone for a moment before grabbing a Coke out of the fridge. He picked up his keys and headed back out to the car, got in, checked his cell phone, and headed down the road.

First he drove past Sandy's house to see if she was home, and then past the bank where she worked. He thought about going in—she was his personal banker after all—but finally decided against it when he couldn't work up the nerve. *Besides, the bank will be closing soon and then she'll call.*

He turned back on the main road and, without thinking about it, was soon heading north out of town toward Spokane. He drove and drove, going through Colfax and continuing north until he came to Steptoe, a little speck of a town on the highway and two crossroads.

At a little convenience store, he bought a fresh Coke before getting back in his car. Hopefully, desperately, he checked his cell phone to make sure there were no messages before turning around and heading back toward Pullman.

He retraced his path, back through Colfax, back toward Pullman, before deciding at the last moment to take the back road through the little bedroom community of Albion. The crooked little paved road wove through the grain fields, finally crossing the Palouse River before it came into Albion. From there to Pullman it followed the river for about a mile before making an abrupt turn of a little over ninety degrees, where it meandered back and forth through the wheat fields again until it reached Pullman.

The fields of wheat and barley had ripened and were golden in color. Large combines were busy going round and round the hills, their headers cutting off the large heads of grain where they fell to an auger that moved them up and into the large, hungry machines.

Jay paused for a moment or two at the main intersection in Albion, then turned and followed the river out of town toward Pullman. He'd gone almost a mile when his cell phone, which was sitting on the passenger seat, started to ring. The display showed Sandy's name and number, and Jay anxiously flipped open the phone before his voice mail could pick up.

"Hello, this is Jay," he said right before the phone slid out of his hand and landed on the floor, on the passenger side of the shifting lever.

Agitated, Jay leaned over and reached around until his fingers closed around the cell phone. He straightened back up and looked back out the front window just in time to see a large white-tailed buck deer, a trophy by anyone's standards, standing in the middle of the road directly in the path of his car.

Cell phone forgotten, Jay grabbed the wheel with both hands, slammed his left foot on the brake and cranked the steering wheel hard to the left. The brakes locked up, squealing loudly as the rear of the car started to slide past the front of the car on the right side.

Realizing he had over-steered the car to the left, Jay let off the brake and cranked the wheel back to the right as hard as he could before reapplying the brakes. The tires turned, squealing and smoking until they slowly gained traction and the front of the car started back to the right. The car was completely on the shoulder of the road when Jay realized he was heading directly toward a large Ponderosa pine. He instinctively braced against the wheel, his legs fully extended as he readied himself for impact. The tree impacted the car at the front door post of the driver's side, causing the air bags to deploy almost immediately. The force of the collision made the rear of the car swing around the tree, almost as if it was being bent in an arc.

Jay's last conscious thought was to wonder whether the loud crash in his left ear was the side window shattering or his skull fracturing as he slowly slipped into a black gloom.

Broken glass and chrome trim lay on the ground at the tree's base as the car bounced off the trunk of the tree almost sideways and skidded in the loose gravel and dirt. The passenger side tires popped as they sank in the dirt on the abrupt embankment. The momentum of the car caused it to roll over before landing back on its wheels against a four-strand wire fence. A cedar fence post exploded into hundreds of pieces, most of them no bigger than a toothpick upon impact with the car.

Scores of sharp barbs on the wire grabbed at the car like little fingers intent on holding it upright. Failing in their attempt, dozens of the barbs penetrated the skin of the car and ripped little grooves into the body as the car's weight and momentum tore through the wire fencing. No more than a foot from the edge of the river, the red Impala rolled again, landing with its top directly in the middle of the slack water of the Palouse River.

Water poured in the broken windows. In minutes, the car settled to the silty bottom of the murky water, leaving less than a third of the left rear tire sticking above the surface. Jay's limp, motionless body hung upside down as swirls of mud settled back down to the roof of his shattered car.

Back on the road, the large buck walked off the pavement, past the tree, and into the brush next to the river. The only discernable damage to the magnificent tree was a small section of missing bark no more than twelve inches square. Clear sap had already begun flowing on the exposed wood as the tree began its healing process. All else was calm.

CHAPTER TWENTY-SEVEN

Chester Ingle, just Chet to his friends and colleagues, was heading home after a long day's work as chaplain for the Whitman County Sheriff's Department, feeling every bit of his sixty years of age. The county was short funded, so Chet was required to pull patrol duty part of the time, and today had been one of those long patrol days. He had just finished his last stretch and had turned around in the little community of Albion to head for home in Pullman. In anticipation of the dinner his wife was preparing, he'd skipped lunch and was famished. He could practically taste the spaghetti and red meat sauce, made with ground sirloin and hickory smoked sausage, which gave it quite a unique flavor. His wife's secret ingredient, however, was a small amount of apple cider seasoned with a little cinnamon. It added a wonderfully intriguing flavor that all their family and friends raved about. He could hardly wait to get home.

Chet followed the road along the Palouse River and started to round the sharp corner as the road veered to the north away from the river.

That's odd, he thought when he detected fresh skid marks on the highway. "*Those weren't there a few minutes ago.* He stopped to get a better look at the skid marks in an attempt to analyze the scene.

A quick scan of both ditches didn't turn up any wrecked cars.

He got out and followed the skid marks clear to the large Ponderosa Pine just off the shoulder of the roadway. A bad feeling hit the pit of his empty stomach as he took in the shattered glass and crumpled chrome trim at the base of the tree and noticed the freshly disturbed soil all the way down to the splintered fence post and broken strands of barbed wire. His gaze continued out into the river, and he was horrified to see part of the right rear wheel and tire of a submerged car.

Chet didn't know if anyone was in the car or not, but he had to assume the worst. He raced back to his car, flipped on the patrol lights, and radioed for a search and rescue vehicle and an ambulance.

The river bank was more than four feet above the water, which forced Chet to move some twenty yards downstream to where the shore was more gradual. He quickly took off his gun belt, removed the wallet from his pants, and slid his wristwatch off his arm.

There was no way a rescue vehicle could get out here in time to help, and he was already resigned to getting wet. So he just said a quick prayer asking the Lord to help him and walked out into the water. When he was about half way to the car, the river bottom dropped off precipitously. The water was over Chet's waist, and he was using his hands to part the slimy green scum from the top of the rank smelling river. The suction from the mud made each agonizing step harder than the one before it. Chet was still frail from an on-the-job injury that had kept him off the force for the past year, and for a long moment he was afraid he wouldn't reach the car.

Grabbing hold of the car just in front of the rear wheel, he paused to catch his breath. He listened for sirens again, hoping with all his might that an officer would arrive to help him.

"What in the world am I going to do now?" he said out loud. "There's no way I'll be able to tell if someone's still in the car."

Part of him wanted to head back to the shore, but he absolutely couldn't leave the car until he knew if anyone was in it. He might be their only hope, however frail. *God, please give me enough strength to see if anyone is in the car,* he prayed.

When he finished his short prayer, he breathed in as much air as his lungs could hold and plunged under the foul surface of the water. He couldn't open his eyes under the water, so he had to rely on his sense of feel. He found the door of the car and followed it to a side window. His lungs felt like they were going to burst, so he surfaced and gasped for air.

This is the passenger side, he realized, momentarily confused since the car was upside down. He worked his way around to the other side of the car.

The water was deeper on the far side, almost up to Chet's chest as he grabbed hold of the submerged undercarriage. "Here goes nothing." Another deep breath, and he ducked under the water again. He could feel the dented, mangled metal and quickly worked his way down to where the side window used to be. He reached inside and was horrified when he felt a body in the car. Out of air, he had to come up one more time for breath.

"I can't do it," he said between gasps. *I have to try, one more time,* he decided with renewed determination.

This time Chet went directly to the window and briefly groped around the person's head, looking for the seat belt release, momentarily forgetting the car was upside down. When he realized his mistake, he reached up where he thought the seat should be and felt for the release button. His lungs were screaming at him now, but he was determined to stay down as long as he possibly could, realizing that this was probably his last chance to free whoever was in the car.

Much to his surprise, his left hand found the button, and the seat belt released immediately, allowing the body to fall to the top of the car. Chet was at the end of his endurance so he grabbed hold of the left forearm of the body and pulled with all his might as he headed back above the surface of the water to the waiting, life-sustaining air he so desperately needed.

The body followed through the window cavity with much more ease than he had anticipated and half-floated, face-down, on top of the smelly water.

Chet turned the person over. It was a young man, probably in his midtwenties. He had seen death many times, never getting used to it, and this man definitely had the look of death. His face was bluish purple, and he appeared to have some sort of head injury.

The young man wasn't breathing as Chet dragged him backward through the slack water to the waiting shore. They quickly reached the edge of the river, and it was all Chet could do to drag the young man halfway up the shore, leaving the legs still underwater. Blood started trickling out the young man's left ear and left nostril as Chet plopped down next to him, exhausted.

"I don't think you're going to make it," Chet said as heaviness filled his heart. "But I have to try to save you."

In all his years of service, he had never actually performed CPR on a real person. Now his ignorance terrified him. "What do I do?" he asked out loud as his hands began to shake. "I have to clear the airway," he remembered, unsure where to start.

He looked around frantically and was near tears when he heard an approaching patrol car, siren screaming as it came to a sliding halt.

More sirens could be heard as additional officers arrived. The search and rescue vehicle and ambulance soon followed. Paramedics came and took over the CPR.

"How long was he underwater?" one of the men asked Chet.

"Somewhere between four and twenty minutes would be a fair guess," Chet answered gloomily.

"Not much chance then," the other paramedic said matter-of-factly.

A couple other deputies entered the water and quickly searched the overturned car. "No more vics," they announced to the now more than dozen emergency personnel.

"Get a tow truck," the senior officer ordered the newly arrived deputy.

Chet lay on the bank of the river, completely exhausted. He said a quick prayer for the young man and rose to his knees.

"His license says he's from Pullman, a Jay Bilston," a deputy said as he raided the driver's license taken from the saturated wallet.

"We have a slight pulse," one of the paramedics finally said as they rolled Jay onto a waiting gurney and strapped him down. "We'll let the hospital deal with this one," he added as they made their way up the bank to the waiting ambulance.

Chet stood up and gathered up his belongings. He gave a brief report to the Sheriff, who was now on the scene.

"Would you like a ride to the hospital?" the sheriff asked.

Chet hesitated as he contemplated the offer.

"No, I'd better get home so I can shower and change. I have a feeling I'll be paying that young man's family a visit tonight," Chet replied sadly before turning and making his way up the bank to his waiting patrol car.

He took a blanket out of his trunk and placed it on the front seat of his patrol car. Tears filled his eyes and ran down his cheeks as he got in the car and headed down the road toward home and his waiting wife.

CHAPTER TWENTY-EIGHT

Jay didn't know whether he was alive or dead, asleep or awake. At first he couldn't see anything but darkness—darker than anything he had ever imagined before. After several confused moments that could just as well have been hours or days, the blackness muted to a smoky brown, and he felt like he was suspended in a cloudy, opaque substance. The substance seemed to be some sort of thick liquid that was neither warm nor cold to the touch.

At first, he was filled with a terror so great he thought it may cause his heart to explode, but it passed. Once he calmed down, he actually found the strange substance oddly comforting. And despite the fact that he couldn't move, he was sure his arms and legs were present. Another comfort.

He couldn't remember anything, much less figure out where he was or how he had gotten there. For some reason the name "Anna" kept resonating in his mind. He focused on it for as long as he could, but he soon slipped back into the beckoning blackness from which he'd just come.

⁂

Jay pulled away from the blackness again, feeling as if he were rising somehow, but from a power source other than himself. The opaque liquid was getting lighter in color as Jay rose up. Or was the liquid settling down around him? He couldn't be sure.

He strained his eyes in an attempt to see something, anything, but could only make out color.

"Anna," "Anna," "Anna," kept resonating in his mind over and over, but he struggled to remember what the word meant. He thought it was a person, or maybe a place.

After some time passed, he could make out strands all around him, three or four inches wide, but paper thin. They appeared to be greenish in color, almost like large translucent blades of grass. They waved back and forth, but Jay couldn't feel a current. The surrounding liquid continued to become lighter in color as Jay rose further up.

Before long, he could make out several indistinct forms swimming in a circle near the surface, ten or so feet above him. As the light improved he was able to discern some sort of strange green men that he was certain he'd seen before, only this time their arms and legs were replaced with fins. Jay watched in fascination as these strange creatures circled round and round, eyes fixed on him.

Some indeterminate amount of time passed with little or no change in Jay's world. The creatures continued circling just below the surface, the grass continued flowing back and forth, and Jay remained suspended, unable to move of his own accord.

Something moved to his left, in the darkness amidst the flowing grass. He could detect it before he could see it. Some sort of presence, gigantic in size.

Jay was afraid of this new presence he was unable to see, but when it came no closer and offered no threat, he forgot it. Instead he continued to focus his attention on the little creatures directly above him. They had a mesmerizing effect that seemed soothing to his spirit. He continued to watch them for some time until the presence caught his attention again. It had gained in stature.

He strained to see what it was with all his might but could see only darkness. Fearful, he continued watching, and after some time, the shape became more distinct. He struggled against the fluid to try and turn, to face the presence, but was unable to move more than a fraction of an inch.

The dark shape continued to grow larger, and now it was moving closer. Jay could make out distinct lines and decided the large shape was some sort of ship. It approached, bow first, but at a slight angle until it was no more than several feet away and slightly above his prone body.

"Anna," "Anna," "Anna," continued its assault on his mind. He couldn't figure out what it meant.

Suddenly, near the bottom of the bow of the large ship, a rectangular door, roughly three feet wide and seven feet tall, flew open. A brilliant white and yellow light blazed through the opaque substance and made Jay squint his eyes in discomfort. The light was broken by the silhouette. A person?

Jay was amazed that the liquid didn't pour into the ship through the open doorway, causing it to sink, but somehow it didn't.

A sound broke the perfect silence. A voice, and by the tone and pitch he decided it was a woman. He strained his ears to make out what it was saying, but the liquid or substance he was in caused the voice to be garbled.

Slowly it grew louder, but remained garbled, leaving Jay to wonder what it meant. Now it seemed the voice was coming from the silhouette inside the doorway of the giant ship. It had gotten close enough for Jay to discern that the figure was definitely a woman. He could see the outline of her shadowy body along with her long, dark, flowing hair.

Something deep inside of Jay stirred. An emotion, a shred of recognition of something or someone, he couldn't be sure which.

The voice continued, reassuring, comforting; yet urgent. He struggled to understand, frustrated and angered that he couldn't. The grass continued to flow, back and forth around him. The strange creatures circled, watching.

Suddenly, almost violently, a moment of recognition and understanding came over the suspended and immobile Jay.

"Anna!" he screamed at the top of his lungs.

The woman in the ship was Anna. It all made sense to him now. She was calling out to him over and over, asking him to save her, to rescue her from the ship.

He struggled with all his might, determined to reach her, to embrace her, to save her. Slowly, ever so slowly, he started to sit up and reach his hands toward her. The pain was excruciating, but he wasn't going to be deterred. Slowly, he closed the distance to Anna, reaching his hands ever so close.

"Can't you reach me?" he screamed out, unsure if she could even hear him. Frustration tore at his heart, his soul.

"Anna, here I am! Grab my hand!" he yelled out as he painfully lifted his left hand and stretched it out to her.

The silhouette seemed to hear, to recognize him. She reached out, but they were still too far apart. Jay concentrated with all his might, but was unable to get any closer.

"Anna," "Anna," "Anna," he whimpered painfully.

A change made Jay look up. The strange creatures continued to circle, but had begun descending down toward him. They were close enough that he could make out their faces, and he was startled to he realize they had large, beaver-like teeth that gnashed back and forth like gigantic scissors, ready to cut him to shreds.

The creatures were all watching him, broad smirks twisting their faces as they approached. Anna forgotten, Jay fearfully tried to move away from them. In slow motion, his body reclined until he was back in a prone position. The creatures continued to descend, illuminated by the light from the ship's open doorway.

Anna's garbled voice grew more and more frantic as the creatures converged downward, toward Jay. He was certain they were going to gnash him up and feed on his body. A terror-induced scream escaped his mouth, only to be suppressed by the liquid in which he was suspended. The creatures were mere inches from him now, circling, circling, and circling. They seemed to delight in his terror as they slowly continued their descent.

The large blades of grass suddenly wrapped themselves around Jay's arms, legs, and midsection and began pulling him downward, back into the darkness. He struggled against them momentarily, but willingly succumbed when he realized they were pulling him away from the strange, vicious creatures and the danger they posed. Slowly, slowly, slowly he sank downward into the black nothingness from which he had emerged. The light from the ship grew smaller and smaller until it disappeared into nothingness.

"Anna," "Anna," "Anna," was the only sound Jay heard as he settled deeper into unconsciousness.

Jay lay on the hospital bed, hoses and machines attached to his body seemingly everywhere. His head was bandaged and misshapen; the machines were thumping and whirring all around him. His parents were the first to arrive and were at the side of his bed, along with the doctor and a couple of nurses.

"My baby, how could this happen to my baby?" his mother kept saying over and over as tears flowed down her cheeks.

His father stood upright, rigid, as tears filled his eyes.

Jay's mom gripped his hand tightly as she rested her head against her husband for comfort. The doctor waited a moment or two before clearing his voice. He introduced himself and asked Jay's parents to please accompany him out of the room so he could have a word with them.

"Mr. And Mrs. Bilston, your son suffered some grave injuries in his accident. He has several fractures of the skull and was underwater for an undetermined, but lengthy, amount of time. His CT scan shows bleeding on the brain along with a slight detachment of the left hemisphere. His heart had stopped for an unknown amount of time before the paramedics were able to successfully administer CPR.

"In short, the outlook for your son's recovery is small. I'm not trying to paint a bleak picture, but I don't want to give you false hope either. In my professional opinion, even if he does emerge from his coma, based on similar brain injuries of past patients, Jay will most likely have brain damage of some sort, most likely severe. I want to stress that every patient is different, thus their recovery from an accident like this varies greatly. But I also want to prepare you for the reality of an injury like this now instead of later. I would also encourage you to have as many family members visit Jay as soon as possible. Other than that, all we can do is wait and pray."

The doctor shook their hands before leaving the room. Jay's mom leaned back in her chair, emotionally exhausted, and sobbed.

CHAPTER TWENTY-NINE

Jay lay in the hospital, his condition unchanged for the next fourteen days. His mother and father, along with Bill, rarely left his side. All of the nurses had come to know them very well, and they all felt absolutely terrible that the family had to go through such pain. The doctor also checked in regularly, but didn't offer them any additional hope after a new CT scan showed very little, if any, progress with Jay's injury.

The church rallied around the Bilstons and flooded Jay's room with cards and balloons wishing him a speedy recovery. An almost steady stream of church members came to visit Jay and to offer moral support to the family. They provided meals for Jay's parents and had the prayer chain going constantly, asking God to please be with Jay and his family.

Curious to almost everyone was Anna's noticeable absence.

It was just past lunchtime at the hospital. Jay's mother and Bill were at his side, his father having just left for home to get some rest. The last two weeks had been hard on all of them, and they were all quite weary. At first they had been overjoyed simply because Jay had survived night after night of uncertainty, but now both their moods and their hopes were fading as he showed no signs of improvement.

PRICELESS

The doctor entered the room with a nurse and simply stood there for a moment. They turned when he cleared his throat and nervously looked first from Bill and then to Jay's mother before speaking.

"Mrs. Bilston, um, I need to talk to you about Jay. In spite of all our efforts, Jay developed a lung infection, which has kept us quite concerned for some time."

Jay's mother grabbed Jay's limp hand.

The doctor, aware that he had raised fresh fears, quickly added, "He's much better now though. As a matter-of-fact, we have just about done all we can do for Jay. His condition is stabilizing, and we are planning on releasing him to a rehabilitation clinic to further his recovery. I would say no more than forty-eight or so hours from now Jay will be stable enough to move. I have taken the liberty to arrange transport for him at that time, barring any changes in his condition."

After a moment of uncomfortable silence, Mrs. Bilston spoke up, anger overwhelming the sorrow in her voice. "So that's it? You're just going to throw him out like some piece of trash or something? Well he's not a piece of trash, he's my son! My baby boy!" she added hysterically.

The doctor stood there patiently and waited for her to calm down.

"Ma'am, we're not throwing him out. You have to realize, we are an emergency hospital. We stabilize patients and save their lives. We're not equipped to continue the rehabilitation of patients. Other facilities are geared to handle cases—people like your son. I'm sorry if it seems harsh, but it's what's best for Jay at this point," he explained slowly.

"Why don't you just say it like it is? You're just sending him to a nursing home to die, somewhere other than here so you don't ever have to think about him again. Well shame on you!" She added furiously before falling into Bill's arms to cry.

"Forty-eight hours," the doctor repeated before awkwardly leaving the room.

Jay's predicament had initiated a wildfire of phone calls. When Anna heard about Jay's pending move, turmoil over their relationship gave way to her love for him and faith in God. She rallied the church in a prayer vigil. People came to the church at all hours of the day for the next two days. Anna was there the whole time, sleeping very little. Her whole existence revolved around the altar, where she prayed almost constantly for Jay's recovery.

Several people from the congregation went to the hospital, where they held an ongoing vigil with Bill and Jay's parents. It was a serious but joyous time as all involved focused their prayers for Jay's recovery. The outpouring was amazing, and it seemed to have a wondrous effect on the people of the church. Despite their sorrow, everyone was excited about the Lord and praised Him for sustaining Jay's life as much as He had. Looking back, most everyone agreed that the terrible tragedy was the spark for a revival in their little community church—a revival that brought hundreds of souls to new life in the Lord.

But now Anna was all alone in the large sanctuary, and her mood had turned dark. There were only two hours left in the timeline the doctors had given Jay. She slowly walked around the empty room, all the while keeping her eyes fixed on the cross at the front.

"Dear Jesus, I'm still here faithfully holding vigil for Jay. I love you and praise you for all the blessings you've bestowed on me over the years. I've been a true and faithful servant, Lord, giving all of myself no matter the task or chore, never complaining, always happy that you would find me worthy of your service. Never once have I failed to obey your wishes or plans for me, and I cheerfully and willingly accepted each and every task, praising you every step of the journey that has brought me here to Pullman to pursue the plans you have set for my life. I'm here before you now to ask something of you, something for myself. I'm here to ask, on the promises of your own word, that you restore Jay's health, not for me Lord, but for him and his family. I would pray that you touch him as only you can do, for the doctors give him virtually no chance for recovery."

Tears were streaming down Anna's cheeks as she continued to pray. Her eyes were closed, and her head was bowed, but she continued to move forward slowly toward the cross.

"And Lord, if for some unknown reason only you in your infinite wisdom can understand you won't restore Jay's health, I ask, I plead with you to take him home to be with you. Please, please, don't allow him to lie there in that state, somewhere between life and death, dream and reality. I don't pray this for myself, Father, but rather for Jay's mom and dad, who are suffering so greatly. Please allow them the opportunity to grieve and begin to heal. I love you and praise you, Lord, all day, every day. These things I ask on your own promises and in your name, Amen."

Anna opened her eyes and raised her head when she was finished. She was surprised when she realized she was no more than two feet from the cross that hung on the wall. She walked up and placed her right hand on the bottom of the crucifix in reverence, moved her hand to her lips and back to the wood, placing her kiss on the cross in a gesture of love for her Lord before returning to the altar to kneel down and continue praying for another she loved.

❧

"Anna," "Anna," "Anna." The words startled Jay, who was lost somewhere in a black void.

"Anna," "Anna," "Anna," and he was awakened a little more.

He strained against the blackness, trying to see something, anything, but sterile black nothingness was all that resulted from his frantic searching. Finally, Jay allowed the black void to comfort him, and he settled down into it, away from anything that may harm him. But after some time, it started to eat at him, ebbing away his very existence.

Jay renewed his struggle against it, but could remember nothing of who he was or where he was, and consequently had nothing to grab on to. A dread started to build up in the very center of him as his straining to leave was met with failure after failure after failure. He wasn't sure how long he struggled and failed, for no time, years, months, weeks, days, hours, or minutes existed in this place. He knew he had purpose, existence, reason. Enough of reality was left that the blackness hadn't stolen from him to discern he was indeed a real and vibrant entity, existing apart from the blackness into which he was now immersed.

"Anna," "Anna," "Anna."

There it was again.

Jay couldn't remember what it meant or where it was, but he reached out and grabbed on to the only shred of himself left in his mind, soul, or body.

"Anna," "Anna," "Anna," it was growing stronger now. He struggled to hold on, keep a grip on the words, the substance, whatever it was he was hearing. He had a new determination, somehow bolstered by those three words that kept resonating somewhere deep within himself. A hope or a joy, something new and good, surged up inside him as he focused every bit of his energy on those three words. "Anna," "Anna," "Anna."

Slowly, slowly, slowly the darkness seemed to ebb away. Slowly it gave over to dark brown and then to brown mixed with tans. Jay kept focusing on the words repeating regularly in his mind, holding on to them out of nothing more than instinct. Somehow a small part of him knew those words were his key to reality, to his existence, so he fought for them, welcomed them, and cherished them.

He continued his ascent, becoming aware some point along the way of the strands of grass that bound his body. They weren't tight or uncomfortable, but they were present. He continued to struggle to see something, anything in the murky substance.

Once again he could sense the presence of the large, dark ship before he could see it. He struggled to reach it, to get closer to it, to touch something tangible and real in his mind. Slowly he remembered the ship and what—who—Anna was. Slowly he watched and waited.

Eventually, just as it had before, a door opened at the bottom of the ship, and a silhouette of Anna could be seen as the brilliant light resonated out around her, shining downward, a spotlight on Jay's suspended form. He could hear her calling to him over and over as he bent forward in a new resolve to reach her, to save her from the large black behemoth. He glanced above to the surface of the much clearer substance, checking for those strange creatures from before, and was relieved there was no sign of them.

Turning his attention back to Anna, he knew he had to reach her, to save her. Somehow he felt this would be his last chance. If he failed now, he'd never again see her, the one he loved, the one who sustained him. He stiffened with resolve and drew on every bit of energy he had.

"I'm coming for you, Anna!" he yelled, unsure if she could hear him.

Slowly, painfully, he inched up toward her outstretched arms. He could hear her garbled pleading but couldn't understand it. He knew she was calling to him, pleading with him to save her.

"Hold on, I'm coming for you, Anna!" he yelled again.

The pain was excruciating now, but he pushed it from his mind. He kept rising up, closer, closer, closer. The strands of grass tightened as if he had reached the end of the slack and held him firmly. He fought desperately against them, no more than three feet away from Anna. Close enough to make out her fine features. There seemed to be tears flowing from her eyes.

"Hold on, Anna, I'm coming!" he called, more determined than ever to save her. He was near exhaustion, and the pain was overwhelming as he continued to struggle, gaining inch by precious inch.

Anna was calling out even more now. He could almost make out her words over the short distance.

I have to save her! he thought over and over. *If I don't, she'll be gone forever.* His own fate was no longer a concern, as long as he could save her.

The pleading voice drove him on, gave him strength when he was certain he had given it all he had. Each inch was an epic battle. The strands that held him were taught and unyielding as he pulled against them and the thick, cumbersome substance he was in.

The blackness beckoned him, promising the rest he so desperately needed and craved. Certain the end was close and would be final no matter the result, he made one desperate last push to reach Anna.

At first, the blades of grass that wrapped around his body held fast, but slowly, ever so slowly they began to yield. The pain was excruciating, greater than any Jay had ever experienced before, yet he pushed on. He could almost touch her outstretched fingers. She was calling to him, more desperate than ever now, almost frantically. Jay strained with all of his might and still came up just short. It was not enough. He was going to fail.

"Anna, I love you, Anna!" he yelled to her as he pushed futilely forward.

"I love you, Jay!" he heard from her, the words plain and clear and beautiful.

The sound of Anna's voice gave him courage and strength to go on, yet the bands around his body held tight.

"Jay, come to me. Reach my hands. I'll save you, Jay. I love you."

Dread struck him a mortal blow. Absolute terror gripped his soul as he realized for the first time, it was Anna trying to save him, not he trying to save her.

Panic flooded his whole being.

"Help me, help me, Anna!" he called out to her. The bands

began constricting around his body. "Anna!" he shrieked in vain as the bands, slowly at first and then more forcefully, pulled him down and away from the ship, from Anna and all that was left of his reality. His reason gave way as the bands pulled him down to claim him as their own, a prize or trophy to keep forever.

Slowly, slowly he descended back through the browns and tans, back through the dark brown, back into the blackness.

"Anna," "Anna," "Anna."

He could hear but not comprehend. The blackness was welcoming. He embraced it, taking comfort in the bleak nothingness that absorbed his pain.

"Anna," "Anna," "Anna."

It meant nothing to him.

"Anna," it was almost gone, almost finished now. He knew it was so and greeted it. He longed for it to end, wanting not to be bothered anymore by whatever or whomever it was.

"Anna."

The sound was so faint it barely stirred him. He pushed it from his mind and turned into the blackness, giving his whole being to it, to nothing, to everything. Only the smallest fraction of his being could even feel the word, barely heard. He was peaceful, still, nothing.

"Anna!"

Suddenly, painfully from somewhere, everywhere, nowhere, he could sense a presence. Slight at first and then stronger as it wrapped itself around him and held him tight, somehow soothing despite the pain of stabbing awareness. It grabbed tighter as Jay struggled to understand.

The presence was warm and real, inviting and reassuring in its touch. Slowly he understood, and he gave all of himself to this new, warm presence. He held nothing back, not one shred of himself for the blackness or for himself. He gave his all to this new presence.

It was Anna.

Somehow, someway she had reached him, come down to him and wrapped her arms around him. She was strong, warm, and loving.

"I'm here Jay, and I'm taking you back with me," he could hear her whisper in his ear. "I love you."

She started her ascent with Jay, back through the blackness, back through the browns, back toward the large ship, away from the nothingness. Jay could still feel the bands around him as they drew closer to the ship, growing tighter, unwilling to yield him to Anna. They were ever so close now, Jay could see inside the great ship. The bands held tight, the pain returning to him, growing stronger by the minute.

"Stop, Anna, I can't go on!" he pleaded with her as the bands pulled against him, the agony reminding him why he had chosen the blackness.

"You're coming with me, Jay. I'm not letting you go," she said as they reached the outer part of the ship.

The light was blinding as they approached the doorway, the pain overwhelming. Jay could feel the bands stretching as they pulled against his body. They were going to pull him apart.

"I can't, it hurts so badly, I can't make it."

"We're not stopping," she said as reassuring as possible, but with unwavering determination. Live or die, Jay was coming with her.

They entered the front of the doorway to the ship. The light was brighter than anything Jay had ever seen before. His pain was proportionally worse.

"Anna!" he screamed out as he was pulled all the way through. A great white light of agony exploded inside of Jay, causing all reality to give way to insanity as the door to the giant ship slammed closed.

Bill sat next to the hospital bed, along with Jay's mother. It had been forty-eight hours with absolutely no change. The nurses had just told them they were going to start prepping Jay for transport to the rehab facility in about fifteen minutes. Jay's father had told him good-bye and left a few hours earlier, completely exhausted.

"Don't worry Mr. B, I'll give Mrs. B a ride home," Bill reassured Jay's father.

Mr. Bilston had gained a new respect and love for Bill over these past few weeks. Bill had been there, positive and reassuring, the whole time. Sometimes it seemed he had been the source of strength for all three of them during these most difficult times.

Now Bill picked up Jay's limp hand and squeezed it gently. "Yo dog, I don't know if you can hear me or not, but I love ya, bro," Bill said as tears rolled down his cheeks. "Hang in there; we're praying for you."

Bill blinked, bleary-eyed, when the little finger on Jay's hand moved slightly. At first he thought he was imagining things, but then it moved again.

"Yo, Mrs. B, Jay just moved his fingers!" he announced excitedly.

Jay's mother rushed to his side, almost afraid to believe this bit of news. She watched as Bill encouraged his friend to do it again. Sure enough, his fingers moved slightly as Jay's mother gasped in shock and disbelief. They looked at Jay's face and were even more shocked when his eye lids opened momentarily and his eyes appeared to scan the room.

"Nurse, nurse, something is happening!" an excited Bill yelled as he ran from the room in search of help.

He returned momentarily with a nurse in tow and explained excitedly what they had witnessed.

"It's nothing, involuntary reflexes," the nurse replied patiently, telling them movements like this would become more frequent with time.

Suddenly the monitors hooked to Jay's body began beeping as their alarm systems went off. The nurse ran to Jay and checked the machines before calling out over the phone, "Doctor, we have a code one, emergency room 312, stat."

Bill didn't know what was going on, but it didn't sound good.

"What's happening? Is he okay, is everything alright?" he asked fearfully as the nurse frantically pushed them from the room.

"You have to leave now!" she ordered as more nurses and the doctor ran past them.

The nurse closed the door as Bill and Jay's mother stood outside the room, trying to understand what had just happened. They listened to the mumbled commotion through the closed door, unsure what they should do until a nurse came and led them off down the hall to the waiting room.

They were scared and crying, holding on to each other, too afraid to do anything but pray.

෴

Anna was startled awake by a gentle shaking. She rose up on her knees, uncertain where she was or how long she'd been there. After a moment, she realized she was in the church, near the altar, as her senses came flooding back to her.

"Anna, it's the phone, it's for you," the pastor said as he handed the cordless receiver to the tired and scared Anna before backing away to give her some privacy.

Anna placed the phone to her ear, afraid to talk, knowing it had to be Bill with some sort of news.

She took a deep breath and managed a shaky, "Hello?"

The voice on the other end sounded foreign at first but she knew it was Bill. "Anna..." he choked out on the other end, emotion filling his voice.

"Anna, it's Bill..." he managed tearfully before emotion overtook him.

Anna knew instantly by the tone of Bill's voice. Jay was dead.

Sorrow overcame her, pain greater than any she had ever known tore at her heart as the tears started to flow down her cheeks. She could hardly breathe. She felt completely helpless. Hopelessness overcame her as she cried silently.

Bill regained some semblance of composure and began again.

"Anna, its Jay..." she could hear the emotion as it rose up in Bill's voice, nearly rendering him speechless.

Bill paused and took a deep breath as Anna screamed "No!" over and over in her mind.

"Anna, its Jay," he sobbed over the line. "He's back! Anna, the Dog is back!"

The phone slipped out of Anna's hands and bounced off the floor as she fell to the floor, arms wrapped around her knees, and sobbed and sobbed.

CHAPTER THIRTY

Jay's recovery was slow and difficult. At first he had no idea where he was or what had happened to him. He only knew his whole body ached like it had never ached before. The doctors and nurses were calling his recovery nothing short of miraculous as they checked on him day in and day out, marveling at his constant improvements. The only lasting ill effect of the accident was a slight paralysis of his left leg, which the doctors assured him would lessen with therapy.

A steady stream of visitors and well-wishers came by day and night, most of them from the church. His whole family rallied around him, becoming closer than they had been for years. They drew strength from this near tragedy as they embraced a new spirit of forgiveness and love.

Bill was at his side almost constantly, prodding him to work harder during the times of therapy when Jay wanted to give up.

Uncle Milton checked in on him every single day, giving Jay a new appreciation for the man.

Conspicuously, Anna never made a single visit to Jay, instead opting to send him a simple card telling him she was thinking of him and praying for him. Jay was confused by her absence at first, but full understanding returned with the memory of their painful last encounter. He desperately wanted to see her, but was afraid to ask anyone about her or to call her. It was clear that she would want nothing to do with him after his last, harsh words to her.

Sandy visited him every day, going so far as to tell anyone who would listen that she and Jay were going out—"practically engaged." At first Jay was polite, but he finally ran out of patience for the pushy young lady. He asked her to not come back a few weeks before he was released from the hospital.

Chet came to visit Jay often, gaining encouragement from the miracle he had had a hand in. He praised God for giving him enough strength in Jay's time of need.

Jay's mother and father fussed over him as if he was a newborn. His mother broke into tears every time she thought about how close they had come to losing her baby.

He was released from the rehab center the first day of November, sixty-four days after the crash. The weather was cold and brisk as his parents helped him into his apartment.

His hospital bill was enormous, but between his health insurance and car insurance, virtually every cent was paid for.

"Your car insurance was incredible!" Jay's father exclaimed. "It reimbursed you the whole cost of your vehicle with no depreciation. It seems you had some sort of gap insurance to cover depreciation. The adjuster told me hardly anyone has the coverage you had. Did you have a premonition this was going to happen or something?"

"Nope, just a good agent," Jay replied.

Jay decided not to purchase a new car to replace the old one. Instead he donated the replacement money to the Pullman Fire Department.

Despite the miracle of his recovery, the days dragged on for Jay. Depression set in and seemed to deepen with every moment. His parents contacted his doctors out of concern for his condition and were informed it was a normal process for someone who had sustained injuries as severe as his. "It's part of his healing process," they told them.

More than anything, Jay missed Anna. He yearned so badly to see her, to talk to her, to hug her, but he didn't have the courage to call her.

Jay still had his money, but that didn't matter much to him anymore. Many, many times he had wished he could go back in time and destroy the stupid letter that had led him to this point. The money was the bane of his existence.

He kept himself locked away in his little house and passed away the time doing absolutely nothing. He was still receiving letters and cards from well-wishers, but had stopped reading those several weeks before.

Occasionally, he'd go out for walks to stretch his legs and get a little exercise, but not very often since he had to use a cane to get around. He was very self-conscious and didn't want people to see him as a cripple. Nor had he been to church since his accident, resisting Bill's constant invitations, vehemently declining, using the excuse he was still short on endurance.

He received the church newsletter weekly and read it front to back, hoping there'd be some news about Anna. He was shocked and surprised when he read there would be a going away party and dinner for her in two weeks. It seemed she had finished work on her doctoral thesis and thus would be going to Colorado Springs ahead of schedule to start the next phase of her life; a phase that didn't have any room for Jay Bilston.

Jay cried himself to sleep the night of Anna's dinner, tossing and turning, thoughts of his lost future haunting him.

He woke up the following morning and made his way to the kitchen, where he made himself a pot of coffee. He looked out the kitchen window and was surprised by the brilliance of the late November sun. Dressing in warm clothes, he grabbed his cane and headed out the door.

The cold air was shocking and he welcomed its bite. He headed out with no destination in mind, wandering aimlessly down the back streets of Pullman. Try as he might, he couldn't get the thoughts of Anna's imminent departure out of his mind, and tears started to flow down his cheeks unchecked. Everything was blurry, and when he wiped the tears from his eyes, he was surprised to find he was standing in front of the little bench he had sat on what now seemed a lifetime before as he watched a couple of squirrels chase each other around a tree. Jay sat on the bench and glanced up the road at an empty driveway littered with windblown leaves, where months before young boys skateboarded back and forth.

He was cold and numb as he sat on the bench. He felt as if he was all alone, without a friend in the world.

"Lord, why didn't you just let me die?" he asked quietly and sincerely.

Jay turned when he heard a vehicle approach. It was a grey cruiser of some sort, and it approached slowly before stopping directly behind Jay. The door to the car opened, and Chet stepped out. "Well look who the cat's drug out," the chaplain said good-naturedly. He walked over to the bench. "Mind if I sit down?"

Jay motioned for him to have a seat, suddenly conscious of his tear-stained face as he turned away from Chet.

"How's it been lately?"

Jay shrugged his shoulders, suddenly unable to talk for fear of crying.

Chet sat there patiently, giving his young friend time to gain his composure before continuing. "You know, you're pretty special to me. It's not very often I get to talk to someone I thought was dead. As a matter-of-fact, you're the first one," he said quietly.

"It'll help if you talk, you know, to let some of those feelings out. It'll make you feel more alive again. Remember, I was in your shoes once."

Fresh tears began to flow. Something about this man was disarming to Jay, almost like a grandparent. He started to talk and Chet listened. He went clear back to when he was a teenager, thirteen to be exact, when at a junior high church camp, God had spoken to him and called him to the ministry. The warmth and love he felt from God's presence was greater than he had ever felt before, or since. At first the joy inside of him had been incredible, but over time it ebbed. "I'm not going into the ministry," he had said in defiance to the Lord.

Jay continued on, pouring his heart out to the chaplain, year by chronological year, explaining to him how ignoring his call to the ministry and in essence, ignoring the Lord, became easier and easier over time.

He told him how he'd met Anna and fallen in love only to push her and the Lord she stood for away in defiance. He told him of the letter, the money, and how he'd spurned her once again in favor of money he'd never wanted or requested.

"I'm so stupid, such a stupid, stupid fool," he said miserably.

Chet patiently listened as Jay continued on in an attempt to unburden his soul. He talked about Anna and how loving she was, always kind and caring to everyone, never holding a grudge when he, or anyone for that matter, wronged her. How the very thought of her was all that tied him to the world when he had been dying. "I love that girl so much," he admitted freely as tears returned to his eyes.

They both sat in silence for a little longer before Jay started again. "Why do you think the Lord allowed that deer to walk out in front of me? It's ruined my life."

Neither one said anything for the longest time, but instead watched as the wind blew leaves around the yard across the street.

After some time Chet cleared his throat. "Well, I don't pretend to have all the answers or to understand all there is about this old world, or our Lord for that matter, but from where I sit, it seems to me you've had it pretty good. You have good friends, family that loves you, and a girl that has stood beside you in spite of yourself. What you do now is up to you. You can either mope around feeling sorry for yourself for the rest of your life, or you can pull yourself up by your bootstraps, so to speak, and make the most of this second chance the good Lord has given you."

"What exactly am I supposed to do?" Jay asked sullenly.

"I think you know what to do, and I think you need to do it." Chet paused for a moment to let his words sink in before continuing. "I've known a lot of men in my life. Some with nothing, some with a million bucks, and some with ten million bucks, and I'll tell you something they all have in common. Every one of those men would give everything they have for a chance at a girl like Anna. Girls like that don't just come along very often. Especially girls that put up with the nonsense we men put them through. You can sit there holding on to that money of yours, making it the most important thing in your life, or you can get up off your rear end and beg, grovel, anything you have to do to get that pretty girl to take back your worthless self. From where I sit, the choice is simple. A girl like Anna is pretty much priceless!"

He paused to clap a sulking Jay on the shoulder before adding, "If you do choose the money, bring it home in cash. Small bills, 'cause when you grow up to be a lonesome old man, it'll come in handy, 'cause, well, small bills will take you longer to count and help to use up your time."

"Yeah, but Anna's gone. She left already," Jay protested.

"There's not one place in this old world you can't be in a day or less, whether it be Colorado Springs, Mexico, Ghana, or anywhere else for that matter. That, my son, is not a viable excuse."

He stood up and took a few steps toward his car before stopping and turning around. "Oh, about your earlier question, I'll take a crack at it. The Good Lord has been known to throw his own to the fishes to shake them up, get their attention." His eyes seemed soft and understanding. "Maybe, just maybe, and I'm no expert mind you, but maybe that deer of yours was the Good Lord throwing you to the fish. Think about it."

Then he turned and walked to his car and drove away.

Jay watched the leaves as they blew around, but mostly he

thought about what Chet had said about Anna. He missed her badly. After fifteen minutes or so, he started to walk.

Before he knew it, he was standing in front of Bob and Nancy's house. He stood and stared up at the room that used to be Anna's as his tears started flowing again. Nancy's car was in the drive, so Jay made his way up the sidewalk, eager to unload his burdens on her. He rang the doorbell and quickly wiped away the tears in an attempt to hide his misery.

Nancy opened the door, and surprised, wrapped Jay in a great big hug. She held him for a moment before moving him away to arm's length to get a better look at him. Concern spread across her face when she noticed his red eyes and swollen, tear-stained cheeks. She ushered him inside to a seat at the kitchen table and bent to making him some hot chocolate, which she placed in front of him along with a plate of her famous brownies.

Knowing exactly how he liked them, she gave him only the crusty edges. Jay thanked her as he slowly ate his brownies. The chocolate was very hot, and he wrapped his cold hands around the mug to warm them. He sipped it for some time and listened as Nancy gave him an update on all that was happening down at the lumberyard. He wondered about Anna, but was too afraid to ask anything and instead nodded and smiled at Nancy's dissertation, answering any questions she had for him with the least amount of words possible.

"Well, I'd better be going." he finally said after an hour or so.

Nancy looked at him for a moment before speaking. "Jay, what's the matter? I know something's the matter. We're all worried about you."

That was all she needed to say. The tears welled up and started to flow down his cheeks. Nancy rushed to his side and placed her arm around him.

"I love Anna so much, and I've been such a fool."

He continued on, telling Nancy everything he'd just finished telling Chet only an hour before. This time though, he added how much he loved her and needed her in his life.

"I don't care about the money. I love Anna, and I love the Lord, and I'm going to start being the man God has planned for me. I can't expect Anna to forgive me, or to love me any more for that matter, but I want her to know how sorry I am and how much I care for her," he said as the tears ran down his face.

"You have to tell her for me, Nancy. Please, won't you tell her for me?" he pleaded.

Nancy pushed back from Jay. "No Jay, you have to tell her for yourself. It won't mean anything coming from me."

Jay sat, stunned and defeated. "She's gone though."

"Well, if you'd been at the going away party, you would've known. The college messed up Anna's transcripts so she had to delay her departure a week. She's right upstairs, and you need to go right up there and tell her what you just told me." She directed him through the doorway and into the living room.

Jay was terrified. He was certain Anna would slam the door in his face merely at the sight of him.

"No, not now," he objected to Nancy.

"Go on, you know what you need to do. Or did you not mean what you said just now about becoming the man God made you to be, and Anna needs?"

Jay swallowed and took his first step. It was dark in the living room, and he had to grab the railing to steady himself as he made his slow climb up to Anna's room. His mind raced, imagining all the different ways Anna was going to reject him and his apology.

Turn around! his mind screamed over and over as he reached the landing near the top of the stairs. It was almost pitch black, so he stopped for a moment to allow his eyes to adjust to the light. He turned to his left to make the last step and froze in his tracks. There sat Anna leaning against the picket guard rail, facing him.

"I heard a familiar voice," she explained quietly.

For a moment Jay just stood there looking at her, unsure of what to do.

"Anna, I have to tell you something," he finally said as his tears started again.

"Sshhhh, I already heard everything," she whispered to him.

Jay sat down on the steps next to her and fell into her arms as they cried together.

CHAPTER THIRTY-ONE

They were married late the following spring in one of Pullman's city parks. All of Jay's and Anna's family were present, as was most of the church. Bill was Jay's best man, and Beth was Anna's maid of honor. It was a simple ceremony performed by the Whitman County chaplain. The bride wore an unpretentious white dress, the groom a black tux on white. Jay's sisters tried to get him to wear a pink tie and cumber bund, but he strongly declined, opting instead for black.

Anna postponed her enrollment at Colorado Springs for a couple years so Jay could take some college courses in construction management along with Spanish language classes. They decided, along with the District Superintendent of their church, that taking the courses would be beneficial to Jay when they went to the mission field.

Their church hired Anna as associate pastor for the remainder of their time in Pullman. Growth was phenomenal as revival spread throughout their church as it never had before. "Yo dog, we're on fire for the Lord," became their adopted theme.

Bill and Beth were married approximately four months after Jay and Anna, who had their turn at best man and bridesmaid. Bill's ministry struggled financially to succeed, but he continued on, never losing the faith.

Jay and Anna presented the Turning Leaf Ministry with a

million dollar plus endowment on the ministry's first anniversary. Jay also gave Bill a list of thirty-four names, encouraging him to contact them. He told Bill only that he was sure those thirty-four people were bound to have a surplus of cash, some of which they could donate to his ministry.

Jay and Anna did keep the new cell phones they had received as replacements for the ones he had lost in the car accident. They were paid for by Jay's cell phone insurer.

EPILOGUE

The midday sun bore down on the tall, dark man standing behind a large juniper tree. From his vantage point he could survey a small compound of houses and businesses more than a hundred yards in front of him. A constant scowl adorned the man's face while a steady fiery rage continued to build as he waited for someone or something to emerge from the complex. Large, dark veins stood out on his neck as he fought to control his anger. Hate surged from his soul. It was a feeling he welcomed as the rush of power from the adrenaline surged through his tense body. Every muscle on his torso trembled as he fought to maintain control. The amount of effort it took to balance on the fine point between immense anger and uncontrollable fury surprised him. A slight smile of anticipation appeared briefly on his dry, sun-cracked lips. The desire to kill was overwhelming.

This was supposed to be a quick little exercise, but it was turning into anything but. His only instructions were; "In, get the information, out—quick as that!"

Fifteen minutes, half hour tops was all the time it should have taken. Now it was dragging on and on, and all he could do was wait. Movement at the gate brought him into a lower crouch. Anticipation welled up inside, fueled by a mix of angry excitement and lustful hatred. It had been a long wait, and someone was going to pay.

The small person slowed with apprehension as the space between the two shrunk to ten feet. A hooded cloak covered the small frame. Slowly, cautiously the hooded individual continued to gingerly approach until no more than a foot separated the two. Without warning, the man's arm leapt from his side in a blur as his rock-laden fist exploded into the side of the hooded head in front of him. Impact lifted the person off the ground with little resistance. Like a rag doll thrown through the air, the feather light body slammed to the ground several feet away.

"Try to run away from me, will you?" the man yelled.

He walked over to the bundle and in one fluid motion, placed a well-aimed kick right in the middle of the body.

"Luis, stop, I'm here. I came back," the informant gasped.

Hearing his name, the dark man hesitated for a moment. "What did you learn?" Luis asked.

The informant remained silent for a moment or two. "In two weeks, the Americans are coming."

"Two weeks," Luis stated. "Two weeks and one of the gringo's will be mine."